Lusa took a deep breath. Leaving the shelter of the pathway, she scurried across the open space. Her heart began to pound again from fear of being in the open. It felt like a long, long way to the safety of the paths on the other side. Before she reached them, she heard the roar of an approaching firebeast. The glaring beams of its eyes swept across her and swiveled back, fixing her in the harsh light. A flat-face shouted something.

Lusa was frozen with fear. Then, as she heard the thump of flat-face paws hitting the ground, she forced herself to run. More shouting broke out behind her. The mouth of the nearest pathway was just in front of her. But as she plunged into the darkness between the dens, she caught a glimpse of a black shape flying in the air over her head. The next moment, something tangled in her paws and she crashed to the ground.

When Lusa tried to get up, she found herself caught in some sort of mesh made out of tough strands like twisted vines. She struggled wildly but only managed to tangle herself further. Frantic to escape, she bit through one of the strands. It gave way, but two flat-faces were already bending over her, one on each side.

"Help!" she squealed. "Toklo! Kallik! Help me!"

SEEKERS

Book One: *The Quest Begins*

Book Two: *Great Bear Lake*

Book Three: *Smoke Mountain*

Book Four: *The Last Wilderness*

Book Five: *Fire in the Sky*

Book Six: *Spirits in the Stars*

RETURN TO THE WILD

Book One: *Island of Shadows*

Book Two: *The Melting Sea*

Book Three: *River of Lost Bears*

MANGA

Toklo's Story

Kallik's Adventure

Also by Erin Hunter

Book One: *Into the Wild*

Book Two: *Fire and Ice*

Book Three: *Forest of Secrets*

Book Four: *Rising Storm*

Book Five: *A Dangerous Path*

Book Six: *The Darkest Hour*

THE NEW PROPHECY

Book One: Midnight

Book Two: Moonrise

Book Three: Dawn

Book Four: Starlight

Book Five: Twilight

Book Six: Sunset

POWER OF THREE

Book One: The Sight

Book Two: Dark River

Book Three: Outcast

Book Four: Eclipse

Book Five: Long Shadows

Book Six: Sunrise

OMEN OF THE STARS

Book One: The Fourth Apprentice

Book Two: Fading Echoes

Book Three: Night Whispers

Book Four: Sign of the Moon

Book Five: The Forgotten Warrior

Book Six: The Last Hope

Warriors Super Edition: Firestar's Quest

Warriors Super Edition: Bluestar's Prophecy

Warriors Super Edition: SkyClan's Destiny

Warriors Super Edition: Crookedstar's Promise

Warriors Super Edition: Yellowfang's Secret

Warriors Field Guide: Secrets of the Clans

Warriors: Cats of the Clans

Warriors: Code of the Clans

Warriors: Battles of the Clans

Warriors: Enter the Clans

MANGA

The Lost Warrior

Warrior's Refuge

Warrior's Return

The Rise of Scourge

Tigerstar and Sasha #1: Into the Woods

Tigerstar and Sasha #2: Escape from the Forest

Tigerstar and Sasha #3: Return to the Clans

Ravenpaw's Path #1: Shattered Peace

Ravenpaw's Path #2: A Clan in Need

Ravenpaw's Path #3: The Heart of a Warrior

SkyClan and the Stranger #1: The Rescue

SkyClan and the Stranger #2: Beyond the Code

SkyClan and the Stranger #3: After the Flood

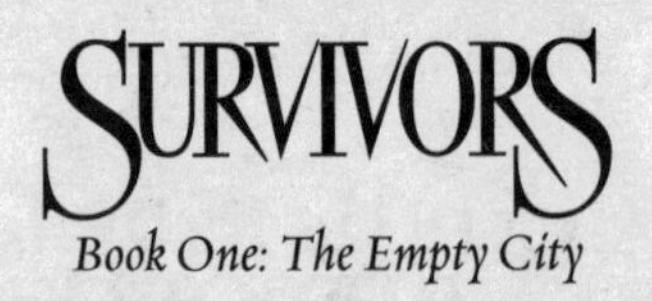

Book One: The Empty City

ERIN
HUNTER

HARPER
AN IMPRINT OF HARPERCOLLINS*PUBLISHERS*

Island of Shadows

Library of Congress Cataloging-in-Publication Data
Hunter, Erin.
Island of shadows / Erin Hunter.— 1st ed.
p. cm. — (Seekers: Return to the wild)
Summary: As the three bears, Toklo, Lusa, and Kallik, begin their journey home, they encounter new friends and dangerous enemies and must decide which they can trust to help them on their quest.
ISBN 978-0-06-199636-8 (pbk.)
[1. Bears—Fiction. 2. Fate and fatalism—Fiction. 3. Fantasy.]
I. Title.
PZ7.H916625Isl 2012 2011009158
[Fic]—dc22 CIP
AC

Typography by Hilary Zarycky
12 13 14 15 16 LP/BR 10 9 8 7 6 5 4 3 2 1
❖
First paperback edition, 2013

Special thanks to Cherith Baldry

Seal Rock
Walrus Rock
Place of the Caribou Flat-faces
Place of Everlasting Ice
LAST GREAT WILDERNESS
BLACKWATER MOUNTAINS
Place of Fishing Flat-faces
Ice Break River
Snowgoose Island
Caribou Valley
Bear Rock
Great Bear Lake
SMOKE MOUNTAINS
Paw Print Island
Big River
The Claw Path
SKY RIDGE
TOKLO'S BIRTHDEN
Bear Snout Mountain
Three Lakes
LUSA'S BEAR BOWL
Great Salmon River

The Bears' Journey: Bear View

0
800 mi
0
1200 km
Arctic Sea
QUEEN
ELIZABETH
ISLANDS
Arctic
Village
Beaufort Sea
BROOKS RANGE
ARCTIC NATIONAL
WILDLIFE REFUGE
Parry
Channel
BANKS
ISLAND
Kaktovik
Atigun
Pass
Alaska
VICTORIA
ISLAND
Fairbanks
Yukon River
MACKENZIE MOUNTAINS
Superstition
Island
Anchorage
Mackenzie River
Great
Bear
Lake
Arctic
Gulf of
Alaska
Whitehorse
Yellowknife
Great
Slave
Lake
Juneau
ROCKY MOUNTAINS
Prince
Rupert
CANADA
Pacific
Ocean
REVELSTOKE
NATIONAL
PARK
Edmonton
VANCOUVER
ZOO
Calgary
Regina
Vancouver
Canadian Pacific Railway
Seattle
Bismarck
Helena
UNITED
Portland
Columbia
River

The Bears' Journey: Human View
GREENLAND
ELLESMERE
ISLAND
BAFFIN ISLAND
Godthab
Iqaluit
Atlantic
Ocean
Circle
Hudson Bay
St. John's
Churchill
WAPUSK
NATIONAL
PARK
Lake
Winnipeg
Quebec
Trans-Canada
Highway
Montreal
Winnipeg
Ottawa
Boston
Toronto
STATES
St. Paul
Minneapolis
New York

CHAPTER ONE

Lusa

Excitement tingled through Lusa's paws as she padded down the snow-covered beach. Ice stretched ahead of her, flat, sparkly white, unchanging as far as the horizon. She didn't belong here—no black bears did—yet here she was, walking confidently onto the frozen ocean beside a brown bear and two white bears. Ujurak had gone, but Yakone, a white bear from Star Island, had joined Lusa, Kallik, and Toklo. They were still four. And a new journey lay ahead: a journey that would take them back home.

Glancing over her shoulder, Lusa saw the low hills of Star Island looming dark beneath the mauve clouds. The outlines of the white bears who lived there were growing smaller with each pawstep. *Good-bye,* she thought, with a twinge of regret that she would never see them again. Her home lay among trees, green leaves, and sun-warmed grass, a long, long way from this place of ice and wind as sharp as claws.

Lusa wondered if Yakone was feeling regret, too. The bears of Star Island were his family, yet he had chosen to leave them so that he could be with Kallik. But he was striding along resolutely beside Kallik, his unusual red-shaded pelt glowing in the sunrise, and he didn't look back.

Toklo plodded along at the front of the little group, his head down. He looked exhausted, but Lusa knew that exhaustion was not what made his steps drag and kept his eyes on his paws and his shoulders hunched.

He's grieving for Ujurak.

Their friend had died saving them from an avalanche. Lusa grieved for him, too, but she clung to the certainty that it hadn't been the end of Ujurak's life, not really. The achingly familiar shape of the bear who had led them all the way to Star Island had returned with stars in his fur, skimming over the snow and soaring up into the sky with his mother, Silaluk. Two starry bears making patterns in the sky forever, following the endless circle of Arcturus, the constant star. Lusa knew that Ujurak would be with them always. But she wasn't sure if Toklo felt the same. A cold claw of pain seemed to close around her heart, and she wished that she could do something to help him.

Maybe if I distracted him. . . .

"Hey, Toklo!" Lusa called, bounding forward past Kallik and Yakone until she reached the grizzly's side. "Do you think we should hunt now?"

Toklo started, as if Lusa's voice had dragged him back from somewhere far away. "What?"

"I said, should we hunt now?" This close to shore, they might pick up a seal above the ice, or even a young walrus.

Toklo gave her a brief glance before trudging on. “No. It’ll be dark soon. We need to travel while we can.”

Then it’ll be too dark to hunt. Lusa bit the words back. It wasn’t the time to start arguing. But she wanted to help Toklo wrench his thoughts away from the friend he was convinced he had lost.

“Do you think geese ever come down to rest on the ice?” she asked.

This time Toklo didn’t even look at her. “Don’t be bee-brained,” he said scathingly. “Why would they do that? Geese find their food on *land*.” He quickened his pace to leave her behind.

Lusa gazed sadly after him. Most times when Toklo was in a grouchy mood, she would give as good as she got, or tease him out of his bad temper. But this time his pain was too deep to deal with lightly.

Best to leave him alone, she decided. *For now, anyway.*

As Star Island dwindled behind the bears, the short snow-sky day faded into shadows that seemed to grow up from the ice and reach down from the sky until the whole white world was swallowed in shades of gray and black. When Lusa looked back, the last traces of the hills that had become so familiar had vanished into the twilight. Star spirits began to appear overhead, and the silver moon hung close to the horizon like a shining claw. The bears trekked between snowbanks that glimmered in the pale light, reaching above their backs in strange shapes formed by the scouring wind.

"It's time we stopped for the night," Kallik announced, halting at the foot of a deep drift. "This looks like a good place to make a den."

"I'll help you dig," Yakone offered. He began to scrape at the bottom of the snowbank.

Lusa watched the two white bears as they burrowed vigorously into the snow. This would be Yakone's first night away from his family, away from the permanent den where he had been raised. Yet he seemed unfazed—enthusiastic, even, as he helped Kallik carve a shallow niche that would keep off the worst of the wind. The white bears' heads were close together now as they scraped at the harder, gritty snow underneath the fluffy top layer. Yakone said something that made Kallik huff with amusement, and she flicked a pawful of snow at him in response.

Lusa turned away, not wanting to eavesdrop. A pang of sorrow clawed once more at her heart when she spotted Toklo standing a little way off, watching the white bears without saying anything. After a moment he turned his back on Kallik and Yakone and raised his head to fix his gaze on the stars.

Looking up, Lusa made out the shining shape of Silaluk, the Great Bear, and close to her side the Little Bear, Ujurak. Seeing him there made her feel safe, because she knew that their friend was watching over them. It helped to comfort her grief.

But there was no comfort for Toklo. All he knew was that his friend, the other brown bear on this strange and endless journey, had left them. His bleak gaze announced his loneliness to Lusa as clearly as if he had put it into words.

"We're here, Toklo," she murmured, too faintly for the brown bear to hear. "You're *not* alone."

She knew that Toklo had been closer to Ujurak than any of them; he had taken on the responsibility of protecting the smaller brown bear. *Toklo felt like he failed when Ujurak died,* Lusa thought. *He's wrong, but how can any bear make him understand that?*

Kallik's cheerful voice sounded behind her. "The den's nearly ready."

Lusa turned to see the white she-bear backing out of the cave that she and Yakone had dug into the snow. Kallik shook herself, scattering clots of snow from her fur. "Are you okay, Lusa?" she asked. "You look worried."

Lusa glanced toward Toklo, still staring up at the stars. "He's missing Ujurak. I wish I knew what to say to him."

Kallik gazed at Toklo for a moment, then shook her head with a trace of exasperation in her eyes. "We're all missing Ujurak," she responded. "But we know that he's not really dead."

"Toklo doesn't see it like that," Lusa pointed out.

"I know." Kallik's voice softened for a moment. "It's hard out here without Ujurak. But think what we've achieved together! We destroyed the oil rig and brought the spirits back so the wild will be safe. Toklo should remember that."

"Toklo just remembers that Ujurak gave his life for us."

While Lusa was speaking, Yakone emerged from the den, thrusting heaps of newly dug snow aside with strong paws. Kallik padded toward him, then glanced back over her shoulder at Lusa.

"Ujurak has gone home," she said. "He's happy now, with his star mother. There's nothing for Toklo or any other bear to worry about."

Lusa shook her head. *It's not as simple as Kallik thinks,* she told herself. *And not as simple as* Toklo *thinks, either. He might not be here on the ground with us, but I think we've still got a lot to learn about Ujurak.*

Movement from the other bears disturbed Lusa, and icy trickles of cold probed her fur. She let out a small grunt of dismay and wrapped her paws over her snout. She wanted to sink back into sleep, as if she were letting herself slip into a warm, dark pool. Waves seemed to lap around her, luring her to sink deeper and deeper.

"Lusa!" A paw prodded her sharply, and she forced her eyes open to see Kallik's face looming over her. "Lusa, wake up!"

Faint light was seeping through the entrance to the den, and Lusa realized that morning had come. Yakone and Toklo had already abandoned their sleeping places, just leaving scoops in the snow shaped like their curled-up bodies. Lusa stretched her jaws in a massive yawn, stumbled to her paws, and followed Kallik out into the open. Yakone was standing just outside the den, while Toklo was a few bearlengths away.

"Sorry," Lusa mumbled. "It's the longsleep again. It's so hard to stay awake." All her instincts told her that she should sleep through the cold, dark months of the suncircle. Her appetite had waned, especially when there was nothing to eat but greasy seal meat, and she seemed to sleep more and more deeply. Lusa longed for the days to start stretching out, for more daylight to travel and hunt by. She couldn't think of anything else that would keep her awake.

"Try rubbing your face with snow," Yakone suggested. "That should wake you up."

Doubtfully, Lusa scooped up a pawful of snow and rubbed it over her muzzle and into her eyes. The icy sting helped to revive her, though her legs still felt heavy and clumsy.

"Thanks, that's a bit better," she told Yakone.

"We'll have to hunt before we go much farther," Kallik said. Her belly rumbled as she spoke.

Toklo gave a grunt of agreement. "I suppose there are seals around here," he said.

"Yes, it shouldn't take long to find a hole," Yakone put in. "You can leave it to me and Kallik."

Lusa winced. *That was the wrong thing to say to Toklo.* The brown bear hated feeling dependent on anyone else for food or shelter. She glanced apprehensively at the brown bear, half expecting him to growl an angry retort at Yakone, but Toklo said nothing. He glared briefly at the white male, then swung around and headed away from the den. Kallik and Yakone shared a quick glance, then followed, and Lusa brought up the rear, still struggling to shake off sleep and make her sluggish paws obey her.

Before they had traveled many bearlengths, they left the snowbanks behind and reached an area where the ice was flatter and clearer and they could see as far as the distant horizon. The dark hump of another island lay in front of them, too far away for Lusa to make out any details.

"Over there!" Yakone called, pointing with one paw.

Following his gaze, Lusa saw the dark patch of a seal hole in the ice. Kallik and Yakone were already heading toward it.

"We'll soon have a seal," Kallik promised as she settled down beside Yakone at the edge of the hole, their pelts brushing.

Toklo watched them and stood fidgeting for a few moments. "They could take all day," he grumbled at last. "I'm going to look for another hole."

Lusa trotted after him, casting anxious glances back at Kallik and Yakone; her belly churned at the thought of getting separated in this unfamiliar place, but she didn't want Toklo to think he had to hunt alone. To her relief, Toklo spotted another seal hole while Kallik and Yakone were still in sight, and he flopped down at the edge of the black circle of water with a grunt. Lusa crouched down a little way off, wishing she didn't feel so useless.

I'm not good at this sort of hunting, she thought sadly. *And I can't even talk to Toklo. He'd be angry with me for making noise and warning the seals.*

Sighing, Lusa tucked her paws underneath her belly and resigned herself to waiting. Sleep crept up on her again, as if she were plunging slowly into deep mud. She jerked back to wakefulness, her heart pounding, at the sound of Kallik's voice.

"Hey, Toklo! Lusa! Yakone caught one!"

Lusa opened her eyes to see Kallik bounding across the ice with Yakone following more slowly, dragging a seal in his jaws.

At the same moment, the water in the hole where Toklo was waiting swirled and bubbled, and Lusa caught a glimpse of a seal's nose popping above the surface. Toklo flashed out a paw, but the seal plunged down again before he could grab it.

Toklo let out a roar of rage. Springing to his paws, he rounded on Kallik. "I nearly had it! Why did you have to make all that noise?"

Kallik halted, looking puzzled. "Sorry," she said. "But there's no need to get angry. Yakone has a seal. There's plenty for all of us."

Toklo bared his teeth in a snarl. "You don't ever waste prey!" he growled.

Lusa rose to her paws as annoyance sparked in Kallik's eyes. "Please don't argue—" she began.

Both bears ignored her.

"It's a waste of prey to kill two seals when one will do," Kallik snapped.

Toklo opened his jaws to make an angry retort, but he was interrupted by Yakone, who padded up and let his prey drop to the ice at Kallik's paws. It was a big, plump seal, with enough meat on it to feed all four of them.

"Here you are," Yakone said. "Let's eat." Suddenly he seemed to become aware of the tension between Kallik and Toklo, and he glanced from one to the other uncertainly. "Is everything okay?" he asked.

"Everything's fine," Kallik replied, glaring at Toklo as if she was daring him to contradict her. "Great catch, Yakone." She crouched down on the ice beside the seal carcass and tore off a mouthful of flesh.

For a moment Lusa thought that Toklo was going to refuse his share. *Don't be so stupid,* she thought, with a pleading glance. *What does it matter who catches the prey?*

"Come on, Toklo," she said aloud, taking a bite in her turn. The seal meat was too rich and greasy for her; her belly was craving nuts and berries. But the long moons of journeying had taught her not to be fussy; bears had to take food where they could find it. *It's been so long since I had proper black bear food; I've almost forgotten what it tastes like.* "Thanks, Yakone," she mumbled around the mouthful.

Toklo hesitated a moment more. Then, to Lusa's relief, he stepped forward and bent his head to tear at the seal. "Yeah, thanks, Yakone," he grunted, as if every word were being dragged out of him. "It's a good catch."

The tension faded as the four bears ate.

But it's not over, Lusa thought. *Toklo will have to learn to get along with Yakone. If he doesn't, how will we travel together? Will we have to split up? Oh, Toklo, don't make me choose between you and Kallik!*

CHAPTER TWO

Toklo

The seal meat in Toklo's belly felt heavy as he hauled himself up. Studying Yakone, he couldn't decide whether the white male's contented expression came from being full-fed, or whether he was feeling smug that he had caught the seal.

I would have caught one if it hadn't been for Kallik.

"We ought to head for the island over there," Yakone said, jerking his muzzle toward the distant smudge on the horizon. "I've never been there myself, but some of the Star Island bears have visited it. We might pick up some prey."

"Great!" Kallik agreed. "It'll be good for Lusa to get onto land for a bit, too," she added with an affectionate look at the black bear. "She can dig down and find some leaves and roots."

Yakone set off, taking the lead without even a glance at Toklo, who bit back a snarl that rose in his throat. "Ignore me, why don't you?" he muttered to himself as he followed.

His belly churned with misery and resentment as he padded across the ice. Everything had changed; everything felt wrong. He was fed up with snow and ice and the waste of endless white that stretched around them in every direction. He longed for forests with tall trees and deep undergrowth, and warm air full of the scents of prey. He wanted long days of sunshine, or even cloud and rain, rather than brief moments of daylight where the sun barely peeped over the horizon.

And instead of Ujurak we have this white bear with us.

Somehow Toklo had never minded taking direction from Ujurak. Almost from the beginning he had realized that the small brown bear knew more than he did about certain things, in particular which way they needed to go. Even though he had protested some of Ujurak's weirder decisions, his friend had never been wrong. Except that at the end of their journey, Ujurak had been killed in the avalanche. Had he known all along that this was his destiny, that this was waiting for him when they reached the end of their quest?

Toklo felt as though every hair on his pelt, every muscle in his body, were groaning in pain because Ujurak had left them. He tried to tell himself that Ujurak wasn't really dead, that he had returned to his BirthDen among the stars. But it didn't help.

We traveled all that way together! Did I really bring him here so that he could gallop up into the sky and become a pattern of stars? Does that mean he wasn't really a brown bear at all?

Toklo had never felt so alone, not even when his mother, Oka, had driven him away and he'd had to learn to survive on his own in the forest. Back then he hadn't known what it meant to have a friend. Only a brother who had died and a mother who had seemed to hate the sight of him.

The night before, he had looked up at the stars and found the shining outline that was Ujurak, but that hadn't helped, either. It only made him realize how far away Ujurak was: skylength after skylength, much, much farther than any bear could travel.

I'd give anything to reach up into the stars and pull Ujurak back down.

Every night Toklo could look up and see his friend in the stars, but he could never hunt with him or talk to him. He couldn't pad alongside Ujurak anymore, or roll him over in a playful wrestling match, or watch his eyes light up when Toklo brought a plump goose or a juicy hare for them to share.

It won't ever be that way again.

The bears traveled on through the gray half-light of snow-sky, but the dark hump on the horizon never seemed to come any closer. A few light flakes of snow began to drift down, growing steadily thicker until they blotted out the island altogether. Plodding after the other bears through the swirling blizzard, Toklo slipped into a half dream. He imagined that he could see Ujurak just ahead of him, a small brown shape slipping easily through the dense whiteness. Although Toklo quickened his pace, Ujurak was always too far ahead. At last Toklo lost sight of him in the spiraling white flakes. His heart quickened as the snowfall started to ease and he could see more clearly ahead of him. He searched for a small brown shape against the new snow, for a trail of pawprints leading confidently on. But Ujurak wasn't there. He had never been there.

I just imagined it. Because I want to see him again, so much.

The snow stopped and the sky cleared as the brief day drew to an end. The island was noticeably closer now, with craggy hills rising dark out of the flat expanse of ice. In the thick snow they had veered away from it; as they turned to head directly for it again, Toklo became aware of his freezing cold paws and the lumps of snow clinging to his pelt. His muscles ached with weariness. Intent on following Ujurak, he hadn't noticed how hard it was to struggle through the blizzard.

"Can we rest for a bit?" Lusa whimpered. "My paws feel like they're about to fall off."

"We may as well stop for the night," Toklo responded, without giving Yakone the chance to reply. "We won't reach the island before it's completely dark." He braced himself for an argument with Yakone, but the white bear just nodded.

"There's nowhere to dig out a den," Kallik warned. "But you're right, Toklo. The island is too far away to make it there in time to find better shelter. Come on, Lusa, you can lie down next to me—but be careful that you don't fall into the long-sleep again."

Kallik and Yakone settled down side by side on the ice, and Lusa curled up beside them. After a moment's hesitation Toklo joined them, checking the wind direction and positioning himself to shelter the small black bear from the worst of the blast. She gave him a grateful look, pushing her muzzle into his shoulder, and the tiny acknowledgment made Toklo feel a little better. Then he spotted Yakone over the top of Lusa's head, and his jealousy came flooding back.

There might be hare or deer on that island, he thought. *Then I'll show that white bear how to hunt!*

In spite of the cold, Toklo was beginning to sink into sleep when Kallik's voice suddenly roused him. "Look!"

Raising his head, Toklo glanced around warily, half expecting to see an enemy approaching—another white bear, or a full-grown walrus. Then he realized that Kallik was staring up at the sky. Over the island, faint streaks of color were stretching upward: gold and ice blue and the green of forest trees. Lusa scrambled to her paws with a squeal of excitement. "The spirits are here!"

As Toklo and the others stood watching, the colors strengthened and became like shining rivers flowing across the sky from horizon to horizon, brighter even than the twinkling stars. The light billowed into huge clouds, reflecting on the bears' fur, bathing them in brightness. Green, blue, gold, orange, red, and then back to green again: Over and over the streams of light rippled through the sky, dancing to a silent heartbeat.

"The Iqniq." Yakone's voice was hushed, awestruck. "We thought they had left us forever."

"So beautiful . . ." Kallik rested her head against Yakone's shoulder. "Nisa is with them; I have to believe that. My mother is watching over me, dancing through the sky with her pelt full of colors."

"Arcturus!" Lusa spoke happily, as if she were greeting an old friend, her head tilted upward and her jaws parted as if she could drink in the sky-fire like clean, clear water.

Toklo felt as though the spirits were swirling around him, swooping down to the ice before rushing back into the sky, trying to draw him into their dance. *Are you here, Ujurak?* he asked silently. *If you are, let me see you. Please.*

But there was no response, only the shining fire that lapped around him. Toklo didn't know how long he stood there as the rivers of light played across the sky. He stared into the depths until his eyes ached, straining to make out the shape of a little brown bear running toward him. At last the colors faded and the sky turned black once more. Sighing, Toklo let himself sink down onto the ice again, huddled beside his companions. Sleep overwhelmed him like the crashing of a black wave.

Toklo paused at the mouth of a narrow cove that led between dark rocky cliffs so steep that scarcely any snow clung to them. Gulls wheeled overhead, letting out their raucous cries, but nothing else moved in the landscape.

Toklo had taken the lead when they had set out that morning across the stretch of frozen sea that still separated them from the island. Now its black cliffs loomed above them, impossible to climb. They would have to follow the cove, but Toklo didn't like the feeling of being closed in by those sharp rocks. They reminded him too much of the gully where Ujurak had been killed by the avalanche. What if another one came? Would he have to watch all his friends die under an ocean of snow?

"Come on!" Lusa exclaimed from behind him. "What are we waiting for?"

"We need to make sure there's no danger," Toklo retorted. "Wait here."

His claws clicked on the ice as he paced forward. For a moment, he had almost forgotten Ujurak wasn't with them anymore; he had almost asked his friend to change into the shape of a bird and fly up to check out the land ahead. Ujurak's ability to take on the appearance of other birds and animals—sometimes at will, sometimes by accident—had gone from being an unnerving, startling incident to something all the bears were accustomed to. At times like this, when a seagull could see much farther than a bear stuck on the ground, Toklo missed Ujurak even more fiercely.

Have you got cloudfluff in your brain? he asked, furious with himself. *We have to manage without Ujurak now.*

There was still no sound as he moved farther into the cove, so he jerked his head as a signal for the others to follow. At first the ice was smooth, a narrow arm of the sea. But soon the cove grew narrower still, until Toklo's fur brushed the cliff face on either side. At its head, a cascade of ice was poised over jagged rocks, frozen mid-waterfall as it plunged over the cliff. There was no other way out of the cove.

"Follow me!" Toklo called. "And for the spirits' sake, watch where you're putting your paws!"

He scrambled upward, trying to dig his claws into the slippery ice. *This will be a river when the sun comes back,* he thought, trying to imagine climbing against the force of water pouring down. *We'd never make it.*

At last, grunting with effort, he hauled himself onto the cliff top, and turned to help Lusa up the last few pawsteps, bending over to fasten his teeth in her scruff and drag her.

"Thanks, Toklo," Lusa panted as she flopped down beside him.

As they waited for Kallik and Yakone to scramble up, Toklo gazed out across a bare plateau, flat and featureless except where it was veined by frozen streams that had gouged down into the soil in warmer weather. A few scrubby bushes grew along their banks, their trunks twisted by the wind, and a ridge of hills rose in the distance. There was no sign of any animals they could hunt, and no prey-scent in the air.

"We need to cross those hills," Yakone announced as he reached the cliff top. "The bears who visited here said that there's a gentler slope to the sea on the other side."

Toklo grunted, then stiffened as he spotted a cluster of flat-face dens farther along the cliff. "You never said there were flat-faces here," he accused Yakone, swinging around to fix him with a glare.

What use is he if he doesn't bother telling us important stuff like that?

"I didn't know," Yakone retorted, sounding defensive. "None of the bears who visited said anything about them."

"Maybe the flat-faces haven't been here long," Kallik suggested, coming to stand at Yakone's side. "Anyway, we can easily avoid them."

Lusa had scraped away some snow from the rocks at the edge of the cliff and was sniffing at the lichen underneath. Tasting it, she made a face. "There's not much here," she commented. "And I don't see any prey for you to catch. I think we should go and check out the flat-face dens. There might be food there."

"No-claw food?" Yakone said, surprised. "I thought you were all wild bears."

"We are," Toklo growled. "The less we see of flat-faces the better."

To his annoyance, Lusa turned away from the lichen-covered rocks to contradict him. "You've been glad enough of flat-face food before now, Toklo."

Before Toklo could reply, Yakone padded up to the small black bear. "Back on Star Island, I remember you telling us that we shouldn't eat the food the no-claws threw out. You said if we did that we'd forget how to be wild bears and catch our own prey."

"I know." Lusa scrabbled awkwardly in the snow with her forepaws. "But that was different. There wasn't enough flat-face food there to feed all of you. And there was other prey for you to catch. But when you're on a journey, you have to eat what's available."

"Lusa's right." Toklo took her side for the satisfaction of arguing with Yakone. "I think we should check out the flat-face dens. But we'll wait until it gets dark."

"It'll be okay," Kallik reassured Yakone. "We've done this before."

Yakone still looked doubtful, but he didn't protest anymore.

Under cover of darkness Toklo led his companions across the plateau toward the cluster of flat-face dens. They were built in rows beside narrow BlackPaths, and a wider BlackPath led away on the far side. Several firebeasts crouched outside the dens.

"I think they're asleep," Lusa murmured, crouching at Toklo's shoulder behind a rock. "I'm pretty sure they haven't seen us."

Toklo nodded. Excitement began to course through him from ears to paws now that they were committed to the raid. *This is better than trekking across bare rocks looking for prey that isn't there!*

Here and there the gaps in the den walls glowed golden, throwing slabs of light onto the ground. Toklo could hear a high, tinny sound coming from the nearest den. But he couldn't hear the sound of flat-face voices or the thump of their pawsteps. He rose from his crouch, only to shrink back behind the rock at the sound of a door opening and slamming shut. Two male flat-faces appeared around the corner of one of the dens and climbed into the nearest firebeast. It woke up with a throaty growl, its eyes blazed out in two streams of light, and it drew smoothly away on round black paws.

"That was close," Toklo breathed, enjoying the tingle of danger.

"Those no-claws were wearing the same green pelts," Kallik pointed out, peering around the rock after the vanishing firebeast. "Just like the ones on Star Island. Why are they all alike?"

Toklo shrugged. "Who cares? They're gone now. Let's go."

He padded across the stretch of open ground between the rock and the first of the dens, with Lusa beside him and Kallik and Yakone a bearlength behind. He could sense Yakone's tension.

"Good," he muttered to himself. "He's going to learn something tonight."

"We need to go around to the back of the dens," Lusa whispered into Toklo's ear. "That's where the flat-faces keep their silver cans."

Toklo nodded. "I remember."

Glancing cautiously from side to side, he led the way across a BlackPath and through a narrow gap between two of the dens. As they emerged on the other side, he spotted three of the large silver cans clustered together near the door of the den.

Lusa gave a little bounce of excitement. "There!"

The scent of rotting flat-face food hung in the air, and Toklo felt the gush of water in his mouth. His belly rumbled as he paused to listen for the sound of flat-faces. The dens on either side were dark and silent. "Okay," he said to Yakone in a low voice, "we have to be really quiet. Dashing in and knocking the cans over will just bring the flat-faces out. Follow me and watch what I do."

Setting his paws down carefully, Toklo crept up on the cans as if he were stalking prey. He pushed at the nearest can until it tilted; Kallik slipped into place to support it as it tipped over, and together they lowered it to the ground. Lusa set her paws against the lid, not letting it come off until the can lay on its side.

"You've done this before," Yakone murmured admiringly.

Pride surged through Toklo. "Let's see what's inside. Yakone, you keep watch and let me know if any flat-faces turn up."

"Toklo, let me—" Lusa began, but Toklo ignored her.

This is my *raid!*

He plunged his head and shoulders inside the can, thrusting his nose into the mass of flat-face waste. His own body was blocking what little light there was, so he couldn't see anything, but the scent of meat was very strong. His muzzle nudged up against something smooth, and he sank his teeth into bone.

Great! Let's see what I've got.

But when Toklo tried to draw back into the open, he found that his shoulders were jammed against the smooth sides of the can. He scrabbled with his forepaws and dislodged more of the waste. The stinking scraps tumbled over his head, and he felt something sticky soaking into his fur. The air was foul, and it was getting harder to breathe.

From outside the can he heard Yakone's voice. "I think he's stuck."

Striking out with his hindpaws, Toklo felt his claws churning up the ground, but his efforts only drove him farther into the can. He fought down panic.

I'm going to be stuck in this thing forever! Or until the flat-faces find me in the morning.

"Toklo, keep still." That was Kallik's voice. "Yakone and I are going to try to pull the can off you."

Toklo stopped struggling. He knew that Kallik was being sensible, but humiliation flooded over him at the thought of being rescued by Yakone, when he had been so proud of taking the lead and teaching the white male something new. He could hear scratching from the outside of the can, and then it suddenly slid off him. He was still gripping the meaty bone in his jaws, and he dropped it to take in huge lungfuls of the cold night air. All kinds of disgusting debris clung to his fur. He stood up and shook himself, sending scraps flying all around him.

Lusa jumped back out of range. "Yuck!" she exclaimed.

Toklo took a deep breath. He wanted to stomp off and hide his shame, but there was nowhere to go in the middle of these flat-face dens. "Thanks," he grunted reluctantly to the white bears.

"Hey, that's okay." Yakone dipped his head toward the bone Toklo had dropped. "Looks like you got something, anyway."

Thick scraps of meat clung to the bone. Toklo's mouth watered again, but he stepped back, gesturing for the white bears to eat.

"If you're sure. . . ." Kallik murmured. "Thanks, Toklo."

Meanwhile, Lusa was poking about in the tipped-over can. "Hey!" she said. "There are potato sticks! They're the best. And fruit!"

"You'd better have those, Lusa," Toklo said. "Is there any more meat?"

"Hang on a moment." Lusa disappeared inside the can, and Toklo heard her rooting around. Then she backed out again. "There you go. Meat."

She dropped a crumpled paper sack at Toklo's paws. Inside, the meat looked as if something had chewed it into little pieces, and there were scraps of tough white stuff holding it together. Toklo buried his snout in the sack and wolfed down meat and white stuff all at once.

"Great, Lusa," he mumbled between gulps. "Thanks."

Yakone raised his head from the bone. "Lusa, this is a really neat trick," he commented. "And you're not scared of no-claws at all."

Lusa ducked her head, looking embarrassed. "Flat-faces are mostly okay. They don't understand about bears, though."

"Lusa's right." Toklo swallowed the last mouthful of meat. "They don't like us near their dens. So we need to get out of here."

With a quick glance around to check for firebeasts, he headed back the way they had come. The others followed. Toklo felt better to be in the lead again, though he couldn't forget the shame of getting stuck inside the can.

And it'll take forever to get the stink out of my fur!

CHAPTER THREE

Kallik

Kallik suppressed a sigh as she followed Toklo out of the no-claw denning area. *Why does he have to be so pushy, and want to lead all the time? What does it matter?*

Toklo had been difficult ever since they left Star Island. Kallik knew that he was grieving for Ujurak, and she had tried to be understanding.

But we all lost Ujurak. We're all grieving. It's not just about Toklo.

Padding in Toklo's pawsteps across the plateau and toward the distant hills, Kallik tried to focus on the good things. They had been faced with so many problems on Star Island: the poisoned seals that were making the white bears sick, and the oil rig that was endangering the wild and cutting the connection with the ancestral spirits.

We fixed it, all of it! That's an amazing achievement. And now we can go home.

Kallik's thoughts flew back to the Frozen Sea, where she and her brother, Taqqiq, had played as carefree cubs, so long ago. Their mother, Nisa, was gone forever, but Taqqiq was still alive; at least Kallik wouldn't let herself think otherwise. Hope welled up in her. *Maybe Taqqiq has gone back there. Maybe I'll see him again.*

She glanced at Yakone, who was striding tirelessly alongside her. "Did I ever tell you about my brother?" she asked.

Yakone shook his head; Kallik was warmed by the interest in his dark eyes.

"I lost him when my mother died. . . ." she began, launching into the tale of how she and Taqqiq had been separated on the ice, how she had finally found him at Great Bear Lake, where all bears gathered to celebrate the longest day of burn-sky, only to lose him again when he decided not to join Ujurak's journey.

"He hung out with some pretty unpleasant bears by the lake," Kallik confided to Yakone. "They used to steal food. Once they even stole a black-bear cub and wanted to keep him so the other black bears would give them their food!"

"That must have been hard for you," Yakone said. "After all, he was your brother, right?"

"It was very hard," Kallik admitted. "He had changed so much from the Taqqiq I knew when we were cubs. He seemed to know what his friends were doing was wrong, but he made a lot of enemies, thanks to them. I just hope he found his way back to the Frozen Sea," she went on, anticipation bubbling up inside her. "I'm going home, Yakone, and I want Taqqiq to be there!"

* * *

The trek across the island seemed to take forever. The cold was no problem for Kallik, but she hated the biting wind that flung ice crystals into her face, and the rock that was hard beneath her paws. There was little prey; Toklo managed to catch a hare, but it was thin and scrawny, hardly enough to feed one bear, let alone four. And when they tried to creep up on the gulls or the snow geese, the whole flock would take off before the bears got near enough to spring, flapping around their heads with harsh cries that sounded like mockery to Kallik.

When they reached the range of hills, they spent a whole day trying to find a path that would lead them through. That night they slept huddled in the shelter of an overhanging rock, and they finally scrambled up to the ridge in the gray light of the next day's dawn.

Kallik shivered, and her heart sank as she gazed out across the view in front of her. Beneath her paws the ground sloped gently away to another expanse of icebound sea, which stretched into the distance, with no more land in sight. That wasn't the problem; it was the state of the sea that troubled her. Close to shore, the frozen surface was sliced through with dark jagged cracks, splitting the ice into separate floes. Kallik could imagine them tilting beneath her feet, pitching her into the hungry waves.

"Are you okay, Kallik?" Lusa asked, looking up at her.

Kallik swallowed. However hard she tried, she couldn't forget how her mother had died: the swirling water between two chunks of ice, and the vicious jaws of the orca gaping to drag Nisa down. "I'm fine . . . it's just . . . it looks as if there might be orca down there."

Lusa pressed comfortingly against her side. "Look how narrow the cracks in the ice are. Even I could jump across those. We probably won't need to swim."

"And if we do, we'll deal with the orca," Yakone promised.

"You have seen orca before, haven't you?" Toklo broke in irritably. "They're not that easy to deal with."

Without giving Yakone the chance to reply, he headed down the slope; Kallik and the others had to trail after him. Kallik remembered that the last time they had encountered orca, Ujurak had been there to help them, turning into an orca himself to drive the great whales away. He wasn't here now, and she had probably made Toklo angry by reminding him.

But we can't examine every word before it comes out of our mouths just in case it upsets Toklo, she argued silently. *He'll have to accept that Ujurak isn't coming back, just like the rest of us.*

When the bears reached the edge of the sea, Kallik was relieved to see that the ice floes were bigger, and the cracks narrower, than she had thought when she'd seen them from the ridge. Lusa was right: It would be easy to leap from one to the next. Her fears began to recede a little, though she still kept a sharp lookout for the telltale fin of an orca cutting through the waves.

Yakone was scanning the water carefully, too. "I was hoping there might be seals, or fish," he explained to Kallik.

"But the sea seems empty."

Kallik shuddered. "Maybe the orca have taken all the prey."

"This is getting to be a hungry journey," Yakone commented.

"They all are," Lusa grumbled.

For once, Toklo let Kallik take the lead as they reached the shore. She listened for a moment before she set paw on the ice, studying the sounds the broken floes were making, the noise of the waves slapping around them. She chose the chunk of ice that sounded heaviest in the water, the least likely to break up again under the weight of the bears. She gathered her haunches underneath her and jumped as far from the edge of the ice as she could. It tipped and rocked beneath her, but she stayed crouched down, and she was close enough to the center to avoid sliding into the dark green water around the edges.

"Follow me closely," she called to the others. "Keep away from the edges, and stay low. The ice will move, but you should be okay."

She noticed that Yakone hung back and waited for Lusa and Toklo to jump first. Kallik guessed Toklo wouldn't like feeling that the white bear was watching out for him, but he had to accept that Yakone was better suited to this part of the journey. Lusa couldn't jump as far as Kallik, but her weight was less, so the ice rocked less disturbingly. The little black bear stayed on her belly and wriggled over to join Kallik in the middle.

Toklo took a short run up and leaped so far that he almost

flattened Lusa. The floe jerked in the water and waves slapped against the sides, but the bears huddled together and the ice quickly steadied. Finally Yakone jumped on, spreading his weight evenly among his four giant paws and only blinking when the ice lurched to one side.

"This is not going to be easy," Lusa commented between gritted teeth.

"The ice will be more solid as we get away from the shore," Yakone assured her. "And you've done great so far. Follow me to the next one." He slid cautiously toward the edge of the floe; Kallik and Toklo shuffled back to balance his weight. There was a jerk as Yakone sprang onto the next chunk of ice, but Lusa headed determinedly after him, grunting with concentration as she jumped over the gap.

"You go next," Kallik told Toklo, spreading her paws farther apart to steady the bucking ice.

Toklo looked at her. "I'll watch out for orca, I promise. I can still keep you safe, Kallik."

Kallik's heart ached. *You have nothing to prove, my friend.* Out loud she said, "I know you can, Toklo. I hope the water here is too shallow for whales, but we need to keep watch, especially when Lusa is crossing the gaps."

Toklo nodded, and for a moment everything felt the same as it had always been: the two larger bears looking out for Lusa and Ujurak, knowing that their strength and size had to keep all four of them safe. Then Yakone called out, "Is everything okay?" and Toklo's gaze clouded again. He slithered to the edge of the floe and jumped heavily across the gap. One of his hindpaws landed close to the jagged cliff that plunged down to the open waves; he grunted and snatched it back before stumbling toward Yakone and Lusa, who were watching him with wide, startled eyes. Kallik silently begged them not to comment.

"Wait for me!" she barked, trying to sound lighthearted. She let her paws slip over the ice until she felt the floe start to dip under her weight; then she pressed down with her hind-paws and pushed herself over the dark gap that snaked through the smooth white ice. She landed with her paws spread wide to keep her steady, but the other bears were already balancing the floe, and it barely moved under her weight. Kallik nodded breathlessly to her companions, then looked past them. Chunks of ice stretched toward the horizon, bobbing gently as the waves moved beneath them. Lusa was right, crossing them wouldn't be easy, but they didn't have a choice. And the sea would close up as they left the shore behind and reached the deeper, colder water.

Kallik shook her fur. "Let's keep going," she said. "We won't want to get caught on the broken ice when night comes."

As the day went on, Kallik began to notice that Lusa was lagging behind. Even though the gaps grew smaller as they came to the deeper water, she seemed to be having problems jumping from one ice floe to the next. Kallik waited on a large, steady floe for the black bear to catch up. She thought she could guess what was wrong. Since the raid on the no-claw dens, Lusa had only had meat to eat, and not much of that.

Out here on the sea, there's no chance of finding any leaves or berries for her.

When Lusa had caught up, Kallik stayed beside her, crossing with her from one floe to the next, until they reached Toklo and Yakone, who had stopped to wait for them a few bearlengths ahead.

"Everything okay?" Yakone asked.

Lusa nodded. "I'm sorry," she panted. "I just feel so tired. My paws don't seem to go where I tell them to."

"She needs to get to land," Kallik told the male bears. "Can we go any faster?"

"Oh, sure." Toklo's voice was heavily sarcastic. "Go faster, when Lusa can't keep up as it is. That's a *great* idea!"

"I just thought—" Kallik began.

"No, you didn't think," Toklo interrupted. "Why can't you just let me make the decisions, and we would all do a lot better?"

It was hard for Kallik not to lash out at Toklo and rake her claws over his ears. "You have no right to order us around!" she growled.

"Some bear has to, when you have bees in your brain," Toklo retorted, fury flaring up in his eyes. "Or you can carry on alone, and see how far you get!"

"We'd be just fine, wouldn't we, Yakone?"

"Stop it, both of you!" Lusa's voice rose into a wail. "This is all my fault," she went on miserably. "I'm holding you back."

"No, you're not." Kallik padded over to Lusa and pressed her muzzle against the little bear's shoulder. "It's harder for you, that's all. I just want to do what's best for you."

"It's not best, when you and Toklo talk about splitting up," Lusa told her in a small voice. "We belong together. You know we do."

"You're right." Kallik felt her anger die. "I'm sorry."

Toklo gave a grunt of acknowledgment, though he didn't meet Kallik's gaze. He gave Lusa an awkward prod with one paw. "Let's go a bit farther," he suggested. "Then we'll find somewhere to spend the night."

He turned and jumped onto the next ice floe. He had adapted to the way the ice pitched and rocked when he landed, and he slithered quickly to the center with his paws spread out to steady it. Kallik's irritation rose again at his assumption that he was still taking the lead, but at least he turned and waited for Lusa, checking to make sure she crossed safely before carrying on.

Thankfully, the chunks of ice grew bigger and the gaps narrower until the surface was solid and unbroken beneath their feet, though there was still no sign of land ahead. Darkness fell, with a thick cloud cover that cut off the light of the moon or stars. With nowhere to make a den, the bears huddled together to sleep.

Missing walls of snow or even of earth around her, Kallik slept uneasily. The wind swept across the ice with a thin, whining sound; she began to imagine that she could hear voices in it. Then she thought that she could hear her name. "Kallik! Kallik!"

Her eyes flew open. Toklo, Lusa, and Yakone slept beside

her, as still as stones. Kallik caught her breath as she spotted a glimmer of starlight far out over the sea. The voice calling her name seemed to be coming from there. Gradually the light grew closer, though Kallik couldn't make out what it was. Cautiously sitting up, she prodded Lusa, who was closest, with one paw. "Lusa!" she hissed.

The black bear didn't move; not even her nose twitched.

Growing fearful, Kallik faced the starry glimmer. It seemed to be moving faster now, and as it drew closer, she could make out its shape. That's when her fear vanished.

"Ujurak!" she barked joyfully.

The brown bear trotted up to her. Stars were entangled in his fur, and his eyes glowed with the silver light of two small moons.

"Kallik," he murmured affectionately, coming so close that she could see his breath clouding in the icy air.

Kallik prodded Lusa again, but still she couldn't rouse the black bear. "Why can't I wake the others?" she asked.

"They will see me soon," Ujurak promised. "But tonight I've come to visit you."

Kallik stared at him. "Why me?"

"Because I need to ask you something," Ujurak told her. "Kallik, please don't quarrel with the others. It makes your journey harder."

"I know." Shame swept over Kallik and she bowed her head. "I'm sorry."

"Toklo isn't the easiest bear to get along with." There was a spark of amusement in Ujurak's eyes. "But you have always been the one to calm ruffled fur and keep the bears together. This is your gift, Kallik."

Kallik nodded, remembering the quarrels she had stopped, the tempers she had cooled, on their long journey to Star Island. It hadn't always been easy, and sometimes she'd almost had to bite her own tongue off to keep the peace, but there was no point getting angry with the bears that you relied on for companionship, food, and shelter. She just had to think outside the moment, to the days and moons that lay beyond them. "I'll try harder," she promised.

Ujurak lifted his muzzle, leaving a trail of sparks hanging in the air. "Good. Because you and Toklo and Lusa must share your destiny—and your journey—for a while longer."

"I'll try," Kallik repeated. "This journey is too important to be risked on a single fight. We're going home, aren't we?"

Ujurak didn't answer. Instead, his eyes flared with dazzling brightness. He took a huge leap into the air and soared above Kallik's head, a streak of silver light heading for the sky.

"Good-bye, Ujurak!" Kallik called, watching him as he rose higher and higher, until he was no more than a point of light among the clouds, and then winked out.

Kallik woke to pale gray light, with a milky line on the horizon where the sun was struggling to rise. Toklo was already awake, standing a couple of bearlengths away and giving himself a vigorous scratch with one hindpaw. Yakone was stirring beside her, though Lusa still slept in a bundle of black fur. Kallik felt a rush of affection for her three companions, warmed by the knowledge that Ujurak wanted her to keep them united and focused.

"Hey!" she exclaimed, springing to her paws. "Ujurak came to me in a dream last night!"

To her dismay, Toklo spun around to face her, his eyes full of pain. "Why would he come to you and not me?" he demanded.

Why wouldn't he visit me? Kallik took a deep breath, determined to do as Ujurak asked and not quarrel. "He said you would all see him soon," she explained. "And his message was for all of us."

"But it was *you* he spoke to—or so you say," Toklo retorted.

He turned away, but not before Kallik glimpsed hurt mingling with anger in his eyes. She wished she knew what to say to him. *I know he's grieving . . . but I couldn't keep Ujurak's message to myself, could I?*

The sound of raised voices had woken Lusa, who struggled to her paws, glancing from Kallik to Toklo and back again. "Ujurak visited you?" she asked Kallik in astonishment. "What did he say?"

"He warned us about arguing with each other," Kallik said, deciding not to mention how Ujurak had told her that she was the peacemaker among them. She didn't want Toklo thinking she had been singled out even more. "He said that our destiny lies together for a while longer."

"I know *that*!" Toklo choked out, not looking at her.

"Well, okay, then," Kallik replied, trying to sound calm. She noticed that Yakone was giving her a bewildered look, as if he didn't understand why a dead bear was visiting her, or why Toklo should be so angry about it.

"I'll explain later," she murmured.

Meanwhile, Toklo was already walking away, not looking to see if the others were following him. His head was down and his shoulders hunched. Kallik sighed. *I guess all we can do is follow.*

The island they had crossed lay far behind them now, and nothing could be seen in any direction but flat white. Kallik's belly growled with hunger, but there was no sign of prey or seal holes. Lusa kept up well at the beginning of the day's journey, as if the news of Ujurak's visit had encouraged her, but as time went on, she started to fall behind again. Kallik could see how hard it was for her to keep putting one paw in front of another.

We all need food. And Lusa needs to get to land. How long can we go on like this? Kallik wondered, her anxiety rising with every pawstep. *We'll never get home at this rate. We don't even know where we are.*

A harsh squawk from overhead interrupted her thoughts. Looking up, she saw a gull, its white wings flashing silver as it circled their heads. Toklo halted to watch it.

"Please," Kallik heard him grumbling as she and the others caught up, "don't come and bother us when we have no hope of catching you."

The bird went on squawking and swooping around them, then headed off in a different direction, only to circle around and come back to them again.

"I think it wants us to follow it," Lusa said.

"Bee-brain!" Toklo snorted. "It's a *bird*."

"I know." Lusa wasn't daunted by Toklo's dismissive tone. "But maybe it's not *only* a bird. I've never seen a bird behave like that."

"We might as well follow it and find out," Kallik suggested, suddenly beginning to feel hopeful. "It can't do any harm."

Toklo let out an exaggerated sigh. "Okay. Have it your way."

Kallik took the lead as the four bears headed after the gull. It kept plunging around them, skimming the surface of the ice, then mounting into the sky again on strong curved wings. Kallik had to break into a trot to keep up.

Suddenly Yakone let out a roar. "I see a seal hole!"

He bounded past Kallik, heading for a dark circle breaking the white surface. Kallik glanced back to make sure that Toklo and Lusa were still following, then hurried after him. By the time she reached the seal hole, Yakone was crouched at the edge, his gaze fixed on the dark water. Keeping back so she wouldn't disturb him or frighten the seals, Kallik looked around again for the gull. She caught a glimpse of it, a silver fleck against the cloud cover, and then it was gone.

At the same moment, Yakone exclaimed, "Yes!"

Kallik glanced back to see that he was already dragging a seal out of the hole. It flopped around on the ice until he killed it with a swift blow to the neck.

"That's amazing!" Lusa breathed out. "We didn't even have to wait for it."

"And it's *huge*! We'll all eat well today," Kallik said, admiring the fat body. "You know," she added more hesitantly, "I don't believe this was just good luck. I think that bird was Ujurak."

"What?" Toklo exclaimed.

But Lusa was nodding eagerly. "I think you're right, Kallik. We really needed food, and the bird came to show us where to find it. That's *just* what Ujurak would do."

"Well, I think you're both cloud-brained," Toklo said grumpily. "We got lucky, that's all."

Kallik suppressed a sigh. She thought Toklo would be anxious to think that Ujurak had come to help them, because he wanted to see his friend so much.

Maybe he doesn't dare let himself believe.

Yakone was looking from one bear to another with a baffled expression on his face. "I thought Ujurak was dead."

"He was, but . . ." Kallik began.

"He rose up into the sky and turned into stars," Lusa interrupted eagerly. "And when he was with us down here, he could change into all different shapes, so I don't see why he couldn't come back as a bird if he wanted to."

Kallik was struck again by how much she missed Ujurak. "I wish he'd come back as a bear. Before he died, he seemed so real."

"He *was* real!" Lusa insisted.

"But he wasn't a real *bear*, right?" Yakone said. "Real bears don't turn into stars."

Toklo let out a disgusted snort, then turned away without speaking.

"He *was* a bear," Kallik replied. "He was just . . . different.

And now he's in the stars, and he's watching over us." She leaned over and rested her muzzle on Yakone's shoulder. "Our memories of him are real, I promise," she went on. "We just never knew that he belonged among the stars."

"I'm glad we didn't," Lusa said softly. "I think it would have made me . . . scared of him."

Yakone glanced from Kallik to Lusa and back again, his eyes still full of confusion. "I see . . . I guess," he muttered. "Can we eat now?"

"Sure we can," Kallik responded. "You made a great catch."

As the bears settled down around the seal and began to tear off chunks of juicy flesh, Kallik realized that Yakone had never really known Ujurak, not the way the rest of them had. Of course he would find it hard to understand how important the star-bear was to them.

But he'll soon learn, if Ujurak is really with us on our journey.

CHAPTER FOUR

Lusa

Lusa's belly ached as they set off across the ice again. She knew that seal meat wasn't the right food for her. But at least she had managed to conquer the worst of her exhaustion. The thought that Ujurak had guided them to the seal hole gave her new hope and helped her to ignore the pain in her belly.

Soon he'll find some food for me! Luscious berries . . . crunchy nuts . . . mmm . . .

Trekking in Toklo's pawsteps, Lusa thought she could hear the roar of rising wind, yet the air around her was barely moving.

"What's that?" she asked.

Toklo glanced around, then shrugged. "I have no idea."

Kallik and Yakone were talking quietly together as they padded side by side, a bearlength behind Lusa. Either they hadn't heard the noise, or they weren't bothered by it. Lusa tried to tell herself there was nothing to worry about, but the noise grew louder until it sounded like thunder rolling overhead.

Eventually Toklo halted. "For the spirits' sake . . ." he muttered.

Lusa stared around until she spotted a brightly colored speck on the horizon, and she jerked her muzzle toward it. "Look—over there!"

Toklo peered in the direction she was pointing. "It could be a firebeast."

Kallik and Yakone halted, too, and the four bears waited for the creature to come nearer.

"With all the ice to choose from, it looks as if it's heading straight for us," Toklo grumbled.

As the firebeast drew closer, Lusa could see it more clearly. The lower part of its body was black, with red stripes down the side. The upper part was the warm reddish brown of earth and it stretched up higher and higher, level after level.

"It's a firebeast in the shape of a mountain!" she breathed out.

The noise was clearer, too. Along with the roaring there was a loud cracking sound, and she could see something dark lapping at the bottom edge of the firebeast. Splinters of ice bobbed wildly on churned-up water, shining with grease. There was a harsh tang in the air, and Lusa remembered the reek of oil they had encountered in the Last Great Wilderness.

Toklo let out a roar. "It's breaking through the ice! *Run!*"

Cold terror paralyzed Lusa for a heartbeat.

"Run, bee-brain!" Toklo charged into her, pushing her away from the route of the firebeast.

At the same moment, she heard the crack of a firestick. Glancing up at the firebeast, she spotted a flat-face leaning over the side, high above her. He was so far away that the firestick in his hand looked no bigger than a twig, but she heard it crack again, and chips of ice spurted up a pawlength from Toklo. The brown bear let out a defiant roar, and fled.

Lusa scrambled after him, her paws slipping on the ice in her panic. The firebeast seemed to be approaching much faster now, the huge red and black shape looming over her. The ice began to break under her paws, slopping water over her legs; she leaped over it and ran on.

"Keep together!" Kallik howled. "We can't get split up!"

The ice was breaking up all around Lusa. The roar and crash of the firebeast filled the air. Her friends' voices, and the crack of the firestick, were drowned in it. Lusa caught a glimpse of Toklo balancing precariously on a tiny chunk of ice, then jumping onto a bigger ice floe beside it, but she couldn't see Kallik and Yakone.

Suddenly Lusa couldn't run any farther. A gap too wide to leap had opened up between her and the more solid ice beyond. The floe where she was standing tossed up and down in the churning water, and she struggled to keep her balance.

"Help!" she wailed.

All around her, chunks of ice were smashing against one another as the water heaved from the passage of the firebeast. Lusa knew that if she fell in, she would be crushed among them. A wave broke over her, soaking her fur. Her paws slipped, and she clawed helplessly at the smooth surface of the ice. She breathed in the stink of oil.

"Help!" she called again.

She felt something bump against her ice floe and let out a squeal of panic. Then she saw Yakone in the water, swimming strongly and pushing her chunk of ice with his muzzle. He propelled it through the tossing waves until it nudged against a more solid stretch, where Toklo and Kallik were waiting.

Lusa jumped off the ice floe, landed awkwardly, and crouched shivering in the snow.

Kallik bent over her. "Are you okay?"

"I think so," Lusa croaked.

Yakone heaved himself out of the water and gave himself a good shake, then padded over to Lusa and touched her shoulder with his muzzle. "Okay now?"

Lusa nodded. "Thank you, Yakone. That was really brave."

Kallik was looking at the white male with shining eyes, while Toklo ducked his head, half embarrassed.

"Yeah, it was great," he grunted. "Thanks, Yakone. Lusa's an annoying little chatterbox, but I'd be sorry if we lost her."

The firebeast was still grinding past, shouldering its way through the ice. Suddenly more ice chips spurted up around the bears' paws; Lusa hadn't heard the crack above the thundering roar of the firebeast, but she could see two flat-faces leaning over the side now, their firesticks pointing toward her and her friends.

"We've got to get out of here," Toklo said roughly. "Fast!"

CHAPTER FIVE

Toklo

Toklo looked around, wrenching his head so fast that his neck hurt. There was nowhere on the ice to take cover from the flat-faces and their firesticks. The ice they were standing on was beginning to split, dark cracks running across it. Toklo could feel it shuddering beneath his paws. His heart pounded as he imagined the huge firebeast swerving to come after them.

"Swim!" Yakone roared suddenly. "We've got to swim!"

He was pointing across the channel through the ice that the firebeast had left behind it. Toklo stared in disbelief at the churning water with the sheen of oil on its surface, and the chunks of ice that tossed and crashed against one another.

"Yakone's right," Kallik said, as another shot from the firesticks whined over the bears' heads. "We need to get to the other side of the firebeast, away from the firesticks."

Toklo understood. But it wasn't as easy as the white bears seemed to think. "Lusa can't swim that far," he objected, glancing down at the shivering black bear. "She's exhausted already. I'm not leaving her."

Lusa raised her head. "I'll be okay," she insisted, but her voice was shaking.

"Sure you will," Kallik said. "We'll help you."

"Toklo, just go!" Yakone growled.

Toklo knew this was no time for argument. Bounding over the crumbling ice, he plunged into the water and struck out strongly for the other side of the channel. Glancing back, he saw that Lusa was swimming with Kallik on one side of her and Yakone on the other.

If there are bear spirits in these waters, help us now! he begged.

The firebeast loomed above him. It was moving away, but Toklo couldn't help expecting it to change direction at any moment and come roaring back to swallow them. At least they were out of the flat-faces' line of fire.

And there won't be any orca, he thought. *The firebeast will have scared anything away for skylengths!*

His paws paddling frantically, Toklo reached the other side of the channel and tried to scramble out of the water. At first the ice broke away under his weight, and the sea surged around him as he flopped back into it. Fighting back panic, he kept going, breaking a new channel until at last he reached a place where the ice was thick enough to support him. He hauled himself out and looked around for his companions.

Kallik had climbed out of the water a few bearlengths farther down the channel. She was leaning over to help Lusa out, while Yakone gave the little black bear a boost on his shoulders.

Toklo bounded over and got a grip on Lusa beside Kallik, helping to haul her over the rim of the ice. Lusa collapsed, water streaming from her black fur. She retched miserably and coughed up a few mouthfuls of the oily water.

"Thanks," she choked out. "I'll be fine."

Kallik stood watching the firebeast as it roared away and the water in the channel gradually grew still. "I think it got fed up with chasing us," she said. "After all, we're not much prey for a thing that size."

Toklo nodded, beginning to relax as the noise died away and the firebeast dwindled into the distance. "Good riddance," he muttered.

Yakone clambered out of the water and padded up. "Hey, Toklo, you're bleeding," he said. "It must have been those firesticks."

Toklo started. "What?"

Yakone angled his snout toward Toklo's shoulder. Twisting his head to look, Toklo saw a furrow through his fur, and a reddish scratch on the flesh underneath. Blood was oozing out of it, trickling through his pelt and dripping into a scarlet puddle on the ice.

"I didn't notice," he said. In the biting cold he could hardly feel the sting of the wound. "It's nothing."

"It's not nothing," Yakone argued. "You might not be badly hurt, but you'll leave a trail of blood, and that could attract hostile white bears."

Toklo took a breath, determined not to lose his temper at being bossed around. Yakone had been right about swimming the channel, and he was right about this. "I'll take care of it," he responded.

"I wish Ujurak were here. He knew all about healing," Kallik fretted.

"Yeah, he'd have known which herb would stop the bleeding," Lusa put in, reviving enough to give Toklo's injury an anxious sniff.

Toklo crushed down the memory of Ujurak and let his gaze travel around the desolate landscape. "Lusa, this is the ice," he pointed out. "There are no herbs. In any case, the scratch will heal soon enough," he added impatiently.

He twisted his head again and drew his tongue along the wound, only to jerk away with a growl deep in his throat. Touching his freezing fur had given him a burning pain in his tongue, far worse than the sting of the scratch.

"Toklo, what's the matter?" Lusa asked.

"It burns," Toklo said. "I won't do that again."

Instead, he scooped up a pawful of snow and packed it down over the wound, hoping that would be enough to stop the bleeding. Cold stabbed through him, but he held the snow in place until it was tightly wadded into his fur. He hoped it would stay there once he started to move.

"Well?" he demanded, meeting his friends' worried gazes. "What are we waiting for?"

This time Toklo let Yakone take the lead as they plodded away from the channel. The firebeast vanished into the distance, and soon the channel it had broken was no more than a dark line behind them on the ice. The reek of oil faded, though some of it still clung to their fur.

When the daylight began to ebb, there was still no sign of land anywhere on the endless ice. Toklo's shoulder ached, though at least his wound had stopped bleeding. Kallik and Yakone quested from side to side, looking for seal holes, but they'd had no luck when darkness put an end to their search.

"Ujurak, are you there?" Toklo heard Lusa speaking softly. "Give us another sign, please."

Toklo glanced up hopefully, half expecting to spot Ujurak's starry shape galloping toward them. But there was no response to the black bear's plea, and his tiny shoot of hope withered and died.

Curled up to sleep in the open, Toklo felt a furry body huddling next to him. A warm tongue rasped busily over his wound. He half opened his eyes to see who it was, but it was too dark to make out more than a humped shape beside him. He let out a grunt of gratitude, then gave a long sigh as he relaxed. The gentle licking continued until he drifted into sleep.

When Toklo woke next morning, it was already light, and the cloud cover overhead was beginning to break up. Lusa was sitting next to him, thoughtfully washing her paws. She glanced over at Toklo as he sat up in alarm.

"Where are Kallik and Yakone?" he asked.

"They went to see if they could find some prey," Lusa responded calmly. "Look, they're coming back."

Glancing around, Toklo spotted the two white bears trekking over the ice toward them. Shame swept over him; obviously his companions had let him sleep so he could rest his wound. It felt much better already, enough for him to be able to help the others hunt.

"Hey, Lusa," he began awkwardly. "Thanks for lying beside me last night, licking my wound."

Lusa looked surprised. "I didn't. I went straight to sleep."

Kallik and Yakone came up in time to hear the exchange. Kallik was carrying a huge fish in her jaws.

"You must have dreamed it," she said, dropping her catch at Toklo's paws.

"I'm glad it was a good dream," Lusa added, with an affectionate look at Toklo.

Toklo shrugged. "Good catch, Kallik. That's a nice change from seal."

But as all four bears crowded around the fish to eat their share, Toklo couldn't shake the memory of what had happened during the night. He *knew* he hadn't dreamed it.

Some bear came and helped me, because I was cold and my shoulder was aching.

He swallowed the last gulp of fish and drew away from the others, looking up into the sky, which grew brighter as the clouds cleared away.

"Was it you, Ujurak?" he whispered, feeling a bit foolish to be talking to the air, but hoping that his friend's starry ears could hear him.

CHAPTER SIX

Kallik

Anxiety, sharp as an orca's tooth, nagged at Kallik as the bears set off again. She could tell that Lusa was weakening, however much the black bear tried to hide it. She could see pain in the smaller bear's eyes and knew that her belly was still aching, too. When Kallik looked around, she could see nothing but the wastes of endless ice.

When are we going to find land?

"Are you okay?" Yakone asked, coming to pad alongside her. "You look worried."

"I am worried, about Lusa," Kallik explained. "This isn't the right place for her."

"But she traveled as far as Star Island," Yakone pointed out. "She should be able to get home again, right?"

"It's not as simple as that," Kallik replied. She glanced across to where Lusa was trudging along beside Toklo. They hadn't been moving long, but already Lusa's paws were dragging, as if walking was a massive effort for her. And Toklo was limping; Kallik guessed that his wounded shoulder had stiffened overnight, even though the skin had already started to heal. "For one thing," she went on, "we're not going back the same way we came. The ice here all looks the same, and I have no idea where we are."

Yakone looked puzzled. "You found your way before."

"But Ujurak was with us then."

Yakone's blank look made Kallik realize that this was no explanation at all, as far as he was concerned. "Ujurak was . . . special." She looked for the words that would make her friend understand. "Sometimes he seemed so young and inexperienced, as if he'd just stepped out of his BirthDen. And at other times he was so wise. When we were with him, we were often lost, but somehow he always seemed to know where we should go next." Her voice shook as she remembered the bright young bear. "And he had such confidence that we would end up in the right place."

"I think I see," Yakone said slowly, though Kallik wasn't sure that he did. "But why is it so different now? This time you know where you're going. Home! It shouldn't be so hard."

Kallik sighed. "I told you, everything looks the same. I don't know if we're traveling in the right direction. For all I know, we've gotten spun around, and we're heading back to Star Island."

"No, not possible." Yakone gave her shoulder a comforting nudge with his muzzle. "If we were going back there, I'd know."

Kallik was slightly reassured by what Yakone said. She wanted to enjoy the journey, and her fur tingled with excitement when she thought of reaching the Frozen Sea again and finding Taqqiq. And it was great to have Yakone with her. But her anxieties outweighed all that.

We might be wandering here forever!

Yakone gave her another nudge. "See that snowbank up ahead?"

Kallik nodded.

"Race you!"

Yakone took off in a flurry of snow and ice crystals. Kallik bounded after him, reveling in the feeling of her muscles bunching and stretching, her powerful legs eating up the distance. She reached the snowbank a bearlength ahead of Yakone. Scooping up a pawful of snow, she spun around and flung it at him. Laughter bubbled up inside her at the expression of surprise on his face.

"I'll get you for that!" he threatened.

"You'll have to catch me first!"

With a growl of mock fury, Yakone launched himself at her. Kallik slipped to one side, and he plowed straight into the snowbank. His paws threw up clots of snow as he scrabbled to get out. Then he turned and in the same movement flung a cloud of snow into Kallik's face.

She ducked, loving the icy spatter of snow on her muzzle and forehead. *I haven't had such fun since I played with Taqqiq!*

"Look, Lusa, we've found a couple of white-bear cubs." Toklo's voice came from behind Kallik; to her relief he sounded amused. "Do you think they'd make a good meal?"

"I'd like to see you try," Kallik challenged him, spinning

around to confront the brown bear. She would have sprung at him and bowled him over for a play-fight, but she remembered in time about his injured shoulder.

Yakone scrambled up out of the snow, shaking it from his fur. "White bears aren't good to eat," he said, baring his teeth. "They're far too tough."

Kallik shot Toklo a swift glance and was relieved to see that the grizzly hadn't taken Yakone's bared teeth as a threat. The two males faced each other with amusement in their eyes. *Good!* she thought. *We'll get along a lot better if Toklo doesn't feel he has to compete with Yakone all the time.*

As the journey over the ice continued, Kallik began to feel as if she had known Yakone all her life. Or was it just that they shared the same instincts, along with the same white fur? When they hunted together, they seemed to know each other's ideas before speaking them aloud. And it was great to share her thoughts with another white bear. However close she felt to Lusa and Toklo, their true homes were under different skies, far from the ice, and she couldn't expect them to see the world as she did.

"It was so hard when the Frozen Sea melted," she remarked to Yakone as they padded together across the ice. "I didn't know how to find food on land. Lusa and Toklo helped me when I got to know them, but for a long time before that I was on my own."

Yakone nodded, with a grunt to tell Kallik he was listening.

"We all met at Great Bear Lake," Kallik went on. "You

remember, I told you how Taqqiq was there with the bears who stole food. You've never seen so many bears all together! White bears and brown and black bears . . . They had all traveled there for the Longest Day, and an old white bear called Siqiniq spoke the words of a ceremony. I wish you'd been there, Yakone!"

"So do I," Yakone replied.

He sounded brusque, as if he didn't want Kallik to go on talking.

Have I said something to upset him? Kallik wondered. *Maybe he's just not interested.*

She cast a nervous glance at Yakone, admiring his strong muscles and reddish-tinged pelt, but asking herself if she really knew him as well as she thought.

A moment later, Yakone exclaimed, "Look—a seal hole!" and cast her a look bright with friendliness before bounding off across the ice.

Kallik followed, still not sure if she had imagined Yakone's brief coldness.

A few sunrises later, Kallik woke with a new scent in her nose. The other bears were still sleeping, huddled around her, and she edged away carefully before rising to her paws and giving the air a good sniff.

Land!

Excitedly she bounded back to the others and began prodding them awake. "There's land ahead! I can smell it!" she announced.

Toklo swatted at her sleepily with one paw. "Okay. Great," he muttered.

Kallik prodded him again. "Wake up, Toklo! Land!"

Lusa had scrambled up and was staring around through bleary eyes. "Land? Where?"

"I can't see it yet," Kallik replied. "But I know it's there."

"Kallik's right," Yakone agreed. He gave the air a deep sniff, then swiveled around until he chose a direction. "That way."

Toklo, awake at last, lumbered to his paws and stood beside him. "I can smell it, too," he said after a moment. He let out a satisfied sigh. "Let's go. I can't wait to get my claws on some real prey!"

Dark clouds were low on the horizon in the direction they were heading, and for a long time they couldn't see anything but the ice stretching out in front of them. At last the clouds began to clear, and Kallik spotted bulky snow-covered hills looming up in the distance.

"That's a pretty big island!" Toklo exclaimed, halting to stare at it.

Though she didn't say so, Kallik thought that the line of the hills looked familiar. *The Frozen Sea could be just beyond that range. I might be really close to home—and Taqqiq!*

The bears bounded forward, running faster and faster in their eagerness to reach the land. Even Lusa somehow found the energy to keep up. Anticipation surged through Kallik as she splashed through pools of melting ice and the shore grew nearer with every pawstep.

But when she was only a few bearlengths away from the beach, Kallik's excitement suddenly died. She halted and let the other bears gallop past her. Her belly hurt as if she had swallowed a stone, and there was a chill underneath her fur. The snowy hills that lay across their path suddenly felt unwelcoming, as if something were warning her not to set paw there.

There's something here that doesn't feel right. Is this how Ujurak felt when he saw a sign?

Then she gave her fur a good shake. *I'm just imagining things. This is the land we've hoped for, with prey and somewhere to shelter and the right kind of food for Lusa. And it* must *be the way to the Frozen Sea.*

But Kallik's paws still felt heavy as she padded forward to join her companions on the beach.

CHAPTER SEVEN

Lusa

As Lusa's paws felt the stony beach under the snow, her belly began to howl for something to eat that wasn't meat. Desperately she bounded across the stretch of pebbles and scrambled up the slope beyond, stopping to scrape the snow aside when she thought there must be soil underneath.

Before she had dug far, she spotted a flicker of movement out of the corner of her eye. Looking up, she saw two black dots against the white background, and she realized that she was looking at an Arctic hare, almost invisible in its white pelt.

"Is that you, Ujurak?" she called, heading toward it. *I knew he would come and help me find leaves and roots. I hope they're tasty!*

As Lusa drew closer, the hare leaped up and began to run. Where it had been sitting she found a hole in the snow, stretching right down to some grass.

"Thanks, Ujurak!" Lusa exclaimed aloud, scrabbling to enlarge the hole.

As she spoke, Toklo sprang past her, racing after the hare. Lusa watched, horror-stricken. "No, Toklo, stop!" she yelled.

But it was too late. Toklo didn't hear her. He caught up to the hare and swiped it with one massive paw. The hare fell to the ground and lay limp.

Lusa bounded over to him and gave the hare a tentative prod. It was definitely dead, its neck broken. "You killed Ujurak!" she howled.

"What? That's cloud-brained . . ." Toklo's voice died away, and he looked up at Lusa, his eyes stricken. "It's a hare!" he insisted.

"I think it was Ujurak," Lusa said quietly. "He showed me a place I could dig down through the snow to find food."

"What? No!"

Kallik and Yakone trotted up. Kallik bent her head to sniff at the body of the hare. "Are you sure?" she asked Lusa.

"Not *sure* . . . but I think it was him."

"But Ujurak is already dead, right?" Yakone put in, sounding bewildered. "So how can you kill him again?"

"Ujurak could take any shape he wanted to when he was with us, so maybe he can still do that," Kallik explained. "I think he was the bird who showed us the seal hole, back on the ice. So I guess if his spirit took the shape of a real animal, he could be killed again."

"He didn't!" Toklo's voice rose to a desperate roar. "It's a hare! It's prey!"

"You can't eat it," Lusa whimpered. She thought her heart would crack with pain at losing Ujurak again and sorrow for the guilt she could see rising in Toklo.

Toklo stood for a moment looking down at the body of

the hare. Then he began scraping at the snow until he had dug a hole big enough to bury it. Taking the hare's fur gently between his teeth, he dragged it into the hole and began to cover it with snow.

"Good-bye, Ujurak," Lusa murmured. "I hope your spirit can find its way back to the stars."

When the hare was completely buried, all four bears stood silently for a moment beside the tiny mound of snow. Lusa glanced at Toklo and Kallik and saw her own sorrow reflected in their eyes. Then without a word they swung around and began to trek away, farther inland. When Lusa looked back after a few pawsteps, she couldn't even distinguish the burial place from the surrounding snow.

Hunger still gnawed at her belly, but the death of the hare-Ujurak had upset her so deeply that she couldn't find the energy to dig under the snow for more roots and leaves. The excitement and optimism she had felt when she was racing toward the island was long gone. It felt as though that had happened to another bear, a long time ago.

Maybe starting out so badly is an omen, she thought. *There must be more trouble ahead.*

The land sloped gently upward; the surface was uneven, as the snow hid rocks or humps in the ground, and here and there a boulder broke the surface like a dark island in a white sea. Looking ahead, Lusa could see a ridge of snow-covered hills lying across their path, and beyond them in the distance the steep slopes of mountains, their sharp peaks cutting the sky.

"I'm pretty sure I recognize those hills," Kallik said hopefully. "The Frozen Sea could be just on the other side."

"But isn't the Frozen Sea much farther than that?" Lusa objected, remembering the long journey they had made to Star Island.

"We're not going back the same way, though," Kallik pointed out. Her gaze was fixed on the hills ahead, but Lusa thought she could make out worry in her eyes. She wasn't as excited as Lusa would have expected her to be if she thought she was really close to home.

Is there something Kallik's not telling me? Lusa wondered. *Does she feel something bad about this island, too?*

As they trekked on, Lusa kept spotting the marks of animals in the snow: bird tracks and the pawprints of hares, and bigger prints that must have been made by other bears.

"The hunting should be good around here," Yakone remarked.

"But how can we hunt?" Toklo demanded fiercely, speaking for the first time since leaving the shore. "Any animal might be Ujurak coming back to us again."

"But . . ." Yakone sounded as confused as he always did when the bears talked about Ujurak. "You said you killed him and buried him back there."

Toklo shook his head savagely but didn't respond.

"If Ujurak could come back once, he could come back again," Lusa explained, though she wasn't sure how to make Yakone understand when she wasn't sure she understood herself. All she knew was that Ujurak hadn't abandoned them when he rose from outside the cave on Star Island and took his place among the stars.

"Well, then, if he comes back, we haven't really killed him," Yakone pointed out practically.

"We haven't killed him *forever,*" Lusa replied. "But it must hurt, being killed. None of us would want to hurt Ujurak."

"No, but . . ." Yakone shook his head, baffled. "His stars are always up in the sky, aren't they? I've watched you all looking out for him at night. So how can he be down here as well?"

"I don't know," Kallik admitted. "When he was with us on our first journey, the stars were always there, too. It's as if he can be in two places at once."

"That's right," Lusa said. "Yakone, Toklo's right when he says that any of the animals we meet could be Ujurak in another shape."

"But how are we supposed to recognize him?" Yakone asked.

"We can't!" Toklo burst out in a frustrated roar, halting and facing the other bears. "Ujurak always caused problems when he was alive, and he's still causing them now that he's dead."

"But that's just it. Is he really dead?" Lusa pressed herself comfortingly against Toklo's shoulder, but the brown bear shied away from her and stood with his back turned, staring down at the snow.

"I don't know," he replied, his voice thick and choked. "Is he? Or has he turned into stars? He's not a brown bear anymore. Maybe he never was one."

Lusa knew that Toklo had tried to hide his grief and the

turmoil in his mind about Ujurak's death. He thought that he always had to be strong.

"Ujurak was our friend," she murmured. "Does it really matter what he was?"

"It matters to me," Toklo snarled. "If he really was that hare, then I killed him!"

"But you couldn't have known," Kallik said, her eyes warm with sympathy.

"I *should* have known," Toklo retorted. "Lusa did."

Kallik glanced at Lusa, shaking her head. There didn't seem to be any way of jerking Toklo out of his grief and anger.

Yakone broke the silence. "None of this helps us decide what to do now," he stated. "We *have* to hunt, or starve."

Toklo swung around on him, his teeth bared. "Then I'll starve," he growled. "You can do what you want. Kill him again. What do *you* care? He wasn't your friend."

Yakone reared back, startled. "Hey, I never said I wanted to kill him."

Kallik sighed, touching Yakone's shoulder briefly with her muzzle. "We'd better go on," she said. "Maybe Ujurak's spirit will find a way to tell us where he is."

Toklo snorted but didn't protest, and took the lead as they set out again toward the snow-covered ridge. Before they had gone very much farther, they came to a swathe of level ground cutting across the rocky landscape, with deep furrows running along it through the dirty snow. Lusa sniffed the air and picked up the faint tang of oil.

"I think this is a BlackPath," she said. "That means there

are flat-faces somewhere nearby."

"Oh, seal rot!" Yakone exclaimed. "Can't we ever get away from no-claws?"

"I think you're right," Kallik told Lusa. "Those furrows could be the marks of firebeast paws."

Lusa dug down into the snow until her claws scraped the hard surface of the BlackPath. "Let's follow it," she suggested.

"Follow it?" Toklo stared at her. "Now I know your brain is full of cloudfluff!"

"No, it's not," Lusa responded. "Don't you see? If we follow the BlackPath, we'll get to the flat-face dens, and then we can find some food."

"No-claw food *again*?" Yakone asked disapprovingly.

Kallik blinked. "Lusa, I really don't want to do that."

"We have to eat something," Lusa pointed out. "And if we find flat-face food, at least we can be sure that it's not Ujurak. It has to be better than starving."

"Well . . . okay," Kallik conceded. "What do you think, Toklo?"

"I think bears and flat-faces don't mix," Toklo replied, then added reluctantly, "but it might be the best plan, for now."

"Okay," Kallik agreed.

Yakone shrugged, but Lusa could tell he was still uneasy.

Cautiously the bears began to pad along the edge of the BlackPath. Lusa kept her ears pricked for the sound of firebeasts, but the only things she heard were the whisper of wind over the snow and the distant cries of seabirds high above. They were still heading for the range of hills, though not by the most direct route. The BlackPath curved around a wide, flat space that Lusa guessed was a frozen lake, then up a shallow slope and more steeply down into a valley beyond.

"There!" Kallik called out as they reached the top of the slope. "I can see the no-claw dens."

Lusa plodded up beside her and looked out across the valley. On the opposite side she could just make out a large flat-face denning area; it was hard to see, because most of the dens had white walls, and snow covered the roofs.

"That's a lot of no-claws," Yakone commented; Lusa thought he sounded nervous. "I've never seen so many dens all in one place."

There weren't many flat-faces on Star Island, Lusa recalled. "We'll only go to the edge of them," she told him. "Just as far as it takes to find something to eat."

Yakone only grunted.

As they drew closer to the denning place, another, wider BlackPath joined the one they were following. Not far past the junction, Lusa heard the roar of a firebeast coming up from behind, and she leaped to one side as it plowed past through the snow, spattering her fur with filthy snowmelt.

"That was huge!" Yakone exclaimed, staring at the firebeast as it growled away toward the denning place.

"At least it didn't take any notice of us," Kallik said.

"Let's get away from here," Toklo growled as the roar of yet another firebeast sounded in the distance. "Now that we can see the flat-face dens, we don't need to follow the BlackPath."

Without waiting to see if the others agreed, he headed

down into the valley, cutting across the open ground toward the nearest dens. Lusa followed, slipping and stumbling down the snow-covered slope, while Kallik and Yakone brought up the rear. By now the daylight was fading, much to Lusa's relief. It would be easier to stay hidden in the flat-face area if it was dark, and there wouldn't be as many firebeasts and flat-faces moving around, either.

The line of hills reared up above the low roofs of the denning area. Lusa thought that they looked ominous, as if they were frowning down on bears and flat-faces alike.

I really *don't like this place,* she thought. *If Kallik's Frozen Sea is only on the other side of those hills, I don't think I want to stay there.*

They had reached the outskirts of the denning area when Lusa heard the roar of another firebeast. She glanced around, but there were no BlackPaths nearby, and the roar was growing louder and louder, battering against her ears.

Then she heard Toklo call out, "Great spirits!"

The brown bear was looking up. Following his gaze, Lusa saw a metal bird screaming across the sky straight for them. But this wasn't like the birds she had seen flying above the Last Great Wilderness, with their whirling metal wings on their heads. This was much bigger; it had rigid wings that stuck out at the sides, and glaring eyes that looked down at her. As Lusa watched, transfixed by terror, curved claws emerged from the underside; she could imagine it swooping down to catch her and carry her off to its nest.

"Run!" she squealed, taking off across the snow.

The metal bird bore down on her. Its screeching filled the

whole sky, and in her panic Lusa had no idea where she was running. She glanced up to see the glaring lights above her head, fell over her own paws, and rolled in the snow. Scrambling up, she ran on again, expecting at any moment to feel those cruel talons meeting in her back.

Suddenly the lights vanished. The screaming of the metal bird began to die away. Lusa halted, panting, and realized that she was standing in a narrow pathway between two flat-face dens. She had fled into the denning area. Her heart was pounding so hard she thought it would burst out of her chest, but for the moment she was safe.

Where did the bird go? Did it catch one of the others?

Lusa forced herself to be calm, to steady her breathing, and to look around for the others. The narrow pathway stretched in both directions; a light shone from one end, and a firebeast rolled past. The other end was dark. Sniffing the air, Lusa caught the tang of firebeasts and a faint trace of rotting flat-face food, but there was no scent of bear. She couldn't see any of her friends.

"Toklo?" she called cautiously, afraid of flat-faces hearing her. "Kallik? Yakone?"

There was no reply.

"I'd better get out of here and find them," Lusa muttered to herself.

Everything was quiet now, except for firebeasts growling in the distance. Lusa had no idea where she was or what route she had followed to get there. The snow on the path was dirty and half melted, so she couldn't even follow her own pawprints back to where she'd left the others.

She was sure that she hadn't crossed a BlackPath, so she headed away from the lighted end of the pathway, clinging to the shadows of the den walls that rose sheer on either side. At the end of the pathway she peered cautiously out from behind the nearest den. An open stretch of ground lay in front of her, bounded on all four sides by more dens. BlackPaths led away from the ground on both sides, and there were two or three other narrow paths like the one where Lusa was hiding.

"I don't remember this place," she murmured. "I don't remember *anything*!" She crept out into the open, only to dart back into cover a moment later at the sound of flat-face voices.

Two male flat-faces appeared from one of the narrow paths and crossed the open space, talking loudly. At first Lusa thought they were heading for her, and she braced herself to run. But then they disappeared into one of the nearby dens, the door snapping shut behind them.

Lusa took a deep breath. *Now or never,* she told herself.

Leaving the shelter of the pathway, she scurried across the open space. Her heart began to pound again from fear of being in the open. It felt like a long, long way to the safety of the paths on the other side. Before she reached them, she heard the roar of an approaching firebeast. The glaring beams of its eyes swept across her and swiveled back, fixing her in the harsh light. A flat-face shouted something.

Lusa was frozen with fear. Then, as she heard the thump of flat-face paws hitting the ground, she forced herself to run. More shouting broke out behind her. The mouth of the nearest pathway was just in front of her. But as she plunged into the darkness between the dens, she caught a glimpse of a black shape flying in the air over her head. The next moment, something tangled in her paws and she crashed to the ground.

When Lusa tried to get up, she found herself caught in some sort of mesh made out of tough strands like twisted vines. She struggled wildly but only managed to tangle herself further. Frantic to escape, she bit through one of the strands. It gave way, but two flat-faces were already bending over her, one on each side.

"Help!" she squealed. "Toklo! Kallik! Help me!"

CHAPTER EIGHT

Toklo

Toklo had fled when the metal bird had come shrieking out of the sky. He had lost sight of his companions, but when the bird swooped out of sight over the rooftops of the flat-face dens, there was no struggling bear shape in its claws. He realized that they had all escaped.

Now all I have to do is find them.

His injured shoulder was stinging, but the wound hadn't stopped him from moving fast when he'd needed to. Looking around, he saw he was standing on a BlackPath in the depths of the denning area. Snow was piled in huge mounds on either side, leaving the black surface clear for firebeasts. Toklo scrambled over the nearest heap and took cover in the shadow of an overhanging den roof.

When he looked up, he could see the line of the hills beyond the jumble of dens, and he realized roughly the direction he would need to take. *I suppose the best thing to do is go back to the place where we split up. I bet the others will do the same.* His belly lurched with fear. *If they can.*

He was turning to pad alongside the BlackPath when he heard a high-pitched squeal of terror. "Help me!"

Lusa!

Toklo froze, trying to work out where the cry had come from. A narrow pathway gaped in front of him, and darting down it, he spotted Lusa at the far end. She was on the ground, struggling; two flat-faces wearing thick pelts were bending over her. Toklo let out a roar and charged toward them.

The two flat-faces straightened up, then backed away. To Toklo's relief, neither of them was carrying a firestick. They shouted something; then one of them turned and ran toward a firebeast crouching at the far end of the pathway.

"Lusa!" Toklo bellowed.

Lusa was still struggling. As he reached her side, Toklo saw that she was tangled in some kind of mesh made out of twisted vines. She was biting through it, but the hole she had made was still too small to crawl through.

Toklo thrust his muzzle close to hers and began tearing through the mesh. "Hurry!" he growled. He knew it wouldn't be long before the flat-faces came back with firesticks.

Suddenly the mesh ripped open in their teeth, and Lusa scrambled free. "Thanks, Toklo!" she gasped.

"Don't talk—run!"

Toklo turned and bounded toward the end of the pathway, with Lusa scurrying behind him. He heard more shouting from the flat-faces, and the pounding of their paws, but not the crack of firesticks. Emerging from the end of the pathway, Toklo shoved Lusa behind one of the mounds of snow. "Keep still!" he ordered.

Peering around the snow heap, he saw the two flat-faces appear from the end of the pathway. They stood a moment looking around, muttered something to each other, then shrugged and vanished the way they had come, taking the torn vine stuff with them.

"Okay," Toklo murmured. "We can go."

"I don't know the way," Lusa said, standing up and shaking snow from her pelt. "Have you seen Kallik and Yakone?"

"No, but I know the bird didn't get them," Toklo replied. "We'll find them." He tried to sound confident for Lusa's sake, though privately he felt doubtful. *What will we do if we've lost Kallik and Yakone?* "I'm guessing they'll go back to the place where we scattered," he went on. "I think it's this way."

He led Lusa alongside the BlackPath, keeping to the shadows and hiding behind the drifts of snow when a firebeast snarled past. Creeping around a corner, Toklo found himself on the edge of an open space where several firebeasts crouched in rows. Harsh yellow light poured down from thin metal stalks that loomed over them. Toklo's paws tingled with apprehension.

"I think they're asleep," Lusa whispered, peering around his shoulder.

"We still have to get past them," Toklo muttered. "Follow me, and if you think they're waking up, run."

Gagging on the acrid tang of firebeasts and oil, Toklo slunk between two of the rows. The ground underpaw was hard, covered in snowmelt with an oily slick on the surface. He tensed at the sound of flat-face voices in the distance, but the firebeasts didn't stir. Relief flooded over him as he reached the dark opening of a pathway at the other side.

Toklo raised his snout to sniff the air, but he couldn't distinguish any trace of bear beyond the overwhelming reek of firebeasts. "Kallik!" He raised his voice into a roar. "Yakone!"

He thought there might have been a faint answering roar, but it was drowned out by flat-face shouting and the thump of approaching footsteps.

"They heard us!" Lusa exclaimed.

"This way!"

Toklo bundled Lusa in front of him and fled down the pathway and around the next corner. The walls of a huge den rose up on one side, flat and featureless. On the other side was more piled snow, lining a BlackPath that seemed to lead to the edge of the denning place.

"Thank Arcturus!" Lusa panted, scrambling through the snow piles toward the pale outline of the hills beyond.

"Lusa! Toklo!"

Toklo spun around at the sound of Kallik's voice. The white she-bear rose from behind a huge snowdrift, scattering snow as she bounded toward them. Yakone followed her more slowly.

"Kallik!" Lusa hurried over to her friend and butted her head into Kallik's shoulder. "I can't believe we found you!"

"Same here," Kallik replied, giving Lusa an affectionate nudge. "We were afraid the big metal bird had gotten you."

Toklo greeted the two white bears with a rumble deep in

his throat. He didn't want to admit how pleased he was to see them again. *At least to see Kallik again.*

"We'd better get out of here," he said.

"What about food?" Lusa asked, glancing back the way they had come.

"You're *not* suggesting going back there?" Toklo growled. "If you want the flat-faces to catch you again, go ahead. The rest of us are heading for the ridge."

Lusa nodded reluctantly. "Okay. I suppose you're right."

Toklo led the way past the last of the dens, picking up the pace until they were moving at a fast trot. He breathed easier with every pawstep that took him away from this unnatural place.

Behind him he heard Kallik ask, "What did Toklo mean, catch you *again*?"

"Two flat-faces trapped me in some sort of mesh," Lusa explained.

"It seems weird that they'd do that instead of hurting you with firesticks," Yakone observed. "But then, no-claws are weird."

"Maybe they wanted to take you to bear jail," Kallik suggested. "I told you about the time I was trapped there, remember? Those no-claws put me in a net to take me to a place with other bears."

"Maybe they were going to take me back to the Bear Bowl." Lusa gave her pelt a determined shake. "But I'm a wild bear now. Thanks for saving me, Toklo."

"Just remember that." Toklo recalled how scared and angry

he had been when he'd seen Lusa trapped. "These flat-faces might not use firesticks. But they're still not good for bears. So let's get as far away from them as we can."

As they left the last of the dens behind, Toklo realized that they had come out of the denning place by a different route, and now they were much closer to the hills. The land sloped steeply upward, with rocks poking up out of the snow and a twisted thornbush here and there. The hills seemed to glower down at them, as if they were guarding the interior of the island against intruders.

Toklo let out a contemptuous snort. *You're getting as bad as Ujurak, seeing signs everywhere!* Pain twisted his heart again as he remembered his friend. The absence of a smaller brown bear padding alongside him was like a gaping wound that refused to heal. Pushing the dark thoughts away, he kept on at a grueling pace, higher and higher into the hills. His legs ached with the effort, and he could hear his companions panting as they followed, but something forced him to keep going.

"Toklo!" Lusa gasped out from behind him. "Can we rest for a bit?"

Reluctantly, Toklo halted and turned to look back the way they had come. Starlight glimmered on the snowdrifts, broken only by their own trail, and cast dark shadows from the rocks and scrubby thorns. The flat-face dens looked tiny at this distance, like pebbles he could have dashed aside with one paw.

Kallik and Yakone stood close together, gazing across the plain they had left behind, while Lusa panted beside them, her sides heaving and her breath billowing into clouds in the frosty air.

Toklo shifted his paws impatiently. His belly was howling with hunger, and he sniffed instinctively for the scent of prey. The harsh tang in the air was unexpected, and he snuffled at his own pelt, wondering if he had picked up the scent of oil from the flat-face dens. But all he could smell there was bear fur.

"I can smell firebeasts," he muttered, half to himself. "But there aren't any BlackPaths for them to run on."

"Maybe it's from that metal bird," Lusa suggested, scanning the sky nervously.

Toklo grunted. He didn't want to think about the bird hunting them down out here on the hillside, where there was no cover. "We'd better move on," he said.

His paws were still driving him onward, but he couldn't keep up the same fast pace as the slope grew steeper still. Soon he had to leap from rock to rock, or grip the twisted thorns to drag himself upward. At one point the snow gave way under his paws, and he slipped back, colliding with Yakone, who was just behind him.

"Sorry," Toklo muttered.

"Don't worry, I'm fine," Yakone responded. "I just hope there's something worth finding at the other side of these hills."

Have you got a better idea, cloud-brain? Toklo forced himself not to say the words aloud. *Yakone just doesn't understand about making a long journey.*

Soon the top of the crags loomed just above Toklo's head. With a last desperate scramble he pulled himself over the edge. In the same heartbeat a storm of white wings battered his head, and he let out a surprised yelp, almost losing his balance and falling back down the slope.

The scent of goose washed over Toklo. Hunger in his belly took control of his paws. He lashed out, snagged his claws in feathers, and landed hard on top of a goose, bringing it to the ground. The rest of the flock wheeled into the air with harsh cries and were gone.

Behind Toklo, Lusa's horrified voice cried out, "Toklo! No!"

Toklo stumbled to his paws, looking down at the goose with mingled shock and fury. It lay motionless, its neck at an awkward angle. *Not again.*

"There was a whole flock of geese," he growled defensively. "How likely is it that I'd snatch Ujurak? And if it was him," he added, "it serves him right for hanging around looking like prey. I'm hungry!"

But it's not Ujurak, he told himself silently. *It can't be. I killed him by the shore, when he was the hare. This just can't be Ujurak, too. He wouldn't be that cruel.*

"I'm going to eat," he announced defiantly. "You can share if you want to."

Yakone crouched down beside the body of the goose. "Thanks, Toklo."

Kallik hesitated a moment longer, then joined them. "I suppose Ujurak might have sent the geese," she murmured, though Toklo wasn't sure she was managing to convince herself. "We won't get much farther without food."

"That's right." Toklo tried to sound as if he believed her. "Ujurak wouldn't let us starve."

Lusa just shook her head sadly, and padded over to a thorn tree growing at the edge of the rocks. A few shriveled leaves clung to its branches; Lusa stripped them off and crunched them, then clawed off strips of bark and began to chew those.

That doesn't look like much of a meal, Toklo thought, with his mouth full of goose. *But it's better than meat for Lusa, I suppose.*

The goose was a big bird, though divided among three it wasn't really enough. Still, it soothed the pain in Toklo's belly and sent new strength into his paws. Raising his head from the remains of the prey, Toklo let out a groan. He had thought that with the last scramble they had reached the top of the hills. He had half expected to see Kallik's Frozen Sea stretching out in front of them. But now he saw how wrong he was.

From the top of the slope they had just climbed, a narrow plain stretched in front of them. Beyond it the hills rose up again, fold upon fold, higher and more daunting than before. A biting wind swept across the plain, swirling up the snow in clouds of ice crystals.

"Is that really the way we have to go?" Lusa whined, joining them again with scraps of bark clinging to the fur around her muzzle. "I'm tired."

"It's that or go back," Kallik said.

"Come on." Toklo heaved himself to his paws. "We'll find

somewhere to make a den for the night. The climb won't look so bad in the morning."

The plain had only a thin covering of snow, and the rocks beneath were sharp underpaw. The wind probed their fur with cold claws; it still carried the faint scent of firebeasts. Toklo's wound had started stinging again after he leaped to catch the goose, but he plodded doggedly forward, scanning the mountains ahead for some sign of shelter. As the hills drew closer, he spotted a narrow valley leading upward, a deep furrow between snowy slopes. "That could be a frozen stream," he said, veering toward it.

"If we go that way, it will make the climb easier," Kallik added.

Toklo could tell she was trying to sound optimistic. By the time they reached the mouth of the valley, Lusa was stumbling along with her head down; Kallik guided her around rocks, letting the smaller bear lean on her shoulder. At last Toklo spotted a gap between overhanging rocks, leading into a shallow cave. Thorns grew in front of it, sheltering it from the wind.

"Over here," he said, staggering toward it.

As he drew closer, Toklo noticed that the snow in front of the cave was churned up, and at one side of the gap was a pile of frozen droppings. Sniffing suspiciously, he picked up the scent of bear, but to his relief it was stale.

"It looks as if this was a bears' den once," he said. "But they haven't been here for a long time."

It was a squeeze for all four bears to fit inside the cave, but bundled up together they were at least warm. Sighing, Toklo let himself relax, and sleep flowed over him like a surging sea.

Toklo woke to see pale sunlight shining on the snow outside the den. His friends were still sleeping. Wriggling out of the cave, he brushed past the sheltering thorn trees and stood looking up the valley.

His ears pricked at the sound of running water. *I was right,* he thought. *There is a stream.* He padded across a stretch of stony ground until he came to the water's edge. Scraping away the snow, he saw dark air bubbles beneath the surface of the ice, and he slammed a paw down hard. The ice crunched under his claws, and he thrust his muzzle into the hole and took a long drink.

Gasping at the cold, he looked up again, with icy drops of water spinning away from his muzzle. Kallik was just emerging from the cave, with Yakone behind her.

"Come and have a drink," Toklo invited her.

"It *is* a stream!" Kallik exclaimed, and added hopefully, "I don't suppose there are any fish?"

Toklo shook his head. "The water's too shallow. There might be a few minnows, but they're not enough to fill our bellies. We'll have to share Lusa's leaves this morning," he added, nodding toward the thorns that sheltered the den.

Yakone gave the twisted branches a shocked look and let out a disgusted snort. "I'm not eating trees!"

Kallik butted his shoulder with her muzzle. "You'll get used to it," she assured him.

Toklo wondered about that. More and more he doubted that the white bear from Star Island would be able to cope with the harsh demands of their journey. *You'll soon find out who's the real leader around here.* Toklo knew he shouldn't feel pleased at the thought of Yakone having problems, but he couldn't quite crush the feeling down.

Kallik roused Lusa, who blundered her way out of the den as if she was only half awake. Toklo felt another twinge of anxiety as he realized that the small black bear was still struggling against the longsleep. *But we have to keep going,* he told himself. *And at least there's better food for Lusa here on land.*

All four bears crowded around to strip leaves and bark from the thornbushes. Yakone kept passing his tongue over his jaws as if he didn't like the taste. "I can't believe I'm eating this!" he grumbled.

After a last long drink from the place where Toklo had broken the ice, the bears set off upstream. The valley led them into the hills at a steep angle, with rocky, snow-covered slopes on either side. The tracks of birds and hares stippled the snow, but Toklo didn't think of hunting. The nagging fear that he had killed Ujurak—and might kill him a second time—never left him.

As the valley grew narrower and the top of the hill drew closer, Toklo became aware of a low rumbling sound that grew louder the higher they climbed. It wasn't continuous, but came and went without any obvious reason. Finally he halted.

"What is that?" he asked.

His companions stopped to listen.

"It sounds like thunder," Kallik said after a moment.

Toklo glanced up at the sky, which was clear except for a few wisps of cloud. "Not thunder," he muttered.

"If I didn't know better, I'd think it was firebeasts," Lusa ventured. "But there can't be firebeasts out here."

Toklo shrugged. "It doesn't seem to be doing us any harm."

The rumbling grew louder still as they plodded upward. Before they had traveled many more bearlengths, Toklo saw that the narrow valley ended in a mysterious dark hole; as they drew closer, he saw that the hole was lined with reddish stones, each one squared and regular.

"Flat-faces made that," he murmured, a prickle of apprehension running through his fur.

"What are no-claws doing out here?" Yakone asked, as if he could hardly believe what he was seeing.

His last words were drowned out by another long rumble, which grew louder and louder until it sounded as if it were almost overhead, then dwindled away into the distance.

"What *is* that?" Lusa's eyes were wide and scared.

Kallik scrambled up the steep valley side until she reached the top. Toklo heard her exclaim, "Great spirits!" Turning to look down at her companions, she added, "You were right, Lusa. That noise is firebeasts. There's a BlackPath up here."

Toklo gaped with astonishment. "What?"

"Come and see," Kallik replied.

Toklo clawed his way up the slope, with Lusa and Yakone just behind. Wind buffeted their fur as they stood on the edge of the BlackPath. It appeared from behind a shoulder of the hills, ran straight past the place where they were standing, then curved away and vanished behind a steep, rocky bluff.

"What do no-claws want up here?" Yakone asked, disgust in his voice. "Isn't there anywhere left for bears?"

"I'll never understand what flat-faces want," Toklo responded, in sympathy for once with Yakone. "All we can do is cross the BlackPath and then get as far away from it as we can."

"Okay." Yakone started forward, only to leap backward as another firebeast roared into view and swept past them, churning up the half-melted snow that covered the surface of the BlackPath.

"Wait till it's safe," Toklo growled.

Yakone didn't reply, too busy shaking off the snowmelt spattering his white fur.

"That hole down below looks as if it goes right under the BlackPath. Maybe we should go that way," Lusa suggested.

"You can if you want to," Toklo replied. "But Kallik and Yakone and I would probably get stuck down there."

"No," Lusa said. "I'll stay with you."

"Wait on the edge," Toklo instructed the others. "When I say 'now,' we'll run."

As he finished speaking, he heard the distant rumble of another firebeast. He waited until it roared past and the sound died away again. When he could hear nothing but the whistling of the wind, he growled, "Now!"

Kallik and Yakone leaped past him, side by side, and Lusa bounded after them. Toklo followed once he was sure that the little black bear could keep up the pace. The other three stopped at the other side of the BlackPath, but Toklo kept running. All he wanted was to leave the flat-faces and their firebeasts far behind him.

Ahead of him stretched a rocky wilderness, a jumble of rocks and snow and thorn thickets, stretching up to yet another fold of the mountains. Its emptiness and peace drew Toklo forward as if his paws had a life of their own.

"Come on!" he called, glancing back over his shoulder at the others. "This way!"

Suddenly full of energy at the thought that he was leaving the flat-faces far behind him, Toklo scrambled up to the top of a boulder and launched himself onto a stretch of unbroken snow. But when he landed on the white surface, his paws broke through into emptiness. There was nothing solid underneath, only billows of snow surging around him as if he had leaped into the sea. Toklo let out a startled roar as he fell with snow pouring down around him. His paws lashed out in a vain effort to find somewhere he could grab on and stop himself. Then he struck something hard, and all the world went black.

CHAPTER NINE

Kallik

Kallik froze with horror as she heard Toklo's roar of alarm and saw him plunge downward in a shower of snow.

"No!" Lusa halted, staring in shock at the place where Toklo had vanished. There was a large hole there now, with snow still crumbling from the edges and falling into the darkness below. "The ground just opened up and swallowed Toklo like he was a beetle!"

"Where did he go?" Kallik asked. She had never seen anything as terrifying as the way the ground had gaped open without warning and eaten Toklo.

"Let's take a look," Yakone suggested, padding forward.

Kallik exchanged a nervous glance with Lusa. "Be careful," she said as she followed Yakone.

Drawing closer, checking that the ground was solid at each pawstep, she studied the jagged hole. As Yakone leaned over, trying to peer into the depths, the snow began to give way under his paws.

"Help!" he roared.

Kallik sank her jaws into the fur on Yakone's flank and dug her paws into the ground as she dragged him back. She realized that Lusa was tugging at him from the other side, but the white bear was heavy, and Kallik could feel her paws beginning to slip. Yakone scrabbled to find firm ground, sending more showers of snow down into the hole. Just as Kallik was beginning to think she couldn't support his weight for a moment more, he found a pawhold and stumbled backward.

"Thanks." Yakone's breath came in huge gasps. "I thought I was gone for sure."

More cautiously, Kallik edged forward and peered down into the hole, Lusa at her shoulder.

"Toklo! Toklo, can you hear us?" Kallik called.

There was no reply from below. Down at the bottom of the hole Kallik could see the glimmer of the fresh snowfall, but no sign of Toklo. She called his name again, but there was no sound or movement.

"I—I'm afraid he might be dead," she whispered, drawing back again from the hole.

Yakone nodded solemnly. "Sometimes white bears are lost if they fall through cracks in the ice. I think Toklo has been lost beneath the ground." He raised his head to look up at the sky. "Spirits, take care of the spirit of our friend Toklo—"

"No!" Lusa exclaimed, interrupting Yakone's prayer. "Toklo *isn't* dead. I won't believe it."

"Lusa . . ." Kallik began.

"You don't see him, do you? So he might be okay," Lusa said. "He might be lying under all that snow, injured and waiting for us to help him."

"You would have to go underground to find him," Yakone objected.

Lusa glared at him. "Then that's what I'll do."

Kallik's heart began to pound with fear, but she knew that if her friend went beneath the earth to find Toklo, that she would go with her. *Lusa's right,* she thought. *I* won't *believe Toklo is dead. Not after all we've been through together.*

Yakone was stamping his paws in the snow and casting doubtful glances at the hole where Toklo had disappeared. "Tell her she's being cloud-brained," he said to Kallik. "You know we can't go down there. It's too risky. If Toklo was hurt in the fall, we could be hurt, too. Or we might land on top of him."

Kallik didn't like disagreeing with Yakone, but she knew that she couldn't turn away and leave Toklo underground. "I'm sorry, but I'm with Lusa," she said. "We have to do something. Toklo needs our help."

"Besides, we're not going to jump down the hole," Lusa added. "That *would* be cloud-brained. We'll have to find another way of getting to him."

Yakone stared at the she-bears as if he couldn't believe what he was hearing. "White bears don't belong underground," he told Kallik. "Our place is under the open sky, or in a snow-den."

"I'm not suggesting we live there," Kallik snapped. "Yakone, I have to do this for Toklo."

Yakone blinked, surprised, and looked away.

Another kind of apprehension tingled through Kallik's fur. *Am I going to lose Yakone over this?* She knew that if she left Lusa and Toklo behind, and journeyed on with Yakone toward the Frozen Sea, she would never forgive herself. "You don't have to come with us," she added.

Yakone let out a gusty sigh. "I had no idea what I was getting into when I started this journey with you," he said, touching Kallik's shoulder with his muzzle. "All right. Maybe my brain is full of cloudfluff, too, but I'll come with you."

Warmth flooded through Kallik. "Thank you!"

Lusa had been shifting her paws impatiently as she listened. "Remember those caves on Smoke Mountain?" she said to Kallik. "They stretched a long way back into the ground. If Toklo's hole reaches farther than this gap at the top—"

"Then we might be able to get to him from a different entrance!" Kallik interrupted, suddenly understanding. "We have to look for a cave opening." Her optimism died as she gazed around at the landscape. As far as she could see, there was nothing but snow-covered rocks and hummocks, with a thorn tree or boulder here and there.

"How are we going to find another hole, unless we fall into it?" she asked bleakly.

"I think I can help," Yakone told her. "I can tell whether the snow or the ground under my paws is thick, or whether it might be hollow."

"You can?" Kallik was astonished. "How do you know that?"

"The older bears on Star Island taught me," Yakone

explained. "They teach all the cubs. I'm surprised you don't know how to listen to your pawsteps."

Maybe I would, if I hadn't lost Nisa when I was so young, Kallik thought, an unexpected pang of loss stabbing through her.

"Can you teach me?" she asked.

"I'll try," Yakone replied. "You have to learn how to sense the differences in the ground through your paws."

Kallik shook her head. She wasn't sure she understood.

"Like this." Yakone brought one paw down on the snow. "Listen and feel what the snow is telling you."

Kallik copied him, but she wasn't sure what she was supposed to hear. "It just feels like snow to me," she confessed.

"Now over here." Yakone carefully approached the hole, though he kept well away from the edge. He brought a paw down again. "Doesn't that feel different? If I'd been listening to my pawsteps earlier, I wouldn't have started to fall."

Kallik tried it, but she wasn't sure that her paws felt any different. "I'm not getting it," she said apologetically.

"I'm not teaching it very well," Yakone admitted. "It's hard to explain. It's just something I've known how to do since I was a cub."

"Do you think we can start looking for another entrance?" Lusa interrupted. "Toklo could be dying down there! And you're up here trying to listen to *snow*!"

"Sorry." Kallik felt guilty for getting distracted. "Yakone, where do you think the best place to start looking for another hole would be?"

Yakone scanned the ground around the hole where Toklo

had fallen, and risked another glimpse into the depths. "It's hard to tell how far the space stretches, with all this piled-up snow," he murmured.

"If it's anything like the caves on Smoke Mountain, it's more likely to curve than go straight," Kallik mused. "Over in this direction, maybe," she added, sketching out a line with one paw.

"Do you think there's smoke and fire underground here, too?" Lusa asked, suddenly alarmed. "Toklo might be burning up!"

"There's nothing coming out of the hole," Kallik reassured her. She sniffed the air for the smell of smoke, and picked up a faint tang that reminded her of firebeasts. "The air smells funny, but in a different way."

Lusa nodded uneasily. "I hope you're right."

"Okay," Yakone said briskly. "I'm going to walk around and see if I can find a place where the ground feels hollow. Maybe you two better wait here. We don't want someone else falling in."

Lusa and Kallik looked at each other. "We want to help," Lusa said. "We'll be careful."

All three bears began testing the ground, but without success. Kallik was concentrating so hard on feeling the snow like Yakone instructed that she began to feel as if every pawstep were an effort. Raising her head to look at the sky, she realized that the daylight was dying.

"We'll have to stop and rest for the night," she said reluctantly. "We can't help Toklo if we're exhausted."

"But—" Lusa scrabbled with her front paws in the snow, then let out a huge sigh. "Okay."

Yakone nodded. "We need to eat, too. I'll go hunt." He strode away.

While he was gone, Kallik and Lusa dug out a den in one of the snowbanks, and Lusa uncovered some roots while she was digging.

"At least we'll eat something," she remarked, "even if Yakone doesn't find any prey."

It was fully dark by the time Yakone came back, a plump goose dangling from his jaws. As the warm prey-scent flooded over Kallik, she wondered whether Ujurak's spirit might have taken goose form, but between her exhaustion and the growls of hunger from her belly she couldn't bring herself to believe it.

Ujurak wouldn't do that to us, she told herself as her teeth sank into the juicy prey. She remembered how certain Toklo had been that Ujurak wouldn't want them to starve.

Lusa crouched beside the white bears, gnawing on the roots she had dug up. Then they huddled together in the snow-den. Not even her anxiety about Toklo could stop Kallik from falling into sleep.

The next morning Kallik awoke with a vague sense that something was wrong. Cold light filtered into the snowy hollow, where Lusa still slept with her paws wrapped over her snout. Kallik blinked, shaking off her drowsiness, and the memory of what had happened struck her like a gust of storm wind.

Then she realized that instead of three bears in the temporary den, there were only two.

We've lost Toklo! And now Yakone has gone, too!

Careful not to wake Lusa, Kallik struggled to her paws. Inside she felt colder than the snow-covered landscape outside the den. *Has Yakone really left us? Was it all too hard for him, so he's gone back to his friends on Star Island?*

Stumbling out into the open, Kallik narrowed her eyes against the biting wind and looked around. She bit back a joyful cry of relief as she spotted Yakone loping easily across the snow toward her. As he drew closer, she could make out a triumphant gleam in his eyes.

"Guess what?" he panted as he drew to a halt in front of her. "I've found a hollow place!"

"That's great!" Kallik yelped, with a sharp twinge of guilt that she hadn't trusted Yakone to stay with them. "Where?"

"Come on, and I'll show you."

"Okay. Let me wake Lusa."

Optimism flooded over Kallik as she prodded the little black bear awake. With Yakone's special skills they would soon find a way underground; it felt as though Toklo were only a few pawsteps away.

"Hurry up, Lusa," she urged as the black bear rubbed snow over her eyes and muzzle to wake herself up. "We're going to find Toklo!"

Yakone retraced his pawsteps to a humped, uneven stretch of snow. He halted at the foot of a snowy bank, where Kallik could see a few scrape marks, as if he had already begun digging experimentally. Kallik walked toward him, trying to listen to her pawsteps to see if she could sense the hollow place, but she still couldn't tell any difference from the rest of the snow.

"Under there," Yakone said, pointing with his muzzle. "We'll need to dig down, but we must be careful. There's a hole there, but I'm not sure how big it is."

Kallik nodded. All three bears began digging cautiously at the snow, pawful by pawful.

"I can feel something!" Lusa exclaimed.

Scrabbling excitedly, she uncovered the edge of a piece of wood. To Kallik's amazement, it wasn't the branch of a tree. It looked as if it had been cut and squared.

"No-claws did that," she said, stopping abruptly with a paw raised to take the next scoop of snow.

Yakone backed off a pace. "No-claws, here?"

"We're not so far from that BlackPath," Lusa reminded him, still scraping vigorously to reveal more of the wood.

Kallik sniffed the air. "I can't smell no-claws," she said. "Just that weird scent—a bit like firebeasts."

She began digging again, and after a moment's hesitation Yakone joined her, pushing the snow aside with powerful paws. Soon they could see that the wood was part of a slab lining a hole with square sides. It led into the side of the snowbank, stretching downward into darkness.

Lusa's eyes stretched wide. "It's not a hole; it's a tunnel!"

Kallik snuffed at the dank air that flowed out of the opening. "It's that smell again," she muttered, wrinkling her nose in disgust. "But it's a lot stronger here. Whatever is causing it must be down there."

"Flat-faces must have made this." Lusa had stepped into the mouth of the tunnel and was peering curiously into the blackness. "But there's no scent of them." She took another pace forward. "Toklo! Toklo!"

There was no response.

Lusa glanced back over her shoulder. "The tunnel is leading roughly the right way, toward where Toklo fell into the hole," she pointed out. "Let's go!"

"No, wait—" Kallik felt uneasy about stepping into the dark, enclosed space when they had no way of knowing if Toklo was down there.

But Lusa paid no attention. She was already heading deep into the ground, her black fur seeming to melt into the darkness. Kallik knew that she had to follow. She couldn't allow her friend to explore the fearful tunnel by herself. But she had to force her paws to carry her forward.

White bears belong in the open, with the sky stretching above us, she thought. *Not cramped up in underground passages, away from the light and the snow.*

"Do we really have to go down there?" Yakone asked, reluctance evident in his voice and the doubtful look on his face.

Kallik detected a hint of jealousy in his tone. "Toklo's my friend," she replied. "And so is Lusa. I can't let them down."

Kallik was building her nerve to head down the tunnel when she spotted four stones a couple of pawsteps inside. Two white stones, very close together. A smaller black stone a paw's width away from them. And farther away still, on the edge of the fading light, a rough brown stone. There was no doubt in her mind that each stone represented a bear. Had Ujurak put them there?

"Look!" Kallik breathed. "A sign! Now I know this is the way we have to go."

With a bewildered Yakone just behind her, she plunged into the tunnel and followed Lusa.

CHAPTER TEN

Lusa

Lusa padded along the tunnel, letting her feet guide her. The hole led straight down with a gentle slope; the floor was made of flat, beaten earth, easy on her paws. The weird smell was all around her, and she shuddered at the thought of it soaking into her fur.

Behind her she could hear the pawsteps of Kallik and Yakone. She felt reassured by the thought that her friends were following her, but when she glanced back over her shoulder, she couldn't see them in the pitch darkness.

"Toklo!" she called again, her voice sounding puny and insignificant in the black depths ahead of her. "Toklo, it's me, Lusa! Are you there?"

Still no reply. Stifling a whimper of fear, Lusa plodded on. For a while she didn't seem to be getting anywhere. She could see nothing, and she could hear nothing except for the pad of her own paws and the paws of her friends behind her, and now and then a drip of water that seemed to echo unnaturally loudly.

Then Lusa began to realize that the darkness wasn't quite as thick as before. A pale gray light was seeping down the tunnel in front of her, growing brighter as she walked forward. There was enough light that soon she could see the tunnel walls and roof, still lined with slabs of wood holding back the earth and stone, and the smooth brown floor that was littered with twisted scraps of metal glinting in the half-light. There was only one creature Lusa knew that would leave behind something like that.

"Why were flat-faces all the way down here?" she wondered out loud. "What were they doing?"

"I don't know." Kallik pressed up close behind Lusa as the light grew stronger. "I hope we don't meet any."

A few pawsteps farther on, Lusa discovered the source of the light. High above her head was a ragged-edged hole, partly blocked with snow that turned the light shining through it to pale silver.

"Is that where Toklo fell through?" Kallik asked. "Why isn't he here?" She raised her voice. "Toklo!"

"No, this can't be the place," Lusa responded. "There hasn't been time for snow to block Toklo's hole again. And there's no fresh snowfall down here. That must be a different hole."

Kallik sighed. "How many holes are there?"

Yakone stretched his neck out and pressed his snout reassuringly against her side. "Don't worry. We'll find Toklo."

For a moment all three bears stood gazing up at the hole, as if it might tell them something. Lusa was the first to break away, though her heart sank as the light began to die away behind them again, leaving them to face the unbroken darkness once more.

Before the last of the light had vanished, Lusa became aware of faintly moving air ruffling her fur, and she halted at a spot where the tunnel they had been following split into two. A slight breeze, barely noticeable, came from one of them.

"Now what do we do?" she wailed, gazing in confusion from one dark hole to the other. "How do we know which way to go?"

Kallik squeezed past her and sniffed at one of the openings, then the other, before turning back to Lusa and shaking her head hopelessly. "There's no scent of bear either way."

Turning back toward the nearer of the two tunnels, she let out a roar. "Toklo!"

Lusa waited, her belly churning with anxiety, until the sound had died away, then tried the other tunnel. "Toklo! Please—answer us!"

But there was no sound except the eerie echoes of Lusa's voice, nothing to tell them which tunnel they should follow.

"Let's think," Yakone said. His calm voice helped to draw Lusa back from the edge of panic. "The tunnel has led us straight so far. . . . That means Toklo should be somewhere in that direction." He pointed with one paw to the nearer tunnel.

"Are you sure?" Kallik asked doubtfully. "I'd have thought he'd be over here." She angled her snout toward the other tunnel. "This is where the breeze is coming from."

Lusa wanted to stamp her paws with frustration. "We can't

stand here forever!" she burst out. "If Toklo's hurt, we don't know how much time he has left. We have to choose."

"That way, then." Kallik pointed toward the tunnel Yakone had chosen. "I'm all confused down here."

Relieved to be moving again, Lusa let Yakone take the lead into the darkness of the tunnel he had chosen. The path sloped down more deeply; a chill tingled through every hair on Lusa's pelt as she thought of the weight of earth above their heads.

Toklo didn't fall this far, she thought worriedly. *We'll never find him down here.*

"Toklo! Toklo!" she called again and again, but the only answer came from the tiny sounds of the tunnel: the dripping of water, the creaking of wood, and now and then the rattle of a falling pebble.

Suddenly Yakone let out a grunt. Unable to see in the pitch blackness, Lusa blundered into his hind legs.

"Sorry," she muttered. "What's the matter, Yakone? Why have you stopped?"

"The tunnel's blocked," the white bear reported.

"What?" Kallik's voice came from behind. "It can't be! What's blocking it?"

There was a pause; Lusa could hear Yakone snuffling, and picked up the strong scent of earth.

"Rock and soil," Yakone replied after a few moments. "It's packed solid from top to bottom. We can't get any farther this way."

"But what if Toklo is trapped behind it?" Lusa asked, horror chilling her to the tips of her paws.

"Then he's trapped." Yakone's voice was flat. "There's nothing we can do."

"Okay, we have to go back to where the tunnel divided, and try the other direction." Kallik's voice was determined, and Lusa found her hope beginning to revive. "Come on."

Lusa stifled a sigh as she began to slog back the way they had come, the tunnel sloping upward this time. There was no point in calling for Toklo; they already knew he wasn't along this path.

It seemed a long time before Lusa could make out Kallik's outline against the faint light from up ahead, and they came back to the place where the tunnel divided. For a horrible few moments Lusa wasn't sure which was the tunnel they had come in by and which was the one they hadn't explored yet. Then she remembered that they had come past the place where the light filtered in, and she headed for the remaining opening, the one that was darker.

"It's this way! Hurry!"

But all three were growing tired, and it was hard for Lusa to keep her paws moving. She couldn't help thinking of how good it would be to curl up against the tunnel wall and go to sleep. It was almost cozy down here, out of the wind and snow. But when she let her eyes close and her knees start to sag, she jerked awake as if cold water had been poured down her neck. How could she go to sleep when Toklo might be in great danger? She couldn't close her eyes until they had found him.

Not far along the new passage, they came to a place where

Lusa felt cold air flowing over her fur again, coming from one side. The light was long gone, but she realized that they must have reached another tunnel opening.

"Maybe we should go that way," Yakone suggested. "It might lead us closer to where Toklo fell."

Lusa stopped herself from pointing out that Yakone had already made one bad choice, when he'd led them down the blocked tunnel. She knew it wasn't his fault.

"I think we should keep to the main passage," Kallik said nervously. "How will we ever find our way out if we keep turning?"

Lusa nodded, then realized that her friend couldn't see her. "You're right," she said out loud. "We'll keep going. But if we can't find Toklo this way, then we'll come back and try this other tunnel."

As they continued, Lusa became encouraged to realize that they were gradually moving upward again; she hadn't liked the deeper pathway at all. Even better, before long she realized that she could see her own paws, trudging steadily along the earth floor. Blinking, she looked up and saw a light shining along the passage ahead.

"Hurry!" she called to the white bears behind her. "This one might be Toklo's hole!"

But as she picked up her pace and drew closer to the light source, she realized that she was wrong. This hole was smaller than the one where Toklo had fallen, and once again there was no fresh snow beneath it. She halted, looking up in frustration.

"We could get out here," Kallik said as she padded up. There was an edge to her voice; Lusa guessed that she was reaching the limit of her willingness to be so far underground.

"We don't *want* to get out," Lusa retorted. "Not before we find Toklo."

"I don't mean we would give up," Kallik said hastily. "Just that we could get out for a moment to see where we are."

"This hole is too small," Yakone commented, looking up. "Not even Lusa could get out that way."

"My head could, though!" New energy flooded through Lusa at the thought of getting some sense of direction in these endless tunnels. "Yakone, stand underneath the hole. I'm going to climb on your back—if you don't mind," she added.

Yakone padded forward until he was directly underneath the hole. "It's fine. Come on."

Lusa scrambled up onto his broad shoulders and balanced there while she thrust her head upward, breaking through the crust of snow that blocked the hole. Blinking, she looked around. The light outside seemed very bright after the darkness of the tunnels, but as Lusa's eyes grew used to it, she realized that the day was already fading. Worse still, nothing looked familiar. There was no sign of the BlackPath they had crossed just before Toklo fell, not even the distant sounds of firebeasts. She was looking out at the familiar landscape of thorns, rocks, and snow, but she couldn't recognize any of it.

She pulled her head in again and slid down from Yakone's back. "It all looks the same," she admitted, her voice full of despair. "We could be close to where Toklo fell, or we could be skylengths away. I just don't know."

"Then we have to keep on looking," Kallik said, lowering her head to touch Lusa comfortingly on her shoulder.

"Okay." Lusa braced herself, then set off once more plodding down the tunnel, with the two white bears just behind. The light from the hole faded until they were left in darkness once more.

This is so hard, Lusa thought as she groped her way forward, trying not to bump against the tunnel walls. She wished desperately that Ujurak were still with them. He could have changed into a rabbit or a worm or a centipede, or some other animal that was comfortable underground, and helped to guide them.

Are you here, Ujurak? she asked silently. *We need you. Please come and help us.*

She longed to see the star-bear in some form, but there was nothing else alive in the tunnels that could possibly be Ujurak.

There's just the three of us, Lusa thought. Then she gave herself a shake. *Just the three of us, and Toklo.*

CHAPTER ELEVEN

Toklo

Toklo let out a groan and opened his eyes. At first everything was dark, and terror washed over him as he stared into the blackness. *Am I blind? Oh, spirits, no!*

Then gradually he began to make out his surroundings. He was lying on a flat earth floor, half buried in dirt and small stones and melting snow. Looking up, he saw the hole above his head, and beyond that the night sky.

What happened? he wondered. *What am I doing down here?*

Then he remembered. He and his friends had crossed the BlackPath, and he had bounded forward into the wilderness, eager to get away from the flat-faces and everything they made. The last thing he could recall was the ground giving way under his paws.

"I fell," he mumbled to himself. "Through that hole and right down here." Toklo blinked up at the hole, bewilderment rushing through him like an eddying stream. *They wouldn't have left me down here.* "Hey, Lusa! Kallik!"

Moving his head sent pain clawing through it, and every

muscle in his body shrieked in protest as he staggered to his paws and shook the snow and earth from his pelt.

"Lusa!" Toklo roared as loudly as he could. "Kallik!"

The only response was more snow dislodging from the edges of the hole and spattering on top of his head. Toklo backed away from the shower. If the snow above him collapsed completely, he could be crushed under it.

"I'd better move," he muttered.

Peering around, he saw a dark tunnel leading away in both directions. The sides were lined by flat pieces of wood, and more thick strips of wood supported the roof, though where he had been lying the wood strips had fallen away. The harsh tang of firebeasts was stronger than ever down here.

"Flat-faces!" he said with a snort of disgust. "This is one of their places. The sooner I'm out of here, the better."

In one direction the tunnel sloped upward, giving Toklo hope that it would soon lead to a way out. He began to pad along it, his paws unsteady at first until his muscles loosened up and the throbbing in his head began to die away.

His mouth felt as dry as a shriveled leaf, and in the dim light he spotted droplets of moisture clinging to the walls of the tunnel. Stretching out his tongue he licked some of them, wincing at the harsh taste that reminded him of firebeasts.

I'd give anything for a long drink of clean water!

The last of the light faded completely as he moved away from the hole, leaving him in total darkness. He felt a stab of fear at the thought of stumbling around in the pitch-black tunnels until he was too weak to go on, but he forced it down.

There must *be a way out!*

His hopes were raised when he felt a faint breeze blowing into his face, and a glimmer of light showed in front of him. Pain stabbed through his muscles as he broke into a shambling run, only to halt in frustration when he came to a place where the tunnels forked. A trickle of light came from a narrow crack in the roof, just enough to show him the two passages leading away from him. One looked bigger than the other, and still led upward; that was where the breeze was coming from. Toklo plunged into it, almost certain now that he was close to the surface and a way out.

But the tunnel went on without a break, farther and farther into the darkness. The upward slope leveled out, and the passage seemed to grow narrower, so that Toklo kept bumping into the walls. Bruised and confused, he was finding it harder and harder to make his paws move.

"I've got to sleep for a bit," he told himself, with a pang of fear that he might never wake up. "Then I'll feel stronger, and I'll soon find a way out."

But as he slumped to the floor and huddled against the passage wall, he had to admit that he didn't really believe it.

A scratching noise woke Toklo. He started up, his heart thumping. For a moment he couldn't remember where he was. Then he realized that he could see: A thin ray of light angled down from a gap in the roof. The sight brought back the memory of his fall and his struggle through the tunnels. He had no idea of how long he had been sleeping.

In one direction the passage stretched away into darkness. In the other it was partly blocked by a pile of rocks and earth. The scratching noise was coming from the other side of the blockage.

"Kallik? Lusa?" Toklo's voice was hoarse. "Is that you?"

There was no reply. Despair surged over Toklo. For a moment he had been certain that his friends had found him.

Scratch. Scratch.

Toklo froze. If it wasn't Kallik and Lusa on the other side of the rockfall, what was it? He tried to sniff it out, but the harsh firebeast tang overwhelmed everything.

Scratch.

Toklo shivered at the sound of small, scrabbling claws. *What sort of creature lives here in the dark?*

Then he shook his head, annoyed with himself. *Stop being ridiculous! You're still a strong brown bear, even if you are underground. And the tunnel's a tight fit, so whatever's there is probably smaller than you.*

Hunger was grumbling in his belly. Water flooded his jaws at the thought that the unseen creature might be prey. He began scrambling over the rockfall, flinching as the sharp stones bit into his pads, and let himself slide down on the other side.

Something white flickered in the near darkness. Toklo made out the shape of an Arctic hare, limping away from him as if it was sick or injured.

It probably fell down here, just like me, he thought, launching himself after it.

His scrapes and bruises, and the suffocating dark of the

tunnels, made his movements stiff and clumsy. The hare let out a squeal of terror and dove away down the passage, but there was just enough light for Toklo to pursue it, guided by its pale pelt. He swiped at it with a paw, missed, and forced his aching legs into a leap that brought him down on top of it. Scrambling up, Toklo kept one paw firmly clamped down on the hare, but it was dead, its neck broken.

"Call yourself a hunter?" Toklo muttered, glad that his friends hadn't seen the awkward catch. Then he crouched down beside his prey and devoured it in a few ravenous bites. He didn't let himself think about the possibility that it could be Ujurak. If Ujurak decided to visit him down here, he wouldn't be stupid enough to come in the shape of prey, not when Toklo had no other source of food.

The hare meat seemed to lie heavily in Toklo's belly, but the food refreshed him, and his legs felt stronger as he set out again along the passage. Blundering along in the darkness, he realized that the tunnel was rising again. He gradually became aware that he could hear something beyond the padding of his own paws: a low, rumbling sound, like distant thunder, except that it grew louder and softer again, then died into silence, without any pattern that he could work out.

Suddenly Toklo realized what he was hearing.

Firebeasts!

Somehow he must have found his way back to the Black-Path that he and the others had crossed before he fell down the hole. By now the sound was almost overhead.

More light was leaking into the tunnel from a jagged hole a

few bearlengths ahead of Toklo. Padding along until he stood underneath it, Toklo saw that another rockfall had opened up a gap, breaking away some of the wooden strips that shored up the roof. Beyond it he could see the night sky. The gap looked too small for him to squeeze through, but Toklo's paws were tingling at the thought of climbing back into the open air.

I can't take another pawstep down in these horrible tunnels! Not without doing my best to get out.

Clambering up on the pile of earth and rocks that had fallen from the roof, Toklo reared unsteadily onto his hindpaws and sank the claws of his forepaws into one of the wooden strips. Grunting with effort, he hauled himself up and thrust his head and then his shoulders through the gap.

A thundering roar sounded as he broke out into the open, and blinding light angled over him. Firebeasts were sweeping up and down the BlackPath; he had surfaced a paw's width from the edge.

But Toklo couldn't wait for the noise and light to die away. The wood he was clinging to wobbled under his weight. He had to use all his strength to force his way out of the hole before it collapsed. Sharp rocks and splinters of wood dug into his sides as he heaved himself upward. His hindpaws scrabbled for a grip on the wood, and he groped with his forepaws at the edge of the hole.

"Nearly there . . ." he panted.

Then he heard the roar of another approaching firebeast. It grew and grew, louder and louder, until it seemed to fill the whole world. Its glaring eyes were fixed on Toklo, and its round black paws pounded the BlackPath.

A shudder ran through the wooden strip that was supporting Toklo. He let out a roar of alarm as it gave way, and he crashed back into the tunnel in a shower of earth and rocks. Pain clawed through Toklo's head, and he choked on soil. Debris was pinning him to the floor of the passage.

As his senses spun away, he remembered how Oka had buried his brother, Tobi, under sticks and earth.

That's the right way for brown bears, he thought muzzily. *Maybe this is how I'm meant to die after all. . . .*

CHAPTER TWELVE

Kallik

Kallik halted, angling her ears forward. A faint roaring seemed to be coming from farther down the tunnel. "I can hear firebeasts!" she exclaimed.

"Then we must be close to the BlackPath!" Though it was too dark for Kallik to see the small black bear, Lusa's voice betrayed her excitement. "And that's not far from where Toklo fell in!"

"Let's hurry," Yakone's deeper voice rumbled.

Kallik strained all her senses as she bounded down the tunnel. She hated the dark passages more and more with every breath she took. She had never felt so far from her mother or the endless sky. But she refused to give up. Somewhere in the darkness Toklo was lying injured, or searching desperately for a way out. She wouldn't abandon him.

Just ahead the passage divided once again, but this time Kallik had some sound to guide her, and she made for one of the openings with scarcely a heartbeat's hesitation.

"Yes!" Lusa panted, scurrying just behind her. "I can smell

new dust this way. Some of the rocks must have fallen."

Kallik drew in the air, though she hardly broke stride to check the scent. "You're right," she replied. "And I think there's a trace of bear."

"Toklo!" Lusa exclaimed happily. "We've found him!"

Kallik wasn't so sure, but her hope mounted as the sounds of firebeasts and the new scents grew clearer. A cold wind was blowing down the passage into their faces. This was surely the way out—and somewhere close by there was a bear.

It has to be Toklo! It has to!

Now faint light was filtering through the passage from somewhere up ahead. Drawing closer, Kallik saw that it came from a ragged hole in the roof, above a mound of earth and stones. Dust still hung in the air, catching in her throat.

"What happened?" she asked hoarsely. "Where's Toklo?"

"Toklo!" Yakone let out a full-bodied roar. "Toklo!"

"Look!" Lusa darted forward, and started scraping soil from the bottom of the mound.

Kallik stared at her in surprise for a moment, then realized that Lusa was uncovering a patch of brown fur. "Toklo!" Lusa gasped. "He's buried!"

Lusa whimpered as Kallik came to scrape beside her. "Oh, spirits, don't let him be dead!" said Kallik.

Kallik's heart thumped so hard she thought it would burst out of her chest. Her paws flung soil and pebbles to one side, uncovering more of Toklo's pelt. Working together, she and Lusa gradually uncovered Toklo's body, while Yakone climbed the mound of debris beside them and poked his head out of the hole.

"The BlackPath is just here," he reported, his voice almost drowned by the roaring of a firebeast. "And the hole should be big enough to get Toklo out."

Kallik finished brushing earth gently away from Toklo's muzzle. His eyes were closed, and at first she thought he was dead. Then she saw the grizzly's breath stirring the dust on the floor where he lay. "Lusa, he's breathing!" she exclaimed. Her legs felt shaky with relief, and she had to pause for a moment. "Wake up, Toklo," she urged him. "It's us. We're here!"

Toklo grunted, as if he had heard Kallik and was trying to respond, but he didn't open his eyes or try to raise his head. His pelt was still clotted with soil, and he was bleeding from countless small cuts.

"How are we going to get him out?" Lusa asked, gazing up doubtfully at the hole where Yakone was still peering out. "He's so heavy."

"Yakone and I will manage," Kallik replied. "Yakone, let Lusa climb out first; then you and I will lift Toklo."

Lusa looked as if she was about to protest, but then seemed to accept that she was too small to lift a brown bear. After hesitating briefly she scrambled up the mound of debris and over Yakone's shoulders, to disappear through the hole.

Her voice came floating down to Kallik. "It's so good to be out of there! Quick, get Toklo out while there are no firebeasts coming."

Yakone followed her out, his body blocking the light from the hole for a few moments. Kallik could hear him grunting and puffing with the effort of dragging himself through the gap. A light rain of soil pattered around her; then light filtered down to her again, and she looked up to see Yakone's head outlined against the night sky as he gazed down at her.

"Can you lift him where I can reach?" he asked.

Kallik began working her shoulders underneath Toklo's unconscious body until she could balance him on her back. At first she thought that his weight would pin her to the ground, but after taking a deep breath she straightened her legs and hauled him up the heap of rubble, every pawstep an effort. Yakone stretched down with one paw and hooked his claws into Toklo's pelt. Leaning farther over at a precarious angle, he sank his jaws into Toklo's shoulder.

"Push!" he urged Kallik, the word choked out around his mouthful of fur.

Kallik heaved upward, almost losing her balance as the mound of earth and stones started to give way underneath her. Suddenly she felt Toklo's weight grow lighter, and she stretched upward to give him a final push as Yakone hauled him through the gap and out onto the surface.

"You did it!" Lusa squealed excitedly.

Kallik scrambled up the disintegrating pile and launched herself at the edge of the hole. Her forepaws sank into snow; she felt herself start to slip, but then Yakone grabbed her pelt in strong jaws and yanked her upward. With one last frantic scrabble Kallik heaved herself through the hole, feeling splintered wood raking along her sides. Then she was standing shakily on the surface beside the BlackPath, taking in huge gulps of the freezing night air. The icy wind that probed at her fur felt wonderful after the stifling darkness of the tunnels.

"Thank the spirits!" she exclaimed.

Lusa was bending over Toklo, and she looked up anxiously at Kallik. "He still won't wake up," she said.

"Give him time," Yakone replied. "He needs to rest. We'd better get him away from this BlackPath before the no-claws spot us."

Glancing around, Kallik spotted a rocky bluff a few bearlengths away, overhung by thorn trees. "That would be a good place," she pointed out.

With Yakone's help, she managed to drag Toklo across the snow and into shelter. Lusa padded alongside, her eyes wide with worry. The brown bear was limp, showing no signs of waking. But Kallik could still see the faint movement of his chest that told her he was breathing.

At the foot of the bluff the ground fell away into a hollow, with only a light covering of snow over tough grass and lichen. Kallik and Yakone tugged Toklo into the deepest part, out of the worst of the wind. The sound of the firebeasts sank to a distant rumble.

"You stay here with him," Yakone suggested. "I'm going to hunt. Food will give us all more energy."

"Okay." For the first time Kallik realized how hungry and thirsty she was; she had cramps in her belly, and her jaws were so dry it was hard to speak. Toklo was right: They had to eat.

They couldn't worry about every piece of prey being Ujurak. Ujurak wouldn't want them to starve.

As Yakone climbed back to the top of the hollow and disappeared, Kallik licked up a few mouthfuls of the powdery snow, then settled down beside Toklo, pressing close to him to keep him warm and feeling the steady beating of his heart.

"I don't think he's badly hurt," she murmured to Lusa. "Just a few bumps and scrapes. He'll be fine when he wakes up."

Lusa still looked anxious. "I hope so." She sniffed at one of the scratches on Toklo's shoulder and saw the bleeding had already stopped. "I wish Ujurak were here. He would know what to do for him."

Kallik was shaken once again by a sharp pang of loss as she remembered Ujurak's knowledge of herbs, but she made her voice sound confident as she replied. "Even Ujurak couldn't do anything for Toklo while he's sleeping. Besides, Toklo is strong. He'll be fine, Lusa; you'll see."

Lusa nodded, but Kallik could see she wasn't convinced. She curled up on Toklo's other side, and soon her rhythmic snoring told Kallik she was asleep.

Kallik tried to stay awake until Yakone came back, but her eyes were heavy, and her muscles ached from the long trek through the tunnels and the struggle to escape. A sound startled her; she jumped to her paws, heart racing, to see Yakone dragging an Arctic fox over the rim of the hollow. Behind him the sky grew pale toward dawn, with one lone star spirit left to look down on them.

"How's Toklo?" Yakone asked as he dropped his prey at Kallik's paws.

"I—I'm not sure." Kallik scuffled her paws in shame. "I must have fallen asleep."

Turning to Toklo, she saw that the brown bear was stirring. He let out a grunt of pain, and his eyes flickered open. He gazed at Kallik and Yakone.

"Are you spirits?" he muttered. "Have you come to take me to the river?"

Kallik exchanged an alarmed glance with Yakone. "It's us, Toklo," she said. "Don't you recognize us?"

Toklo raised his head and let it flop down again. "I was buried," he went on. "Sticks and earth . . . that's the right way for brown bears."

"Toklo!" The sound of his voice had roused Lusa; she sprang up with a cry of joy. "You're awake! How do you feel?"

Toklo didn't reply. Blinking in confusion, he gazed from Kallik to Lusa and back again, but he still didn't seem to know who they were.

Cold fear gripped Kallik's heart. *He must have hit his head,* she thought. "I'm Kallik," she prompted him. "And this is Lusa."

At last recognition flowed into Toklo's eyes, but it was followed by a terrible grief. "Then you're dead, too," he murmured. "And we're here together in the place of the spirits. I'm sorry you had to die."

"Toklo, we're not dead," Kallik assured him.

"Then why did they bury me?"

"You fell into tunnels under the ground." Lusa faced Toklo,

forcing him to meet her bright gaze. "We followed you and found you, and I think you must have fallen again, trying to get out. But we're all safe now. We're all alive."

Toklo let out a long, bewildered sigh. "I thought I was dead. My head hurts."

"Have something to eat," Yakone invited, pushing the body of the fox toward Toklo. "That should make you feel better."

Moving stiffly, Toklo worked his paws underneath him so that he could crouch beside the fox. He sniffed at it uncertainly, then began to eat, but slowly, as if he had lost his usual ravenous appetite. He couldn't finish his share of the prey, turning his head away with a grunt.

"We should keep moving," Kallik said, feeling apprehensive as she wondered if Toklo would be fit to travel. "We're too close to the BlackPath here. Sooner or later the no-claws will find us."

"Yes, they might come after us with vines," Lusa said, swallowing a last mouthful of lichen. "Let's go!"

Toklo heaved himself to his paws, but then looked around vaguely as if he had forgotten where they were going and why. Kallik's doubts deepened, until she felt as if she were sliding down into another dark hole. "It's not right, seeing him like this," she whispered to Yakone. "He always wanted to take the lead, but now . . ."

"He'll be okay," Yakone reassured her, touching her shoulder lightly with his snout. "He just needs time."

Kallik brushed her pelt against his. "Come on, Toklo," she said out loud. Kallik tried to keep her voice cheerful. "We have to cross these hills or we'll never get home. This way."

Toklo glanced at her, blinked, then broke into a lumbering walk. Kallik padded beside him, with Lusa on his other side, while Yakone took the lead.

Kallik looked up at the mountain ridge, a dark outline against the rapidly brightening sky. All her misgivings about this place seemed to be coming true.

Spirits, please let there be something better on the other side.

CHAPTER THIRTEEN

Lusa

Lusa kept casting uneasy glances at Toklo. The brown bear was plodding along with his head down, as if it took a massive effort for him to put one paw in front of the other.

I wish Ujurak were here, Lusa thought. *He would be able to find some herbs to help Toklo. There must be something that would bring the old Toklo back to us.*

She tried to remember the herbs Ujurak had used while they were traveling, but the only ones she really knew were the leaves she had helped him find to cure the bears on Star Island who were sick from eating poisoned seals.

And Toklo isn't sick like that, is he? Could he have eaten something poisoned down there in the tunnels?

Passing a clump of low-growing thorns, Lusa stripped off a mouthful of leaves and took them to Toklo. "Try these," she suggested, dropping the leaves at his paws. She didn't know what they were, but figured they might help and couldn't do any harm.

She was nervous in case Toklo roared at her, furious with

her for trying to take Ujurak's place. But Toklo just gave her a bleary glance, then crunched up the leaves without protest and trudged on. Somehow his obedience was even more troubling to Lusa than anger would have been.

Toklo hardly ever does what other bears tell him!

Lusa watched anxiously to see if the leaves had any effect on Toklo, but the brown bear didn't change. He didn't even talk to the others, just shambled along with his eyes on his paws.

When their path led between lichen-covered boulders, Lusa clawed off some of the lichen and brought it to Toklo. *I guess it's worth a try,* she thought, trying to force down her growing desperation. Once again Toklo licked up the lichen without objecting, his eyes dull and uninterested.

Lusa imagined how Toklo would have reacted once: *What's this stuff you're giving me? It's not the right food for a brown bear!* She almost wanted him to be angry with her, just so she could have the familiar Toklo back again.

The sun began to dip toward the horizon again, the short day of snow-sky already coming to an end. The mountain ridge seemed as far away as ever. Lusa's paws were so cold she could hardly feel them, and her legs ached from the effort of climbing. Her breath was coming in rapid pants, and she wondered how long she could keep going.

"Let's make a den for the night," Yakone suggested; Lusa wondered if the white bear could see she was struggling. "We all need to rest."

"Okay." Kallik veered across the hillside to where a single

thornbush straggling from the top of a bank offered a bit of shelter.

Lusa nudged Toklo to get him to follow, and the brown bear slumped down with his nose on his paws, staring at nothing. She touched his ear affectionately with her snout, but he didn't react.

While Kallik and Yakone began digging a makeshift den out of the snowbank, Lusa peeled some of the bark from the trunk of the thorn. "Here, Toklo, try this," she suggested. "It might help."

Toklo nibbled the bark, then turned to Lusa. It was the first time he had met her gaze since he had come out of the tunnels, and she felt that at last he recognized her.

"You should have left me down there," he growled softly. "It was my destiny to stay there, underground in a den where brown bears belong."

Lusa shook her head. "Are you completely bee-brained?" she hissed. "I belong in trees, but there aren't any here—not proper trees," she added, with a disdainful glance at the twisted thorn. "That doesn't mean I'm giving up. It just means we have to keep going until I find some."

Toklo blinked thoughtfully, as if she might have managed to reach him, but his only reply was a grunt. He closed his eyes; Lusa had to prod him and push him to make him retreat into the den. Lusa curled up beside him, but for once it was a long time before she was able to sleep.

"Lusa! Lusa!"

The voice called Lusa out of a disturbing dream, where

she wandered alone over a snow-covered landscape, endlessly searching, though she couldn't remember what she needed to find.

"Lusa!"

Opening her eyes, Lusa gazed past Toklo's sleeping bulk to where a small brown bear was poking his snout into the entrance of the makeshift den.

"Ujurak!" she gasped.

The star-bear's gaze was warm as he jerked his head, beckoning her to join him outside. Lusa scrambled past Toklo, briefly wondering if she ought to wake him, then skirted the mound of white fur where Kallik and Yakone were curled up together, and burst out into the open.

Ujurak was standing a bearlength away, waiting for her. Starlight misted in his fur and glittered around his paws. Above him the stars blazed, so close and bright that Lusa felt she could almost reach up and pluck them out of the sky like a pawful of berries.

"I . . . I'm still dreaming, aren't I?" she asked, her heart sinking in disappointment. "You aren't really here."

Ujurak's eyes gleamed. "Yes, you're dreaming," he replied. "But that doesn't mean I'm not here."

"Oh, Ujurak, I've missed you so much!" Lusa exclaimed. "We all have, especially Toklo. And we've been so worried, because we thought Toklo killed you again when you were an Arctic hare."

Ujurak looked puzzled. "An Arctic hare? No, that wasn't me." His eyes suddenly danced with mischief. "Lusa, I'm always with you, but if any of you think you're fast enough to catch me, you're making a big mistake!"

Lusa let out a huff of relief. "I'm so glad! Can you visit Toklo, too, and reassure him?" she added. "He's been hurt, and he really needs you now."

"Toklo's time will come," Ujurak promised. "And you can tell him he shouldn't be afraid to hunt. Meanwhile, I know what he needs. Come with me." He turned and padded off, leaving no tracks in the snow, only a faint silver glimmer that faded as Lusa followed him.

Ujurak led her around the contour of the hill until they reached a place where the snow had been scraped away. A clump of leaves was growing there; Lusa plunged her snout into them, snuffling up their strong smell. "Are these herbs for Toklo?" she asked. The brown bear nodded.

"Ujurak, thank you! I tried to help him, but I didn't know what to give him," Lusa admitted. Carefully she nipped off the stems and picked up the bundle in her mouth. Ujurak padded beside her as she headed back to the den. Toklo was still sleeping.

"Don't wake him," Ujurak advised. "He needs to sleep, and so do you. The morning will be soon enough for him to eat them."

Lusa set the herbs down and lay down next to Toklo again. To her delight, Ujurak curled himself around her; blissful warmth began to spread through her, and she felt herself sinking more deeply into sleep.

"Thank you, Ujurak," she murmured. "I wish you could stay with us always."

Lusa woke to the sound of Kallik and Yakone stretching and pushing their way out of the den. Toklo was still asleep. Ujurak had gone, but Lusa could still smell the strong scent of the herbs.

"I wonder if I could find—" she began, and broke off, her jaws gaping with astonishment. The small bundle of herbs still lay where she had left it, close to Toklo's snout.

Then it wasn't a dream? She gave herself a shake. *Ujurak came to me and showed me what I needed to help Toklo!*

"Come on, Toklo," she said aloud, giving the brown bear a hefty prod in the side. "Wake up. Look what Ujurak sent you."

Toklo let out a groan. His eyes flickered open with a flash of interest that quickly faded, and then closed again. "Leave me alone," he muttered.

"No, sorry. Not going to happen." Lusa pushed the bunch of leaves against Toklo's snout. "You have to eat these. They'll help."

Toklo sniffed, and his eyes opened again. He looked slightly more interested. "Hmm . . . they smell good." He licked up the herbs and chewed them, his jaws moving rhythmically. "Satisfied?" he asked when he had swallowed. "Now can you let a bear get some sleep?"

He's sounding better already, Lusa thought, rejoicing at the trace of the old grouchy Toklo in the brown bear's tone. She left him to rest and scrambled out of the den to find Kallik standing alone and sniffing at the chilly dawn air.

"Yakone has gone to hunt," she said. "How's Toklo?"

"Better, I hope," Lusa replied. "Kallik, you might not believe this, but last night . . ." She settled down beside her friend in the mouth of the den and told her about her dream visit from Ujurak.

"He really came!" Kallik blinked happily. "He still cares about us!"

Thin flakes of snow began to drift down as the two she-bears waited for Yakone. Not much later Lusa heard a snort behind her, and Toklo came to join them. His eyes looked brighter, and he seemed to be moving more easily.

"How do you feel?" Kallik asked.

"Not too bad," Toklo replied. Lusa had to stop herself from bouncing up and down with glee to hear him sounding like himself again. "I'm not aching so much," he went on. "I don't know what that was you gave me, Lusa, but it worked."

"Ujurak showed it to me in a dream," Lusa explained, briefly anxious that Toklo would be angry that his friend hadn't come to him. "And he told me that he wasn't the hare you killed. We can hunt freely again."

Toklo gazed at her, letting out a long sigh of relief. "The prey had better watch out!" he said. "I'm going to hunt—"

A sudden squeal of terror interrupted him. An Arctic hare burst through the screen of falling snow, dashing straight past Kallik's paws. Yakone appeared in furious pursuit, but the hare was dodging from side to side, skimming over the ground as if it weighed nothing. The white bear was too slow changing direction, and it looked as if the hare would escape.

"Oh, for the spirits' sake," Toklo groaned, heaving himself to his paws.

He headed away from the den, wading through the freshly fallen snow, his gaze fixed on the hare. Then he bounded off at an angle, so that when the hare dodged again, it almost threw itself onto his paws. Toklo gave it one swipe, and it fell to the ground as Yakone came panting up.

"*That's* how you catch a hare," he growled.

Yakone let out a huff of embarrassment, but Lusa and Kallik exchanged a delighted glance.

"It's good to have you back, Toklo!" Lusa exclaimed.

CHAPTER FOURTEEN

Toklo

Toklo's sense of triumph at killing the hare faded as he shared his prey with his friends. He could see that Lusa and Kallik thought he was back to his old self, but they were wrong. His aches and pains were fading, but his sense of belonging with Lusa and Kallik was gone, and he couldn't see the point of their journey anymore.

None of us knows where we're going. I don't know why we're bothering.

Even his satisfaction at showing Yakone how to make a kill didn't mean much to Toklo now. He couldn't remember why he had thought it was so important to challenge Yakone all the time. *Let him take the lead and be responsible for us all. Maybe he'll be a better leader after all.*

Toklo no longer believed that he had been a good friend to Lusa and Kallik. How could he have been, when he had made so many mistakes? *If I'd been that good a friend, Ujurak wouldn't have left. I'd have found some way to save him.*

The snow was falling more thickly now. As he and the others retreated into the den, Toklo decided that he would stay with Kallik and Lusa until they were safely home, or at least until they had found a place where they could settle.

And after that? Who cares? It's not important.

Toklo brushed through rich undergrowth, enjoying the feeling of soft moss under his pads and the warm air scented with green, growing things. Tantalizing prey-scents wafted over his nose, but his gaze was fixed on the brown bear ahead of him. He caught only fleeting glimpses, as the other bear whisked between trees and arching clumps of bracken, but Toklo knew with every hair on his pelt who he was pursuing.

"Ujurak!" he panted. "Wait for me!"

But Ujurak was drawing farther ahead, leaving Toklo to blunder helplessly in his pawsteps. Soon Toklo could barely see him in the shadows where thick foliage blocked out the sunlight.

Skidding to a halt, Toklo let out a roar of anger, loss, and frustration. "You're leaving me behind!"

Suddenly Ujurak's voice sounded in Toklo's ear, as if the star-bear were standing right next to him. "You cannot follow me, Toklo." His tone was tinged with regret. "You have your own journey now. Remember what matters most."

His voice faded as he spoke the last few words. The sunlit forest faded, too, and a blast of icy wind ruffled Toklo's fur. Its touch wrenched him out of the warm forest, and he blinked open his eyes to see the snowbound plains that lay beyond the entrance to their den.

Toklo lay still for a moment longer, trying to recapture the dream. Part of him was comforted by the vision of Ujurak and the way his friend had spoken to him.

"But why can't he say what he means in a way that a bear can understand?" Toklo growled softly to himself. "*Remember what matters most.* Well, Ujurak, I'd do that, if only I knew what it was."

Heaving himself to his paws, Toklo peered out of the den. The landscape had changed overnight, the bumps and hollows smoothed out under a thick white covering. The sky was gray, the clouds heavy with more snow to come.

"I don't think we should travel in this," Yakone said, coming to crouch beside Toklo at the entrance to the den. "We'll all feel better if we rest until the weather improves. What do you think?"

Toklo grunted. He wasn't sure this was the best plan, when they didn't know how good the hunting would be here. And he didn't want Yakone thinking he was too weak to carry on. But he couldn't be bothered to argue.

Soon the snow began to fall again, whirling down in a dense white screen that blotted out the landscape. The bears spent the day huddled together in the makeshift den, sleeping until the pangs of hunger roused them.

"We've got to hunt," Kallik declared. "Yakone and I will go. It's not so bad out there now."

Toklo glanced out at the drifting flakes of snow. He still couldn't see more than a bearlength from the entrance. "All the prey will be hiding down in their holes," he pointed out discouragingly. "And if there are other bears around here, they'll know all the best places to look."

"Well, we've got to try," Yakone responded. "Come on, Kallik."

Toklo watched the two white bears go, then settled down beside Lusa, who was still sleeping. Anxiety pricked him like a thorn; if Lusa had to stay stuck in this den for much longer, she would fall into the longsleep.

And then what will we do?

When the snow eased off a little, Toklo left the den and clambered up the bank to fetch some twigs and leaves from the thorn tree for Lusa. Setting them down beside her, he prodded her awake.

"Oh, thanks, Toklo." Lusa stretched her jaws in a huge yawn. "Where are Kallik and Yakone?"

"Hunting," Toklo replied shortly. "They'll be back soon."

Privately he was getting worried. Kallik and Yakone had been gone for long enough to find prey, if there was any prey to find.

What if they've fallen into those tunnels again?

But Lusa happily accepted what Toklo told her, crunched up the thorn twigs, and curled up to sleep again.

Kallik and Yakone returned soon after; Kallik was carrying a scrawny-looking goose.

"This was all we could find," Yakone said. "I think its wing was hurt; it couldn't take off with the rest of the flock."

"It's better than nothing," Toklo replied, mainly because Kallik was looking so depressed. He had known prey would be hard to find, but it wouldn't help to say so.

Days went by and there was no lull in the falling snow. Toklo, Kallik, and Yakone went out to hunt, but prey seemed to be even scarcer as time went on. *It won't be long before we've hunted everything in this area,* Toklo thought. *And Lusa will have eaten the whole thornbush!* He was beginning to lose track of time, except for the hunger in his belly that roared louder and louder.

"We can't go on like this," he stated finally, after having been out all day and most of the night without making a catch. "There isn't a sniff of prey left around here. We have to move on."

Kallik and Yakone glanced at each other; then Yakone slowly nodded. "You're right. If we wait much longer, then we'll be too weak to move at all."

"I just wish the snow would stop," Kallik said. "It's Lusa I'm worried about. She's sleeping so much, and I'm not sure she'll be able to get through the snow now that it's belly deep."

"She has to," Toklo snapped, anxiety for the small black bear making him brisk.

"I'll carry her," Yakone said, surprising Toklo with the offer. "She's not much bigger than a cub, anyway."

Kallik nudged Lusa awake and explained to her what they were going to do.

"Whatever," Lusa muttered blearily, clambering onto Yakone's back. She blinked several times; Toklo could see her determination to stay awake. "Thanks, Yakone."

Toklo took the lead as they left the den and started trekking through the snow. Dawn light was beginning to trickle over the landscape. The bitter cold probed deep into his fur with icy claws, and he sank into the freshly fallen snow, which reached almost up to his belly fur. Kallik and Yakone plodded along behind him, with Lusa drowsing on Yakone's shoulders.

Before they had been traveling for long the wind rose, whipping snow into their faces. Toklo had a pang of regret for the den they had left behind, but he knew they had made the right decision. They would have starved to death if they had stayed there much longer.

Hunching his shoulders, he headed into the depths of the blizzard. Snow clotted in his fur and weighed him down. The mountain slopes stretched in front of them, higher and higher, the ridge invisible now beyond the eddying snow. There was no sign of shelter. Toklo began to think they would go on forever, trudging into the featureless white. Then he spotted something disturbing the surface of the snow, a couple of bearlengths to one side. Curious, he veered over and peered at the marks.

"Look at this!" he called to Kallik and Yakone, his excitement rising as he realized what he was seeing. "Pawprints!" he continued, as the two white bears waded through the snow to his side. "I'd guess they were made by brown bears." He made a pawprint of his own beside the ones he had just found, and demonstrated how alike they were.

"Brown bears, here?" Yakone sounded dubious. He bent his head and sniffed at the marks in the snow. "You could be right," he admitted.

Looking more closely, Toklo realized that there were

several sets of pawprints. A whole group of brown bears had passed this way, and not long before, or the snow would have covered the prints.

"We ought to follow them," he said eagerly. "These other bears might know where to find food."

"But who knows if they'll want to share it with us?" Yakone pointed out. "They might be hostile."

Toklo felt a sudden stab of irritation, partly because he was afraid Yakone might be right. He had fought before with brown bears who were angry that he was invading their territory. But his excitement was stronger. Finding bears like himself in this desolate place was worth the risk.

"I'm following them," he told Yakone. "You can do what you want."

"You know we can't split up," Kallik said.

"I agree with Toklo," Lusa put in, peering down from Yakone's shoulders. "At least it gives us something to aim for. It's better than just wandering around in all this snow."

Yakone hesitated, then shrugged. "Okay. But if we all get our fur ripped off, don't blame me."

Toklo immediately set off in the direction of the pawprints. As if at a signal, the wind died away and the snowfall faded to a few drifting flakes. The prints stood out clear against the white ground. They led straight on, over a gentle hill, across a frozen stream, and up a steeper slope beyond. Toklo's hopes rose; it looked as if the bears knew where they were going. At every pawstep he hoped to see familiar brown shapes ahead of him, but as the light of the short day died, he had seen nothing moving in the landscape.

"We'll have to stop," he said reluctantly, as it grew so dark he couldn't see the pawprints anymore. The sky was still covered with cloud, too thick for the light of moon or stars to penetrate. "We'll carry on in the morning."

"Stop here?" Yakone sounded disgusted. "We should be looking for somewhere to make a den."

"If we do that, we might not be able to find the pawprints again," Toklo pointed out.

Kallik let out a sigh and flopped to the ground. "All right. I'm too tired to argue. But this had better be worth it, Toklo."

Lusa rolled off Yakone's back, shivered as she huddled down beside Kallik, and was asleep almost at once. Toklo felt another pang of anxiety; what the black bear needed was warmth and the right sort of food, and she wasn't getting either out here.

Maybe the brown bears will be able to help, when we catch up to them, he told himself as he settled down on Lusa's other side. Yakone stood looking at the others for a moment, then let out a snort and lay down beside Kallik.

Toklo slept fitfully, worried that another fall of snow would wipe out the pawprints. But as the sky gradually grew pale and he woke from his troubled sleep, he saw they were still there, a clear line stretching across the snow.

"Come on!" he urged the others, giving Lusa and Kallik a prod. "It's time we were on our way."

"Oh, yeah," Kallik yawned, stumbling to her paws and shaking snow off her pelt. "Following brown bears who might be friendly or might not. I can't wait."

Ignoring the grumbling, Toklo headed off, tracking the line of pawprints. Kallik and Yakone came after him, with Lusa once more riding on Yakone's back.

All the bears were cold, hungry, and bleary-eyed, but rising excitement was spurring Toklo on. He stood waiting when the others insisted on stopping to rest, his paws shifting impatiently. He didn't even want to make time to hunt, though he chased a hare that happened to cross their path, and he helped Yakone creep up on a flock of geese and bring one down. All the while the dark line of pawprints seemed to be beckoning to him.

Toklo wasn't sure how many days they spent following the trail. He was afraid that snow would fall again and blot it out, but the sky stayed clear. Only the wind swept across the snow, blurring the edges of the pawprints. Once or twice, trekking across bare rock, Toklo thought that they had lost the trail, but he managed to pick it up again, always leading upward.

His companions didn't even protest anymore; he could see in their eyes that they were resigned to following him. *And why not? One way is as good as another. Besides, I want to see my kin.*

The trail was leading up a steep hillside now, zigzagging across the slope. A stronger wind was rising, blowing down from the ridge ahead, carrying flakes of snow with it. As the snow grew heavier, it began to fill the pawprints, and the wind erased the last of them.

"Now what do we do?" Yakone asked. "We've lost the trail."

Toklo raised his muzzle and sniffed. "I can pick up their

scent on the wind," he reported. "It's telling me what I've known all along: Brown bears are at the end of the trail. Come on—I don't need the pawprints anymore."

Gathering the last of his strength, Toklo leaped and scrambled through the whirling snow, up the last few bearlengths to the top of the ridge. Kallik and Yakone kept pace with him, gripped by the same urgency.

Panting, Toklo reached the peak and looked down the other side. He was aware of Kallik next to him, her pelt brushing his. A rocky slope led down to a narrow, snow-covered valley. At its foot, crouching behind a boulder as if he was trying to hide, was a small brown bear. He was shaking, and his eyes were wide with fear as he gazed up at Toklo and the others.

"Great spirit!" Toklo exclaimed. "What's a brown-bear cub doing all by himself out here?"

CHAPTER FIFTEEN

Kallik

Kallik followed Toklo as he headed down into the valley. Lusa and Yakone brought up the rear. The small brown bear tried to back away as they approached, pressing himself against the boulder.

"No!" he squealed. "Don't hurt me!"

Toklo halted, well out of range; Kallik could see that he didn't want the younger bear to feel threatened. "Don't be afraid," he said.

But the bear wasn't looking at Toklo. His terrified gaze was fixed on her and Yakone. "White bears!" he whimpered. "Big white bears! Keep them away from me!"

Blinking in bewilderment, Kallik stopped just behind Toklo and exchanged a glance with Yakone. She had no idea why the young bear should be so afraid of white bears. Looking at him closely, she realized he wasn't the cub she had thought at first. He was smaller than Toklo, but looked only a little younger than the rest of them.

As he stood shivering in the snow, Kallik began to think that there was something different about him; something about his head and shoulders didn't look quite right for a brown bear. *I'm probably imagining things,* she told herself with an inward shrug. *It's been a long time since I've seen any brown bears other than Toklo and Ujurak.*

The strange bear was slowly backing away, sidling around the boulder as if he was about to make a run for it.

"The white bears won't hurt you," Toklo reassured him. "None of us will. We'll give you help if you need it, but we can't do that if you run away from us."

The brown bear stopped, his fearful glance flickering from one bear to the next. Kallik saw his eyes widen in shock as he spotted Lusa; she guessed he had never seen a black bear before.

Behind her Kallik heard Lusa mutter, "What's made him so scared? He doesn't look hurt. . . ."

Toklo slowly padded forward. The smaller bear trembled, but he stood his ground, until Toklo was close enough to bend down and touch him on the shoulder with his muzzle. "Why are you so frightened?" he asked softly.

Kallik's heart beat faster as she heard the protective tone in Toklo's voice. *He sounded like that with Ujurak. . . .*

"Tell us your name," Toklo went on.

"It's . . . it's Nanulak."

"And what happened to you? Did you get lost in the blizzard?"

Nanulak blinked up at Toklo. "White bears chased me and attacked me," he whimpered. "I had to hide to get away from them."

"Why would they do that?" Yakone's voice was a deep rumble. "Did you steal their prey?"

Kallik saw Toklo shoot a reproving glance at Yakone.

"No!" Nanulak glared indignantly at Yakone. "I would never do that. They just came out of nowhere and jumped on me!"

Kallik felt a stab of guilt and discomfort. She knew that white bears could be fierce, but she found it hard to imagine they would attack another bear without being provoked. Then she remembered how Taqqiq and his friends had kidnapped the black-bear cub at Great Bear Lake. She knew not all white bears were as honorable as Yakone.

"You poor thing!" she murmured. "I'm so sorry. No wonder you were scared of me and Yakone."

"But why are you all by yourself?" Toklo asked. "What happened to your family? Why couldn't they protect you from the white bears?"

Nanulak shuffled his forepaws in the snow, not looking at Toklo. "My family doesn't want me," he explained in a small voice. "My mother and my half brother and sister drove me away because there wasn't enough prey for all of us."

Kallik heard an outraged gasp from Lusa, and she saw Toklo stiffen. Of course, he knew exactly what it was like to be driven away by your mother. But before Toklo could speak, Yakone stepped forward.

"What about your father? Didn't he help you?"

Nanulak shook his head. "No. He's a white bear, you see."

"What?" Kallik stared at Nanulak for a moment, hardly understanding what he had told them. If his father was a white bear and his mother was a brown bear, did that make him half of each? She hadn't realized that brown bears and white bears could have cubs together. But now that she looked more closely at Nanulak, she could understand the puzzlement she had felt earlier. His head and shoulders were shaped more like hers and Yakone's, even though his pelt was brown.

"Where's your father now, Nanulak?" she asked.

"I don't know." Nanulak sounded desolate. "He doesn't live with us anymore."

Kallik stretched out her neck, intending to press her snout gently against the young bear's shoulder, but Nanulak flinched away, and Kallik left the movement unfinished, unable to show how much she sympathized with him. She felt much closer to him now that she knew he was half white bear.

"Then you can come with us," she announced. "We'll look after you. We won't let the other white bears harm you."

Toklo nodded. "You can trust us."

Nanulak stared at them, his brown eyes round like Toklo's. "Do you really mean that?"

"Of course we do," Lusa said.

"And you'll really protect me if the white bears come back to get me?"

"Just let them try," Toklo growled.

"Thank you." Nanulak took a step forward, so he was

standing close beside Toklo. "The white bears hate me because I'm half white bear and half brown bear."

A low rumble came from Toklo's throat. "That's ridiculous!"

"Even before my family drove me away, the white bears used to attack us," Nanulak went on. "All my family, but especially me. And now that I'm on my own, I'm too small to fight them." He gave Toklo a long look and stretched up as if trying to make himself equal size. "I'll be fine now that I'm with you."

"Who were these white bears?" Yakone prompted. "Do you know where they are now?"

"No." Nanulak's voice quivered. "I ran away and hid. I don't know where they went."

"Can you describe them?" Yakone persisted. "So we have some idea what to watch out for?"

"I told you, I don't know!" Nanulak's voice rose to a high-pitched squeal of terror. "I was too busy hiding. They were white bears! Big white bears!"

"But—"

"Back off!" Toklo snarled, pushing himself between Yakone and the cowering brown bear. "Can't you see you're upsetting him?"

Yakone stepped backward. "Okay, okay. I just want to find out what happened. If we're going to protect him, we need to know what we're protecting him *from*. I'll never believe that any white bear would just attack a cub."

Toklo pressed his muzzle comfortingly against Nanulak's

shoulder. "Ignore Yakone," he said. "No bear is going to hurt you."

Kallik stood watching the two brown bears close together for a moment, surprised to see how quickly Toklo had leaped to the smaller bear's defense. *Yakone was only trying to help.* She felt a light touch on her shoulder and turned around to see Yakone. There was a doubtful look in his eyes.

"Are you sure this is a good idea?" he murmured, too softly for any bear but Kallik to hear him. "Do we really want to take responsibility for this bear? There must be other bears around here—his kin—who can look after him better than we can."

"His mother drove him away," Kallik pointed out. "And his father has gone off somewhere. He doesn't have any bear to take care of him."

Yakone shook his head slowly. "I don't know. . . . We'll have to take him all the way to the Frozen Sea . . . or farther."

"Then that's what we'll do," Kallik retorted.

"But only white bears live on the Frozen Sea, or so you've always told me. Would Nanulak even *want* to travel there?"

"When we get there, he'll go with Toklo." Kallik forced herself not to add "cloud-brain." She was disappointed that Yakone would even consider leaving Nanulak behind, when the small bear needed help. And she was exasperated by the way that Yakone and Toklo always had to argue with each other. "He's coming with us, and that's that."

Toklo set out, the younger bear still huddling close to his side. Yakone crouched down for Lusa to scramble onto his shoulders, and Kallik brought up the rear. Even though she had spoken so firmly in favor of taking Nanulak along, she realized that Yakone had a point. Another member of the group, especially one as needy and vulnerable as Nanulak, might be more than they could handle.

Then she remembered her own family, how Nisa had cared for her and Taqqiq, and how she and her brother had played together on the ice. It had felt so wonderful to belong to them and be part of a family.

"We're a kind of family," she murmured to herself. "A strange one, but a family all the same. Nanulak will fit in. We can't possibly leave him behind."

CHAPTER SIXTEEN

Lusa

Lusa glanced around uneasily, wondering if the white bears who had attacked Nanulak were still in the area. The snow was falling so thickly their white pelts would be almost invisible until they were up close. Though she couldn't imagine abandoning the small bear, she knew that they were all in danger while he was with them.

Her mind was in a whirl. *I can't believe this! Bears attacking Nanulak for no reason, except that he's half white and half brown?* She knew about bears fighting for territory or prey, but this was completely different. *And his family driving him away into a blizzard! Thank the spirits we found him before the white bears did.*

I wonder what Ujurak would do, she asked herself. *I'm sure he would want to look after Nanulak.* But she wasn't certain that she and her friends would be able to fight off the hostile white bears if they came back and attacked them as well.

Looking down from Yakone's shoulders at Nanulak trotting beside them, she tried to push these worries out of her mind. "I'm Lusa," she called down to him. "The white bears are Kallik and Yakone, and the brown bear is Toklo."

Nanulak just gave her a brief nod. Lusa guessed that she was still too unfamiliar for him to be friendly. She didn't suppose he had ever seen a black bear before. He wouldn't even look at her.

"We're traveling to the Frozen Sea," Toklo told Nanulak. Lusa was surprised at how gentle he sounded, his voice full of concern. "Is that okay with you?"

Nanulak looked confused. "I don't know where that is," he replied, "but I guess it's okay. All I want is to get off this island. I don't care where I go after that, so long as the white bears can't find me."

"Wait—we're on an island?" Kallik pressed up to Nanulak, making the little bear flinch away into the shelter of Toklo's flank.

"I knew I was right," grunted Toklo.

Kallik cast her gaze into the distance, confused. "But . . . I thought the Frozen Sea was just over these hills."

"No. I told you." Nanulak's voice grew sharper, and Lusa thought she could detect a trace of anger in his eyes. "I've never heard of this Frozen Sea," he went on. "This is an island, but it's a long way to the other end."

Kallik and Yakone glanced at each other.

"So we have to cross another ocean," Kallik said bleakly.

Lusa felt her heart sink. She knew that they would have to travel beyond the Frozen Sea before she would find the right place for black bears: a place where the sun shone and there were berry bushes and stones where delicious grubs were hidden. If they were still a long way from the Frozen Sea, there would be a lot more ice to cover first. She sighed.

"Maybe it's a good thing we met you," Toklo said to Nanulak. "You can help us find the quickest way off the island."

"I'll try," Nanulak responded, sounding a tiny bit more confident. Toklo bent down and nuzzled his ears, deliberately shortening his strides to match the smaller bear's.

Lusa blinked. For a heartbeat she had thought that she was watching Toklo and Ujurak, traveling side by side as they had done for so long.

Is this bear going to take Ujurak's place in Toklo's heart?

As they trekked on through the heavily falling snow, Kallik and Toklo started ranging from side to side, searching for prey. Nanulak still stayed close to Toklo.

Toklo might find it hard to hunt if Nanulak doesn't give him a bit of space, Lusa thought.

But the smaller bear's nervousness didn't become a problem, because there was no prey to hunt, just the empty landscape stretching in all directions. *All the animals are in their holes,* Lusa realized, licking a snowflake off her nose. *And we can't dig for moss and leaves in the middle of a blizzard.* She huddled down into Yakone's fur, trying to forget the gaping hollow in her belly.

Lusa was soon drowsing, in a half dream of luscious berries and plump grubs, when she was roused by Kallik's voice.

"Over there! Look—no-claw dens!"

Peering through the snow, Lusa could just make out walls and roofs, almost hidden behind piled-up drifts. One or two yellow lights shone out from the windows as the daylight faded.

"What are flat-faces doing out here?" Toklo demanded. "Nanulak, do you know?"

The smaller brown bear shook his head. "I'm a *bear*," he pointed out. "We know about the no-claws, but we don't go near them."

"But we need food, and they might have some," Kallik said. "Lusa, should we give it a try?"

Lusa caught a surprised glance from Nanulak, as if he hadn't expected Kallik to consult her. *I may be small,* she thought with a faint stirring of annoyance, *but I know a bit about flat-faces.*

"Why not?" she replied to Kallik. "We won't find anything else to eat until the snow lets up."

Yakone veered toward the flat-face dens, taking the lead so that Lusa could get a good view of what lay ahead. The others followed.

"Keep a lookout for firebeasts," Lusa warned them. "They're probably asleep in this weather, but we can't take chances."

Snow had blotted out any BlackPaths, and Lusa couldn't spot any firebeasts as they drew closer to the dens. There was no sign of flat-faces moving around, either. Clearly the snow had driven them inside.

"Follow this wall," Lusa instructed Yakone as the first snow-covered den loomed up ahead of them. "Toklo, keep a lookout behind."

"Why is she telling you what to do?" Nanulak asked. "She's only a black bear."

It was Kallik who replied. "Because she knows the most about no-claws."

"And what's with all this creeping around, anyway?" Nanulak went on impatiently, as if Kallik hadn't spoken. "Why don't we just run in and grab what we want?"

Lusa felt her annoyance rising, but she clamped her jaws shut and tried to concentrate on figuring out which of the weird humped shapes under the snow around the den might be a metal can with food inside it. Kallik had already crept up to the nearest and was scraping at the snow to reveal what was underneath.

"We don't want to disturb the flat-faces." Toklo scanned their surroundings as he explained to Nanulak in a low voice, "We'll just slip in and out without any trouble."

"What?" Nanulak's voice was a squeal of outrage. "Slip in and out? Without any trouble? I can't believe you just said that!"

Yakone had halted, glancing back, and when Lusa looked over her shoulder she saw Nanulak and Toklo confronting each other.

"Said what?" Toklo asked. "Why would we want to bother the flat-faces if we can get food without?"

"Because that's not what brown bears do!" Nanulak retorted. "We're bigger and stronger than the no-claws, so we should take what we want."

Toklo took a step toward Nanulak, shaking his head exasperatedly. "Listen, Nanulak, we've done this before. You haven't."

"Are you a coward, or what?" Nanulak challenged Toklo. "You're a *brown bear*! Brown bears aren't scared of no-claws. No-claws should be scared of us."

Lusa remembered how terrified Nanulak had been when they found him. *I can't believe* he's *accusing Toklo of being a coward. Toklo isn't afraid of anything!*

"It's not cowardice; it's common sense," Yakone pointed out.

But Nanulak and Toklo still stood facing each other, their gazes locked together.

"I'll show you if I'm a coward!" Toklo growled.

"Toklo—" Lusa scrambled down from Yakone's shoulders and floundered through the snow to Toklo's side. "Please don't do anything bee-brained. You know—"

The sound of an opening door interrupted her. All the bears spun around to see a flat-face emerging from a nearby den. He closed the door behind him and trudged off through the snow, heading for a more distant nest. He was muffled up in thick pelts and was carrying a big bundle in his arms.

"What's that?" Kallik asked, sniffing.

"Meat!" Toklo swiped his tongue around his jaws. He narrowed his eyes, his gaze following the flat-face, who began to trudge through the snow to one of the other dens. Then he turned and thrust his snout into Nanulak's face. "You want meat? I'll get you meat!"

"Toklo, stop!" Kallik shouted as the grizzly bounded off through the snow toward the flat-face. "Come back!"

"Now see what you've done!" Yakone snapped at Nanulak. "You've put Toklo in danger. You've put us all in danger."

The small brown bear cowered away from Yakone. "Don't come near me!" he whimpered.

"Yakone, don't scare him." Kallik thrust herself between Yakone and Nanulak. "He doesn't understand."

Toklo let out a roar as he approached the flat-face, who spun around, momentarily frozen with shock at seeing a brown bear charging at him through the blizzard. With a yell of terror he hurled the bundle at Toklo and fled up to the nearest den, still yelling, and hammered on the door with his fists. The door opened. Yellow light flooded out onto the snow, and two other flat-faces appeared in the gap.

"Toklo, run!" Lusa squealed.

"On my back—now!" Yakone told Lusa, crouching down beside her.

As Lusa scrambled up, Toklo headed for the bundle of meat. But before he could grab it up in his jaws, Lusa saw more flat-faces pouring out of the den.

"Firesticks!" she gasped, as she spotted the familiar thin shapes in the flat-faces' paws. "Toklo, leave it! Run!"

As Toklo whirled around, scattering snow, Yakone turned and took off, his muscular legs eating up the distance. Kallik kept pace with Yakone, shoving the terrified Nanulak ahead of her. Firesticks cracked, and Lusa felt the sting of snow spraying up as the hard pellets hit the ground. Frantic with worry, she looked over her shoulder and saw Toklo galloping behind them, steadily catching up.

Gradually the falling snow hid the flat-face dens from the fleeing bears and the sounds of firesticks and flat-face shouting died away.

Eventually Yakone halted, letting out a huge puff of air. "We made it!"

Lusa slid down off his back, feeling her legs shake with the sudden release from fear. She wanted to roar at Nanulak and Toklo for being so bee-brained and spoiling her quiet raid.

Before she could say anything, Nanulak spun around, gazing back in the direction of the flat-face dens. Anger was smoldering in his eyes. "What were those things?" he demanded. "Can they hurt a bear?"

"Firesticks," Toklo replied, struggling to get his breath. "The flat-faces were trying to kill us."

"*Kill* us?" Nanulak echoed in horror. "What if the no-claws come after us? We have to take care of them."

"Flat-faces don't usually—" Lusa began, but Nanulak ignored her.

"We should strike first!" he insisted.

To Lusa's horror, Toklo responded with a grim nod. "You're right. We only wanted some food. There was no need for the flat-faces to start shooting their firesticks. We should go back and teach them a lesson."

Kallik stepped forward to confront him. "Toklo, are you completely cloud-brained? That won't get you anywhere except—"

She broke off as Toklo shoved her away. "Don't tell me what to do!" he snarled.

Instantly Yakone strode up to Kallik's side, thrusting out his snout until he was nose to nose with Toklo. "Keep your paws off Kallik!" he growled. "She's right. You and this sorry excuse for a bear nearly got us all killed!"

Toklo opened his jaws to reply, but before he could get a word out, Nanulak spoke. "You want to fight?" he demanded. "Good! We'll show you what brown bears can do!"

"Calm down!" Lusa felt her anger swelling as she raised her voice. "What are you going to do? Kill every flat-face on the island? Do you have any idea how ridiculous you're being?"

For a few heartbeats Toklo and Yakone stood facing each other, the flame of anger in their eyes. Their chests heaved, and low snarls came from their throats.

What if they fight each other? Lusa wondered, terrified. *What will happen to us all then?*

Abruptly Toklo turned away with a contemptuous flick of his ears. "Come on, Nanulak," he growled.

For one heart-stopping moment Lusa thought that Toklo intended to go back to the flat-face dens. But then she realized that he wasn't headed in that direction. Instead he was making for the hills again.

Kallik gave Yakone a nudge. "Let's go. It'll be okay. Toklo is never angry for long."

Yakone hesitated, then gave a reluctant nod, pushing his muzzle briefly into Kallik's shoulder fur. The two white bears followed Toklo, padding so close together that their pelts brushed. Lusa watched them for a moment, then followed.

Is Nanulak just going to cause trouble? Can we really make it to safety without splitting up? she wondered as they trudged silently through the snow. *What would Ujurak do?*

CHAPTER SEVENTEEN

Toklo

"Why can't we go after the no-claws—I mean, flat-faces?" Nanulak asked as he padded beside Toklo up the hillside. He growled the words; Toklo could tell he was still angry. "Are you saying it's okay for them to attack us with firesticks?"

"No, it's not okay," Toklo grunted. "But Lusa's right. Even if we killed one or two flat-faces, the others would come after us. There are always more of them than there are of us."

Nanulak just snorted; Toklo knew he didn't agree, but the smaller bear didn't protest anymore. Toklo guessed that he was too tired to go on arguing; his paws were heavy, and his head drooped. That was fine; Toklo didn't want to talk. He was disappointed that the raid had failed, and troubled by the fight with his companions.

They should let Nanulak make suggestions, and listen to him, he thought angrily. Then a small voice seemed to speak inside him. *Suggestions like going to attack the flat-faces? Is that really what you want to do, Toklo?*

Toklo jerked his head as if he were flicking away a

troublesome fly. Now that his frustration had cooled, he realized that going back to the flat-face dens would have been a bee-brained thing to do. If he hadn't been so angry and scared, he would never have considered it.

The ridge they were heading for was still some way off when Toklo spotted a thornbush jutting out of a snowbank. "Let's stop here," he said gruffly. "We'll dig out a den."

Nanulak waited, looking exhausted, while Toklo scraped a hole in the snow. The two brown bears crept into it together and lay down.

"I'm hungry," Nanulak complained.

"We'll hunt tomorrow," Toklo promised.

Darkness had fallen, but the star spirits gave enough light for him to see Kallik and Yakone plod up and begin to dig out another den a couple of bearlengths away. Lusa caught up, her pawsteps wavering with weariness, as the white bears huddled into their den.

"Come on, Lusa," Kallik said, shuffling to one side. "There's room for you here."

"Thanks," Lusa muttered as she squashed into the den.

Before the others were settled, Nanulak was asleep, snoring with his nose on his paws, his warm breath melting a little hole in the snow.

But for a long time Toklo couldn't sleep. He lay looking up to where thin cloud drifted over the sky, blotting out the stars, then letting them shine out again. A sense of loss griped deep within him as he tried to make out the shape that was Ujurak.

Are you watching us now, little bear?

* * *

When Toklo woke, Nanulak was still asleep, tucked cozily into his side. In the other den the white bears were stirring. Toklo watched them for a moment through half-open eyes, then let out a sigh. Careful not to wake Nanulak, he wriggled out of the den and padded over to the others.

As he approached, Kallik and Yakone both emerged from the den and shook snow from their pelts. They turned to face him; Toklo hesitated when he saw the coldness in their eyes, then made his paws carry him on.

"We have to keep together," he announced awkwardly. "I won't do anything unless we all agree."

At once Kallik nodded, relaxing as if she was willing to forget their quarrel, but Yakone's gaze was unforgiving. "Okay," he agreed grudgingly after a moment. "For now, we'll travel together."

"But stay away from flat-faces with firesticks," Kallik added.

Toklo muttered that he would. His pawsteps lighter, he returned to his own den and prodded Nanulak gently to wake him. "Come on, it's time to go," he said.

Nanulak raised his head and stretched his jaws wide in an enormous yawn. "Can we hunt first?" he asked, stumbling to his paws.

Toklo glanced at Kallik, who gave him a brisk nod. "We'd better," she said. "We're all starving."

While Kallik went to rouse Lusa, Toklo padded away from the dens, his snout raised to sniff the air. Nanulak stayed close to his side.

"I can smell a hare!" he announced after a moment.

"Then keep quiet about it," Toklo murmured, halting to see if he could pick up the same scent. It was there, but very faint. "Well scented," he added.

Nanulak's eyes shone with pride. "It's over there," he whispered, pointing with his snout.

Toklo looked, but he couldn't see anything. Suddenly Nanulak launched himself across the snow. At the same moment an Arctic hare leaped up from a dip in the ground and bounded away, with Nanulak hard on its paws.

Racing after them, Toklo was ready to trap the hare if it changed direction. But Nanulak seemed to have an instinct for which way the hare would dodge. He veered to one side and intercepted it, and Toklo heard its shriek of pain cut off abruptly as Nanulak closed his jaws on its throat.

Picking up his prey, Nanulak trotted back toward Toklo. "I got it!" he announced, his voice blurred by the mouthful of fur and flesh.

"Well done!" Toklo barked, feeling as much pride as if he had caught the hare himself.

He let Nanulak take the lead as they headed back to the others. Nanulak padded up to Kallik and Yakone and dropped the hare at their paws.

"Sorry about yesterday," he muttered. "Here—you eat first."

"Thanks," Kallik responded. "Great catch!"

Yakone said nothing; Toklo could see that he was still reluctant to forgive Nanulak, though he nodded in acknowledgment as he bent his head to take a mouthful of the hare.

"You're a good hunter, Nanulak," Lusa said warmly. "I wish you could scent out some leaves for me!"

Nanulak pointed with his snout toward the thorn tree overshadowing the dens. "If you dig down beside that tree, you should be able to get at the roots," he announced. "They're quite shallow."

"Oh, wow! Really?" Lusa bounded off to the tree and started digging down through the snow. Soon she was chewing happily.

"Thanks for helping Lusa," Toklo murmured to Nanulak as he took his own share of the prey. "She finds it hard out here. Black bears need leaves and roots and berries."

"That's okay." Nanulak's eyes shone. "See? You should listen to me more often!"

He really knows about this place, Toklo thought. *Maybe he will fit in after all.*

When they had devoured every last scrap of the hare, the bears set out again. The snow had stopped and the sky cleared. The air was crisp and cold. Strengthened by the food, even though his share hadn't been enough to fill his belly, Toklo strode out with new energy as he and his friends headed farther into the mountains.

Kallik and Yakone were still walking close together, while Nanulak stayed beside Toklo. Lusa followed a bearlength behind. Toklo was aware that the divisions of the previous night still hung in the air like mist, but at least the bears weren't snarling at one another anymore.

As they climbed higher, Toklo spotted the flat-face denning area, tiny now at this distance. A BlackPath led toward it, and Toklo reminded himself to be careful, in case it crossed their path some way ahead. Intent on the view, he failed to watch where he was putting his paws. Suddenly he felt the ground give way under his feet. Letting out a startled yelp, he slid downward in a shower of snow. For a moment he was terrified that he was falling down another hole; then he stopped with a thump on something hard.

Shaking his head to clear snow from his eyes, Toklo realized that he was lying at the bottom of a narrow ditch. He guessed it was the course of a small stream, and he had landed hard on the frozen surface. A bearlength above his head Lusa was gazing down at him.

"Toklo, you have snow on your head!" she exclaimed with a gurgle of amusement.

"He's almost a white bear," Kallik added, padding up beside Lusa. Yakone peered interestedly over her shoulder with a gleam in his eyes.

"I can still see some brown bits," Lusa responded. "I can fix that, though." Her eyes sparkling mischievously, she flipped more snow down on top of Toklo.

"Hey!" Toklo growled in mock anger. Scrambling to his paws, he heaved himself out of the ditch. "I'll make *you* into a white bear."

Lusa squealed with excitement as Toklo chased her, charged into her, and rolled her into a deep snowdrift. Lusa floundered around, waving her paws, her belly shaking with laughter. "I'll get you for that, Toklo!" she threatened.

"You can try!" Toklo retorted.

As he waited for Lusa to scramble out of the drift, Toklo noticed that Nanulak was standing a little way away, underneath a thorn tree. The small brown bear had a strange expression on his face, as if he didn't understand what was going on.

Poor Nanulak, Toklo thought. *Maybe his family never played with him.*

"Hey, Nanulak!" he called. When Nanulak turned toward him, Toklo galloped closer, scooped up snow in his paws, and flung it into the smaller bear's face.

Nanulak jumped with surprise. For a heartbeat he looked outraged. Then he reached up to the lowest branch of the tree above him and shook off all the snow. He was aiming for Toklo, but at that moment Yakone barged past, running from Kallik, and the snow caught him full in the face.

Yakone halted; the smaller bear shrank back a step. Toklo was ready to step in, worried that the white bear was angry, when suddenly Yakone spun around.

"Great idea!" he exclaimed. "Let's do it to Kallik."

"Oh, no!" Kallik swerved away. "You won't catch me like that."

The warmth of fun and companionship spread through Toklo as if he were standing in the sun. Then he heard a distant rumble and realized it was firebeasts on the BlackPath he had spotted earlier.

"That's enough," he said, intercepting Yakone as he tried to chase Kallik. "We can't stay here playing all day."

Kallik halted and padded back, her panting breath billowing into a cloud in the cold air. "You're right," she said regretfully. "It was fun, though."

"That's where we've got to go, right?" Toklo pointed his snout at the next ridge of hills.

"Right," Yakone agreed. He gave Kallik a friendly nudge. "I'll get you next time. Just you wait."

Walking closer together now, the bears fell into an easy stride. As they climbed higher, Toklo kept casting glances at Nanulak, padding along at his side. It felt good to be traveling with a brown bear again. Having Nanulak by his side eased some of his pain over losing Ujurak.

Maybe Ujurak guided me to Nanulak, so I could look after him. Is that what he meant about remembering what truly matters? Looking after your own bears?

"You must have seen so many different places," Nanulak said after a while. "Is there a lot of snow like this where you come from?"

"No, there's not much snow at all," Toklo replied, casting his mind back to his BirthDen, where he had played with Tobi among trees and grassy meadows. "There are forests, as far as you can see in all directions. And rivers—"

"What's a forest?" Nanulak interrupted.

Toklo gave him an amused look. "Of course, you've never seen one. Well, you see that thorn tree?" He angled his head toward the stunted tree they were just passing. "Imagine that it was really big, stretching right up into the sky, many bearlengths above your head."

Nanulak nodded, his eyes wide with wonder.

"Now imagine a lot of them—more than a bear could ever count—so many that you could walk for days and not get to the end of them. That's a forest."

"Oh, wow! I'd like to see that!" Nanulak exclaimed.

"You will, one day, if you stay with me. I'm going back there."

The smaller bear let out a happy sigh. "I'm so lucky that I met you! Tell me more," he went on eagerly. "Tell me about when you were a cub."

Toklo hesitated for a moment. There was so much that he didn't want to remember about those days—about how Tobi had gotten sick and died, and how Oka had driven him away because she was afraid that he would die, too. But there were other stories that he could tell Nanulak: stories of sunlight and games and the things his mother had taught him before her despair made her turn on him.

"I remember how my mother taught us to stalk prey," he began. "She would walk ahead of us through the trees, and then hide in a thicket . . ."

Nanulak could hardly get enough of the stories, or of Toklo's descriptions of what it was like to live in the forest as a brown bear.

"But then I met Ujurak," Toklo went on, when he was running out of early memories. "And he wanted to journey to the place where the spirits dance. So we—"

"No, tell me more about the forests," Nanulak interrupted.

"Okay . . . but we did really exciting stuff on our journey." Toklo was surprised at how uninterested Nanulak seemed about Ujurak.

"That's all behind you," the smaller bear argued. "You're going home now. When we get there, will you teach me how to catch salmon?"

"Sure I will," Toklo responded. "I'll bet you'll be good at it, too."

Nanulak gave a little bounce, plopping down again into the freshly fallen snow. "I'll be the best brown bear in the forest!" he boasted.

Toklo's paws prickled with excitement at the thought of teaching the younger bear. He wanted to push on faster, to get back to his familiar trees.

That's the right place for brown bears. Nanulak and I could carve out territories for ourselves, side by side. Then we could look out for each other all the time. . . .

Reaching the top of a ridge a little way ahead of Kallik and Yakone, who was carrying Lusa on his back again, Toklo looked across a shallow valley to the slope beyond. Covering the whole summit of the mountain was a mass of ice, glimmering in the pale light of snow-sky.

"Ice!" he exclaimed.

"Yes," Nanulak said. "It covers the top of the ridge in the middle of the island. It's great up there."

Toklo gave him a doubtful look and suppressed a shiver. The wind was already probing its cold claws deep into his fur; it would be colder still up on the frozen mountaintop. He didn't think he had ever seen a bleaker place, unless it was out on the Endless Ice.

"More snow's coming," Nanulak said suddenly, sniffing the wind. "Lots of it."

"Are you sure?" Toklo asked. The sky was still clear, though cloud was beginning to build up behind them.

"Positive. Can't you smell it?"

Glancing at Nanulak, Toklo saw his head and shoulders outlined against the sky, his muzzle raised. His silhouette looked like Kallik or Yakone, not like a brown bear at all. White bears could scent snow. Nanulak wasn't just a brown bear, Toklo realized—he had all the instincts, and some of the appearance, of a white bear, too.

"My paws are falling off!" Kallik exclaimed as she joined Toklo and Nanulak on the ridge, closely followed by Yakone with Lusa. "We should think about making a den for the night. There's more snow to come and we'll want to be well rested."

The way that Kallik unconsciously confirmed what Nanulak had just said made Toklo feel uneasy. He had been thinking of Nanulak as a brown bear; now he was powerfully reminded of his new friend's white-bear heritage.

Beginning to pad down into the valley, Toklo wanted to fire questions at Nanulak. *Do you think of yourself as a brown bear or a white bear? If you could choose, would you rather be just one?* But he couldn't form the words. Nanulak's brown-bear kin had driven him away, and white bears had attacked him. Toklo couldn't imagine that he wanted to talk about any of them.

Maybe he doesn't know what *he is,* Toklo reflected. *Just the way Ujurak used to be.*

Down in the valley, Kallik and Yakone found a dip in the ground sheltered by boulders, and they started to dig out a den. Toklo located a half-buried thornbush and scraped away the snow to uncover the leaves and bark for Lusa.

"Thanks, Toklo," she muttered drowsily, stripping off a pawful of leaves and cramming them into her mouth until she could barely speak. "It's . . . so . . . good."

"Why does she prefer that stuff to meat?" Nanulak asked, staring at Lusa with undisguised curiosity.

"She's a black bear. That's what they like," Toklo replied.

"Weird!"

Toklo was glad that Lusa was too tired to react to Nanulak's tactless comments. "We've all eaten roots and leaves and bark before," he pointed out. "It's better than nothing."

Nanulak puffed out his chest. "I'm a brown bear. I *hunt* for my food!"

Toklo just grunted, undecided whether to be amused or annoyed. "Okay, let's go and hunt now," he said. "We'll see if we can catch something before Kallik and Yakone finish the den."

Nanulak's eyes gleamed with enthusiasm. "Great!"

Toklo told the others where they were going and led the way across the valley to a stretch of tumbled rocks and thorns. The tracks of other bears crisscrossed the snow, but they were blurred, as if the wind had already begun to sweep them away.

Toklo couldn't pick up the scent of any strange bears.

"This looks like the sort of place where prey might be hiding," he told Nanulak. "But I suppose you know that as well as I do."

Nanulak nodded. "All sorts of little animals might live in the cracks," he replied. "They're no more than a mouthful, though. If we're lucky—" He stopped suddenly, raising his muzzle and sniffing.

Toklo caught the scent at the same moment. "Fox!" he breathed out. He drew in a long breath, trying to pinpoint the scent.

Nanulak angled his head toward a thorn thicket. "In there."

Toklo gazed at the thorns for a moment, fighting frustration. Their pelts would be ripped off if they tried to go in after the fox. They would have to wait for the fox to come out.

"I know what to do," Nanulak suggested. "I'll creep around the other side of the thorns and scare the fox. It'll run out this way, and you can catch it."

"Good idea!" Toklo said.

Nanulak slid away, plowing through the snow until he disappeared around the thicket. Toklo stayed where he was, poised to attack. Suddenly a loud roar erupted from the opposite side of the thorns. An instant later the branches parted and the fox darted out into the open.

Baring his teeth, Toklo leaped at it with a roar of his own. Terrified, the fox spun around, only to see Nanulak galloping toward it from behind the thicket. The fox tried to flee, but before it had taken a single pawstep Toklo was on it, swiping a forepaw across its head. The fox collapsed, a limp heap in the snow.

"Got it!" Toklo exclaimed.

"We did it together," Nanulak responded. "We make a terrific team, Toklo."

Nanulak dragged the fox back to where Kallik and Yakone had finished hollowing out the den. Lusa was already curled up inside.

Kallik padded up to give the fox an admiring sniff. "Did you catch this, Nanulak?"

"We both did," Nanulak replied. "Come and share it."

As they gathered around the prey, Toklo was happy to see Nanulak making more of an effort to get along with the white bears. *He's bound to feel closer to me because we look most alike,* he thought. *But it's good that he wants to be friends with Kallik and Yakone, too. He has to learn to trust all of us equally if he wants to travel with us.*

The snow that Nanulak and Kallik had predicted began to fall shortly after they set out the following morning. The soft white flakes grew thicker and thicker, and a wind rose, until the bears were battling their way into the teeth of a blizzard. Yakone carried Lusa on his back again. Toklo felt as if the cold were a huge bear fastening its claws around him, dragging him backward. Every pawstep was a massive effort. The white bears handled it better, though Toklo noticed that even they were shivering. Nanulak plodded on uncomplainingly, more at home in the snow than Toklo.

"This is hopeless," Yakone said. The white male had taken

the lead; now he turned and waited for the others to catch up. "We've got to find some shelter and wait the storm out."

Toklo gazed into the whirling snow. "I can't see a bear-length in front of my nose," he complained. "How are we going to find shelter in this?"

"We'll just have to keep going until we do," Kallik said resignedly.

Toklo hunched his shoulders and faced into the biting wind. "Come on, then." To his relief, before they had taken many more pawsteps, he spotted something dark looming through the snow. "There's something up ahead," he said.

A little farther, and he could see that their path was blocked by a sheer cliff face. Rocks jutted outward, forming a shallow cave underneath.

"There!" Kallik exclaimed, bounding past Toklo to stand under the overhang. "We can wait here until the storm dies down."

Toklo stumbled after her, thankful to be out of the buffeting wind. Nanulak pressed in beside him, and Yakone followed, letting Lusa slide from his back to the ground.

"The snow's thin back here," Kallik went on, exploring the back of the overhang. "Why don't we scrape it away? It'll be so much warmer if we do that."

Toklo wanted to grumble that he was already asleep on his paws, but he bit the words back. It would be worth a bit of extra effort to be comfortable, especially if the storm kept them stuck here for days. He attacked the nearest snow pile, thrusting it out into the open with powerful sweeps of his claws. All the others—even Lusa, who was yawning widely as she scraped—joined him, until they had exposed the bare face of the rock and the sandy floor of the cave.

"Look at this," Lusa said, sounding suddenly more alert. She was pointing at the cave wall with one paw.

Toklo craned his neck to see what she had found. His pelt prickled with shock as he recognized markings on the wall, like the ones they had found in the cave on Star Island, the Place of the Selamiut. These weren't as clear, though, as if bad weather had scoured them away. He could only just make out spiky figures that he thought represented flat-faces.

"Why are they here?" Kallik asked, a trace of awe in her voice. "Are they supposed to tell us something?"

Toklo felt a touch of the same awe as he remembered the markings in the other cave. In the Place of the Selamiut were images of flat-faces and their dens, and pictures of caribou. Most amazing of all, there were images of the four of them: Lusa and Kallik, Ujurak and Toklo himself. But the images here were faint; Toklo couldn't tell if they were meant to be bears, let alone pictures of him and his companions.

"I don't think they mean anything," he grunted. "I can't even see what they're supposed to be."

"What are they, anyway?" Nanulak asked, going up to one of the nearest marks and sniffing at it.

"Images," Kallik explained. "We think no-claws made them."

"Oh, no-claws!" Nanulak turned away dismissively. "Who cares about them?"

Toklo examined the marks for a moment more, but he still couldn't see any meaning in them. He let himself flop down onto the cave floor; the others huddled around him at the back of the overhang, listening to the storm raging outside.

"The wind sounds angry," Lusa murmured from where she was curled up between Toklo and Kallik. "It's like a huge voice, roaring at us."

"You shouldn't imagine things," Kallik warned. Toklo thought she sounded edgy, as if she couldn't help agreeing with Lusa, even though she wouldn't admit it. "It's only wind."

Toklo was just grateful to have found somewhere to rest. Doing his best to ignore the gaping hole in his belly, he closed his eyes and tried to sleep.

Waking from an uncomfortable doze, Toklo was first aware of the silence. The wind had dropped. He opened his eyes on a glare of white snow-light; when his eyes grew used to the brightness, he saw that much more snow had fallen overnight. Huge powdery drifts had blown in under the overhang, sealing him and his companions into the cave.

"It's a good thing we weren't sleeping outside," he muttered as he began rousing the others.

Together they thrust their way through the fresh snow and into the open. A shallow valley, now a vast expanse of white, stretched in front of them, glittering under the pale, low sun. Thin clouds drifted across an icy blue sky.

Suddenly Nanulak stiffened, staring past Toklo with wide, frightened eyes. "White bears!" he whispered.

Toklo turned to gaze across the valley. A group of white bears—a large male, a couple of females, and a half-grown cub—were walking toward them, plowing their way through the snow.

"They're looking for me!" Nanulak whimpered. "Don't let them get me!"

"Are those the bears who attacked you?" Yakone asked.

"I don't know," Nanulak replied, shivering. "I don't remember. But all the white bears on this island are really unfriendly. They fight with the brown bears all the time."

"Then get back into the shelter and stay there, Nanulak," Toklo ordered.

Nanulak ducked behind the mounds of snow, while Kallik and Yakone moved to screen the gaps they had made as they pushed their way out.

Lusa came to stand beside Toklo, blinking worriedly. "Do you think the white bears would attack us to get to Nanulak?" she asked.

"We'll make sure that doesn't happen," Yakone said grimly.

It was the first time Yakone had spoken up in Nanulak's defense, and Toklo flashed a glance of respect at the white bear. Kallik was gazing at him admiringly, and she moved a little closer to him so that their pelts brushed.

"I'm not going to be told what to do by strangers," Yakone added.

Toklo turned to face the group of bears as they drew closer, fixing the male, who was in the lead, with a fierce glare. *If they're looking for trouble, they can have it. They're not going to hurt Nanulak!*

But the bears had veered aside and didn't seem to notice Toklo or the others. They padded past, several bearlengths away. Even so, Toklo remained braced for an attack, and he didn't relax until they were well away, heading farther down the slope into the valley.

"Good riddance," he muttered.

Nanulak crept back outside to watch the departing bears. "They're gone!" he said with a sigh of relief. "You were so brave, Toklo!"

The younger bear's praise warmed him, even though he knew he hadn't done anything. "They weren't a problem," he said gruffly. "Anyway, it's all over now. I'm going to hunt."

"I'll come with you," Nanulak said instantly.

"No, stay here." Kallik padded up and nudged him back toward the cave. "You don't want to meet the white bears when you're alone with Toklo, do you?"

"Toklo would look after me," Nanulak muttered, resisting Kallik's gentle push.

Even though Toklo was pleased that the younger bear trusted him, he knew Kallik was right. "I can't fight every white bear on the island myself," he pointed out. "It's far better for you to stay in hiding. Lusa had better stay here, too."

"But I'd like to hunt with you today," Lusa objected.

"In all this snow?" Toklo butted her affectionately in the shoulder with his muzzle. "We'd lose you in a drift and never find you again."

Lusa bared her teeth in a mock snarl. But she didn't protest again before heading through the gap, back into the cave.

Nanulak stayed where he was, looking sulky.

"You too," Toklo ordered, not in the mood for any more argument.

To his relief, Nanulak seemed to accept that, and followed Lusa with no more than a disgusted snort.

"Kallik and I will hunt this way," Yakone said, pointing his muzzle in a different direction from the one the white bears had taken.

"Great. Good luck," Toklo replied. He decided to follow the line of the cliff, beside the overhang, still keeping well away from where the white bears had disappeared. *We were lucky that they didn't spot us. I want to keep it that way.*

Toklo floundered through the deep, powdery snow, which rose higher than his belly. The thick white stuff masked any possible prey-scents. Looking around, Toklo realized that the whole landscape was different. Briefly he was afraid of getting lost, until he realized that he could follow his own trail back to the cave.

He was beginning to despair of catching anything when he picked up the scent of some small animal and spotted its tracks, tiny prints that told him the creature wouldn't be nearly enough to fill even one bear's belly.

But it's better than nothing.

Toklo set off after the animal, flinging the snow aside as he thrust his way through it. "Spirit-cursed drifts!" he muttered to himself.

Finally Toklo spotted the creature, skittering light-footed across the surface of the snow. It was something he'd never seen before, brown and furry, like a big mouse. Launching himself through the snow, claws outstretched, he pounced.

But instead of feeling his paws close around his prey, Toklo found himself swallowed up in a fluffy white sea. Snow was in his mouth, his eyes, his nose, and he thrashed helplessly. Above his head, he heard the creature let out a triumphant squeak, and he pictured it running away to safety.

Seal rot!

Then Toklo heard another sound above him: the deep bark of a strange bear.

"You'll never catch anything like that."

CHAPTER EIGHTEEN

Toklo

Toklo managed to wedge solid snow beneath his paws and struggle out of the drift. Blinking ice crystals from his eyes, he saw a white she-bear looking down at him from an outcrop of rock. Her eyes glimmered with amusement.

"Haven't you ever seen a snowdrift before?" she called.

"I'm not used to so much snow," Toklo replied crossly. "I'm not from around here."

The white bear jumped gracefully down to a rock on the same level as Toklo. Looking more closely at her, Toklo recognized her as one of the group who had passed by the cave earlier.

"I thought you were one of the brown bears from the other side of the island," she said.

Toklo's fur tingled as the white bear drew closer, and he braced himself for the hostility Nanulak had warned him about. "No," he grunted. "I'm just passing through."

The she-bear blinked in surprise. "We don't get many visitors here."

Toklo was wary of telling her too much about himself. He didn't want to attract her attention to his friends, especially to Nanulak. For all he knew, these white bears were the ones who had attacked the cub.

"I'm not surprised," he responded, "if it's impossible to catch prey when it snows."

"Well, of course you can't hunt in a snowdrift," the white bear said. "Don't you know anything?" Beckoning him with a jerk of her head, she added, "Come up here; it's easier."

Toklo still didn't trust the she-bear, but he was glad to get away from the level of the overhang; he was still too close for comfort to the cave where Nanulak and Lusa were hiding. Toklo hauled himself up to stand beside the she-bear. At once he realized that the snow was thinner here; he could feel the rock beneath his paws. The white bear watched him closely; he was conscious of laughter in her eyes as he panted from the effort of climbing.

"I'm Tikaani," she said.

"I'm Toklo," he puffed, dipping his head.

"So," Tikaani went on, "I'd better give you a lesson in hunting, or you'll starve before you get where you're going."

Though she seemed friendly, Toklo still couldn't shake off his suspicions. "What about your friends?" he asked.

There was a flicker of surprise in Tikaani's eyes, and Toklo wondered whether he should have let slip that he had seen her with the other white bears. Then she shrugged gracefully. "They can hunt for themselves. It's easier to hunt alone, anyway." Glancing around, she added, "Are you traveling alone?"

"Yes," Toklo replied quickly. "I . . . I heard there were brown bears here, so I came to see them, but I don't want to stay here forever."

The explanation sounded clumsy in his ears, but Tikaani seemed to accept it. Her gaze was focused on the white expanse in front of her. "When the snow's this deep," she began, "you have to keep to the higher, more exposed ground, where there won't be so many drifts. Trying to hunt below that overhang is the worst thing you could do."

Toklo nodded. *I already found that out!*

"And you can't chase prey when the snow is this deep," Tikaani went on. "Instead you have to wait, as if you were at a seal hole—though I guess you wouldn't know about those."

Oh, no? Toklo thought, though he said nothing. *I know all about catching seals!*

"Let's see what we can find," Tikaani said. She led the way over the rocks, finally halting beside a small hole in the snow. Stretching out her neck, she sniffed carefully. "There's a lemming down there," she murmured.

"A lemming?" Toklo had never heard of that animal before. From the size of the hole, it couldn't be that big.

"Like the one you were chasing," Tikaani explained. "Now, don't get too close to the hole, or it might realize we're here. We have to wait for it to come out."

She settled down beside the hole, and Toklo did the same. *It's* exactly *like waiting for a seal to pop up!*

"When it comes, it's yours," Tikaani added in a low voice. "Make sure you're ready!"

She remained completely still, her gaze fixed on the hole, and Toklo did his best to imitate her as he resigned himself to a long wait even though there was an itchy place behind one of his ears that he desperately wanted to scratch, and he thought that Tikaani might be able to hear the rumbling of his belly. Suddenly Tikaani looked up and gave him a swift nod.

Has she heard something? Toklo wondered, impressed. *She must have really good ears!*

A moment later the lemming popped its head out of the hole. Toklo waited a heartbeat until it emerged onto the surface of the snow: a small, plump creature with long fur in mottled shades of brown. Then he pounced! He wasn't used to catching anything that tiny, and he thought at first it would slip through his paws. To his relief, he felt his claws sink into it.

I did it!

"Here," Toklo said, pushing the lemming toward Tikaani with one paw. "It's your prey, really."

The she-bear shook her head. "Thanks, but you caught it," she replied. "And I guess you need it more than I do. I'll be able to catch another." She paused, then added, "Will you be okay now?"

Toklo gave her a grateful nod. "Do you live near here?" he asked her.

"My family moves around," Tikaani answered. "We come to the mountains in the really bad weather, because there are more places to shelter, and it's easier to hunt on the exposed rocks." She put her head on one side thoughtfully, then continued, "Would you like to stay with us for a while? My family wouldn't mind, and there's room for you in the den."

Surprised, Toklo shook his head. This wasn't the hostile reception he'd been expecting based on Nanulak's warnings. "No, thanks, I'll be fine." *I just wanted to know where you are so we can avoid an attack,* he added silently to himself.

Tikaani shrugged. "Then maybe I'll see you again tomorrow," she said. "If you're still around?"

"Maybe," Toklo responded.

He stood still and watched her go, leaping gracefully from rock to rock. Then he picked up the lemming and jumped down again to the level of the cave. His heart was pounding, and he felt hot inside his fur.

What's the matter with me? He decided that it must be from the tension of knowing that there were white bears around who could attack at any time. *The one I met was pretty nice, but the others might be hostile, like Nanulak said.*

Toklo kept a wary eye out as he followed his trail back through the snow, and he checked that no strangers were watching before he ducked back under the overhang and through the gap in the snow that they had made earlier when they'd pushed their way out.

Lusa and Nanulak were hiding in the farthest corner of the cave, their eyes wide with anxiety, gleaming in the half darkness.

"You've got food!" Nanulak exclaimed, edging forward.

"You weren't attacked?" Lusa added.

"No," Toklo replied. "Everything was fine." He decided not

to tell the others about Tikaani. He didn't think that she was a threat, and he wanted to avoid scaring them with talk of a white bear so close to their cave.

Just then Toklo heard the sound of pawsteps approaching the gap through the snow. He swung around, then relaxed to see Kallik and Yakone; Kallik was carrying a goose.

"You've done well," he said. "Did you have any problems?"

Yakone shook his head. "We spotted one of those white bears at a distance, but I don't think he noticed us."

"Good," Nanulak growled. "I hope we can keep it that way."

The light outside was ebbing away as Toklo settled down with the others to share the prey. Warmth soaked through his pelt and into his belly as he ate. "Are there many white bears on the island?" he asked Nanulak.

"Too many!" Nanulak snarled. "They're always causing trouble for the brown bears, stealing fresh-caught prey and attacking their cubs."

Toklo was puzzled. Tikaani had seemed quite friendly when he'd mentioned the other brown bears on the island. And she had been generous with the prey; he couldn't imagine her stealing, or attacking defenseless cubs.

"I wouldn't care if I never saw another white bear," Nanulak went on. "I'd like it if every last one of them was wiped out!"

Kallik and Yakone exchanged an offended glance; Kallik looked as if she couldn't believe she had just heard that. Yakone was opening his jaws to reply when Lusa stretched out a paw and touched him on the leg, shaking her head. She was blinking unhappily, but she said nothing.

"There's no need to get so worked up," Toklo said to Nanulak. "You know now that not all white bears are bad, and we'll protect you from the ones that want to hurt you."

Nanulak snorted. "Would *all* of you fight white bears if they attacked me?"

"It's time we got some sleep," Lusa interrupted, shoving Nanulak aside so that she could lie down between him and the white bears. "I'm so tired I can't keep my eyes open, and I don't want to listen to any more arguing."

"I'll sleep next to the entrance," Toklo volunteered. "If any hostile white bears find us, they'll have to get past me first."

As he settled down, he heard a disgruntled huff from Nanulak, but then nothing more as the younger bear curled up and wrapped his paws around his nose. Lusa was already snoring.

Kallik and Yakone lay down side by side; Toklo heard Yakone muttering something into Kallik's ear, but he couldn't make out the words. *I really thought Nanulak was learning to get along with Kallik and Yakone,.* Toklo mused. *I hope Kallik and Yakone can be patient with him.*

The sun dazzled on the surface of the snow the next morning as Toklo set out to hunt again. No more had fallen overnight, and as Toklo started walking, he realized that the drifts had collapsed under their own weight, making it easier to move around.

We'll be able to leave soon, he thought, and wondered why he felt regretful about that. *Maybe it* would *be better to stay here for a while. The cave is a good place to sleep, and there seems to be plenty of prey, if you know what to look for.*

"Hello again!"

The greeting came from a nearby outcrop of rocks, and Toklo spotted Tikaani outlined against the sky. She bounded over to him.

"I hoped I'd see you today," she confessed.

Shuffling his paws in the snow with embarrassment, Toklo wasn't sure what to say. But if Tikaani noticed his awkwardness, she didn't comment on it.

"I want to show you how to hunt birds. They're trickier because they can fly," she explained.

Toklo's embarrassment vanished in a spurt of amusement. "You don't say!" he teased.

Tikaani let out a huff of laughter and butted him in the shoulder with her snout. Leaping back, Toklo scooped up a pawful of snow and flicked it at her, then froze, wondering if she would be offended. But Tikaani just flicked snow back at him, the crystals glittering in the sunlight.

Toklo wanted to keep playing like this all day, but a moment later Tikaani was practical again. "Okay, we need to find a special sort of thorn tree," she said. "Let's try that thicket over there."

Toklo followed her, and watched her nudge her way through the thorny branches until she could tear a large seed pod from one of the trees. The seeds inside rattled as she tugged it free.

"That won't feed us," Toklo objected, though he wondered if it might make a tasty snack for Lusa.

"No, silly, it's not for us," Tikaani responded, rolling her eyes. "Watch."

Delicately she clawed the seed pod open and scattered the seeds on the snow. Then, beckoning to Toklo to follow her, she withdrew into the shelter of the thorns.

"Now we wait until the seeds tempt a bird down," she explained. "Remember, pounce where you see shallow snow, not a deep drift to fall into."

Toklo nodded, wishing he had Tikaani's skill of being able to tell the depth of the snow from just looking at it. As they settled down to wait, Tikaani began heaping snow on top of Toklo.

"Hey, what's that for?" he asked as the cold began to sink into his pelt.

"To hide you, cloud-brain!" Tikaani replied. "Your brown pelt really stands out. When you're on your own, you could try rolling in snow."

"Okay." *But I hope a bird comes down quickly.* Toklo had begun to think he would turn into an ice bear when he heard the flutter of wings and a goose landed on the snow. It started to eat the seeds with its back to Tikaani and Toklo.

Both bears leaped in the same heartbeat, but Toklo felt the snow give way under his hindpaws as he took off, and Tikaani reached the prey first, snapping its neck cleanly with a single swipe.

"Yes!" Toklo roared. "Great catch!"

For a moment his gaze met Tikaani's, and they stood in silence.

"You're good at this, too," the she-bear said. Then, after a moment, "You should stay here. Other brown bears have."

Toklo felt his breath grow short. "I can't stay," he replied; for some reason he felt as if the words were being wrenched out of him. "This isn't my home."

"It could be."

Toklo blinked. "I've heard brown and white bears don't get along on this island," he ventured.

"Some of them do," Tikaani said. "Some of them have even had cubs together." Then she sighed and added, "And some of them don't. But it doesn't have to be like that forever."

Suppose I did stay? Toklo asked himself in rising excitement. *Maybe we could all settle here. Nanulak might get along with these white bears.*

Then he spotted something behind Tikaani, a faint outline that took the form of a small brown bear.

Ujurak!

His friend's voice echoed inside Toklo's head, filled with sadness. *Remember what really matters.* Ujurak's eyes held Toklo's as his image slowly faded away again. Toklo was reminded of the tall trees and the rushing rivers of his true home.

Regretfully, Toklo shook his head. "I'm sorry, Tikaani. I can't stay." He felt guilty to see the disappointment in Tikaani's eyes. "But thanks for the hunting tips! And really, if I could stay, I would." He wished he could tell her everything, about his companions, the journey they had made to Star Island, how he had dreamed for so long of finding a forest with brown bears just like him, and delicious prey to hunt.

A territory, with borders—a *home*. Why did those plans suddenly seem such a long way off? He could be just as happy here, couldn't he, with Tikaani?

"Well, if you change your mind, come back," she said. "I'll be here."

Toklo nodded. "I'll remember that," he promised. He stretched his head out, and they touched muzzles, briefly but just long enough for him to taste the sweetness of her breath and feel warmth through his fur. He closed his eyes. *Why is it so hard to remember what matters most sometimes?* He heard a rustle of snow and opened his eyes to see Tikaani walking away, leaving a trail of pawprints on the rocks. Toklo's heart sank. He would be loyal to his companions whatever happened, but right now it felt as if he were losing a little part of himself.

He headed back toward the cave, carrying the goose, a parting gift from Tikaani. He cast one glance back to see her poised on top of a rock, watching him go. Then he lost sight of her as he rounded a thorn thicket.

He felt encouraged by the discovery that not all the white bears on the island were hostile. But he knew that he had to put Nanulak first. If the younger bear felt so threatened by the white bears that he refused to live on the island, then they had to keep going until they all found somewhere they could live safely.

That's what I have to do, Toklo decided. *But I'm sorry that I won't see Tikaani again.*

CHAPTER NINETEEN

Kallik

Kallik plodded through the soft snow, glad to stretch her muscles again after the couple of days' rest in the cave. Toklo had taken the lead, seeming eager to get going, and even Lusa looked brighter, wading determinedly through the snow.

Toklo is himself again, Kallik reflected. *I hated when he was so different after we rescued him from the tunnel. Now he's almost as comfortable here as a white bear, and he's really good at hunting in snow!* She remembered how she and Yakone had tried out the tricks Toklo taught them, catching a goose even bigger than the one Toklo had brought back when they tempted it with seeds.

Maybe because they were all well-fed for once, Kallik felt that the mood had lifted. Even Nanulak was high-spirited, forgetting his fear of white bears as he pestered Toklo for stories about rivers and forests.

But even though he seemed to be himself again, Toklo was quiet today, responding only briefly to Nanulak's flood of questions. Kallik quickened her pace and caught up with him. "Are you okay?" she asked.

Toklo glanced at her; for a heartbeat his gaze looked unfocused, as if he was expecting to see some other bear. "Yes, I'm fine," he replied.

For days the bears had caught glimpses of ice glimmering on the horizon ahead of them, and now a tough climb, scrambling among snow and rocks, brought them to the edge of it. It was like a frozen ocean perched on a ridge of mountains. Kallik took in a long, cold breath of air. Ice stretched ahead as far as she could see, broken up by dark rocks that poked through the surface. Wisps of cloud drifted across it.

"It's so beautiful!" she whispered. "I never dreamed there could be so much ice at the top of a mountain."

Yakone stood still, his snout raised and his gaze fixed on the expanse of ice. "It's quite something."

"Do you think it's a frozen sea?" Lusa asked, her berry-bright eyes wide with wonder. "We've never seen one of those so high up before."

"There are a lot of things we've never seen before," Toklo pointed out.

"It's just a stretch of ice," Nanulak informed them, fluffing out his fur importantly. "There's no sea underneath it. Sometimes it melts in burn-sky, and there's nothing underneath but rocks."

Kallik took a few steps forward, reveling at the feeling of ice beneath her paws again. "It's worth all the struggles to get up here, just to see this," she murmured.

"It should be easier going now," Yakone commented, then looked over at his companions. "At least, it will be for me and

Kallik. Sorry, I forget that brown and black bears aren't used to traveling on ice."

Toklo took a few exploratory steps out onto the ice sheet. Kallik could see that he was having trouble balancing, just as he had before when they'd crossed the Endless Ice. They had been traveling on land or snow-covered ice for several moons, and Toklo had clearly lost the knack of ice-walking. Nanulak followed him and instantly started slipping, waving his legs around and letting out a high-pitched yelp as he landed hard on his rump.

But his paws are more like mine and Yakone's than Toklo's, Kallik thought. *He should be able to manage just fine on the ice. Is he trying to act like a brown bear, to be like Toklo?*

"Don't forget that there won't be any seals under this ice," Toklo said, retracing his pawsteps to help Nanulak up. "And I can't imagine hares and foxes making their dens in it. We'll have to stay near the edge to catch prey, and to find leaves and twigs for Lusa."

The little black bear stifled a massive yawn. "Yes, please."

Kallik felt momentarily disappointed. As soon as she'd set eyes on the massive ice sheet, she had longed to explore it.

"We could head across the ice for a little way," Yakone suggested. "Just me and Kallik, I mean. Some bear ought to check it out, in case there's anything dangerous."

"That's a great idea!" Kallik exclaimed.

But Toklo was looking doubtful. "I don't like the idea of splitting up."

"We won't go far," Yakone promised.

"Well . . . okay." Toklo gave a reluctant nod. "I think I'll rest for a bit, and then maybe hunt. Lusa, are you going with them?"

"No way! I'll stay with you and get some sleep . . ." Her words ended in another huge yawn.

"Nanulak?" Kallik would rather have spent the time alone with Yakone, but she didn't feel that she could deliberately leave Nanulak behind. "Do you want to come and explore the ice?"

Nanulak gazed at her, a scared look in his eyes. "No, I'm staying with Toklo," he replied. "There might be white bears up here." Turning his back on Kallik and Yakone, he followed Toklo back to the edge of the ice and huddled close to his side.

Maybe he doesn't trust us yet, Kallik thought.

Toklo glanced down at Nanulak and touched him reassuringly on the shoulder. "We'll meet back here, then," he said to Kallik. "And for the spirits' sake, be careful."

Kallik dipped her head in agreement before turning and heading out across the ice beside Yakone. Exhilaration welled up inside her at the cold, the drifting cloud, and the familiar sensation of gliding across the ice.

"You know," Yakone said, breaking into her mood, "Nanulak acts like a helpless cub around Toklo. You'd never think that he was nearly as old as us."

"But he's just lost his family," Kallik reminded him. When she remembered how terrible it had felt to lose her mother and Taqqiq, she couldn't help feeling sympathetic toward Nanulak.

Yakone shrugged. "Whatever. I still think he should be able to look after himself. You and Lusa and Toklo all had to. What's so special about Nanulak?"

Part of Kallik wanted to agree with Yakone. Nanulak wasn't the only bear who had suffered loss and hardship. But she still felt a certain protectiveness toward the younger bear. *Maybe it's because I had to leave Kissimi behind,* she thought, remembering the tiny white cub she had left with his kin on Star Island. *I miss him, and I miss taking care of him, too, even though he would never have survived the journey.*

"Let's run," Yakone suggested. "I haven't had a chance to stretch my legs properly for a long time."

He took off without waiting for Kallik's response. Pushing thoughts of Nanulak out of her mind, Kallik raced after him. It felt great to run, to feel the smooth, unyielding ice beneath her paws and the cold air flattening her fur to her sides.

This is a good place, she thought. *Maybe life would be better here, instead of going back to the Frozen Sea.*

Yakone slowed and halted, panting, and turned to Kallik as she caught up with him. "That was great!" he exclaimed. Then he paused for a moment and touched Kallik's ear with his snout. "Are you okay?" he asked. "You look as if something's bothering you."

"Not really," Kallik replied. "I was just wondering if we're doing the right thing, heading back to the Frozen Sea."

Yakone blinked, surprised. "Why shouldn't we?"

"It's just . . . life will be hard there. The melt season comes earlier and earlier every year. It's difficult for white bears to find enough food before they have to head for land."

"I see." Yakone looked puzzled. "But I thought you wanted to find your brother there."

"Taqqiq might not even be there!" Kallik burst out, giving voice to her fears for the first time. "And if he is, he might not want to see me," she added miserably, remembering how hostile Taqqiq had been when she'd met him beside Great Bear Lake.

Yakone pressed himself comfortingly against her side. "If your brother's that cloud-brained, it's his loss," he said. "Besides, you've got me now."

"I know." Kallik thrust her muzzle into Yakone's shoulder fur.

"I think we should head for the Frozen Sea," Yakone went on. "I'd like to see it, when you've told me so much about it. And if it doesn't work out, we don't have to stay there. We could come back here, or go back to Star Island."

The tight knot of worry inside Kallik relaxed and dissolved into nothing. "Of course we could. We could go anywhere!"

"And right now we'd better—" Yakone began.

A loud, angry roar interrupted him. Kallik spun around to see a huge white bear pacing across the ice toward them. He was an older, full-grown male with ragged yellow fur; his jaws gaped to show a mouthful of broken teeth.

"Get out! This is my place!" he growled.

"Sorry, but we—" Yakone started to explain.

"I saw you with a brown bear," the old bear interrupted. "*And* one of those spirit-forsaken mixtures."

"Is that a problem?" Yakone asked calmly. "Surely there's room here for every bear?"

The old male bared his teeth in a snarl. "White bears should be white, and brown bears should be brown. Now, are you going to leave, or am I going to teach you how a real white bear fights?"

"There's no need for—" Yakone began.

A roar of fury burst from the old male, and he lashed out with one paw, raking his claws down Yakone's foreleg.

For a moment Kallik froze with shock. *What did we do?* Yakone was gaping as if he couldn't believe the old bear's hostility. A heartbeat later Kallik pulled herself together. She gave Yakone a shove, just as the old bear lashed out at him again. "Don't talk—run!"

Shoulder to shoulder, she and Yakone fled back across the ice. The old bear let out another roar and galloped after them. When she glanced back over her shoulder, Kallik thought that he was gaining. With his injured leg, Yakone couldn't move so fast, and Kallik wouldn't leave him behind.

"I could stop and fight him," Yakone panted.

"No, cloud-brain! What if you got badly hurt?" Fear welled up inside Kallik. "Then you couldn't travel." Though she didn't look back again, Kallik imagined that she could feel the old bear's hot breath on her neck. The edge of the ice was in view; Kallik could pick out the shapes of Toklo, Nanulak, and Lusa, but they seemed a long way off.

We shouldn't lead this bear toward them! she thought desperately. Then she spotted a stretch of broken ice, where jagged shards jutted upward, glinting in the sunlight.

"That way!" she gasped.

With Yakone hard on her paws, Kallik pelted toward the broken ice, then at the last moment veered aside and skirted it. A couple of heartbeats later, a bellow of pain and fury sounded behind her. She risked another glance back to see the old white bear in the middle of the broken stretch. He had obviously charged right into it; now he was limping as he headed for the edge.

Yakone gave her a swift nod. "Good plan!"

As they drew closer to the end of the ice, Nanulak trotted out to meet them. "Toklo caught a goose," he announced, as proudly as if he had made the catch himself. "We saved some for—"

He broke off with a squeal of protest as Yakone gave him a shove, nearly knocking him off his paws. "Run!"

For the first time Nanulak spotted the old white bear, who still hadn't given up the chase, though he was lumbering along more slowly now on sore paws.

Nanulak's eyes widened in horror. "A white bear!" he shrieked. "It's coming to get me!"

Kallik bundled him off the ice to where Toklo and Lusa were waiting.

"What happened?" Toklo demanded.

"We didn't do anything!" Kallik replied. "We've got to get out of here."

"But Yakone's hurt," Lusa objected, blinking worriedly as she gazed at Yakone's leg, where blood was trickling out of a deep scratch and dropping onto the snow. "And I don't know where to find herbs up here."

"I'll be fine," Yakone said. "Let's go."

Kallik boosted Lusa onto Toklo's shoulders. Grim-faced, Toklo pushed Nanulak ahead of him, then led the others away at a gallop. Bringing up the rear, Kallik dared to look back, and she realized that the old bear had halted at the edge of the ice.

"Don't come back!" he roared.

Indignantly Kallik watched as he snatched up the remains of Toklo's goose. *That was ours!* she thought, hunger griping in her belly. Suddenly the ice cap that had seemed so welcoming had become a dangerous and frightening place. Kallik couldn't imagine ever wanting to make her home there.

Nanulak told us the white bears here were dangerous, she reflected sadly. *He was sure they were out to get him. And it looks as if he might be right.*

CHAPTER TWENTY

Lusa

Lusa sniffed deeply, her nostrils quivering as she picked up the faint scent of lichen. Nanulak had taught her how to detect it through the snow, and now she felt quite proud of herself as she followed the trail. Her jaws watered as she thought of digging down to expose the crunchy flakes.

They had traveled for half a day since the old white bear had chased them away from the ice, and Toklo had decided to stop while it was still light so that Yakone could rest his injured leg. They had managed to find a safe place for a den in the middle of some thorns; Toklo and Kallik had gone hunting, leaving Yakone to keep an eye on Nanulak.

But the lichen scent soon petered out. Lusa snuffled in a circle but couldn't pick it up again. "I'm not as good at this as I thought," she muttered aloud. Glancing around, she realized the sun had gone and twilight was gathering. She jumped at a creaking sound under her paws and thoughts of the tasty lichen faded. Trying to ignore her grumbling belly, Lusa began to hurry back toward the den. She had wandered farther than she'd meant to, and she wanted nothing more than to see a friendly face.

But following her own trail back was difficult in the half-light. Rocks and stunted trees cast weird shadows, and she couldn't see where she was putting her paws. The wind was rising; Lusa could imagine hostile voices in it as it whined over the flat landscape.

Suddenly the snow gave way beneath her; Lusa let out a squeal of alarm as she felt herself sliding into a shallow concealed hollow. She landed with a thump at the bottom, feeling sharp stones underneath the covering of snow.

"Stupid bear!" she scolded herself. "That's what happens when you try to go too fast."

A sharp pain stabbed through one of Lusa's hindpaws when she tried to scramble up. Awkwardly she turned to peer at it and realized that her paw was jammed between a rock and a thick sheet of ice, evidence of a stream that had once flowed here. Lusa tugged hard, but she couldn't move her foot.

Now what do I do? she wondered, fear surging over her. She wrenched hard at her paw again. The ice sheet must have shifted as she'd broken through it, trapping her. Cold started to seep into Lusa's fur. She stretched up so she could see over the banks of snow on either side.

"Help!" she called, not sure if any of the others were in earshot, or whether they could hear her above the blustering of the wind. "Toklo! Kallik! Help me!"

But no bear answered her cries. Lusa waited, still struggling vainly to free herself, then called again. "Help me!

Over here! I'm stuck! Help!"

Still there was no reply.

They're bound to find me eventually, Lusa told herself. *After all, we found Toklo underground. Only . . . I wish they'd be quick about it!*

Darkness had fallen, and the sky was thickly strewn with glittering stars. Lusa looked up to see Ujurak's shape and felt reassured, knowing that her friend was watching over her.

Please, Ujurak, she begged silently. *Send some bear to find me!*

Almost at once she heard the sound of pawsteps approaching through the snow. Glancing around, she spotted a brown bear skirting a thicket of thornbushes a few bearlengths away, his head down as if he was following a scent trail. At first she thought it was Toklo, but as he drew closer, she recognized Nanulak.

"Nanulak!" she called out, her voice shaky with relief. "Nanulak, help me! I'm stuck!"

Nanulak raised his head, looking around as if trying to find the source of the noise.

"Over here!" Lusa shouted, though her voice was almost drowned out by birds shrieking overhead; she wondered if she had disturbed Nanulak's prey.

Nanulak turned his head, and Lusa was sure he had seen her. "Thank you, Ujurak!" she exclaimed.

But a heartbeat later Nanulak veered away from her and headed back past the thornbushes, picking up the pace until he was running.

Lusa froze with shock. "Nanulak!" she cried. "Nanulak, don't leave me!"

But he had gone.

Lusa wrenched at her paw in a panic, scraping it against the ice in her efforts to free herself. A flurry of wings sounded overhead; she looked up to see birds circling around her, flying lower and lower, until one of them darted down to peck at her.

Lusa lashed out a paw at it. Though she missed, the birds drew off a little way, only to fly down again a moment later. Their wings buffeted her head, and their beaks flashed out, pecking at her shoulders.

I'm going to die here! The birds will eat me alive! Lusa thought, terror flowing through her body like ice.

Then Lusa heard more pawsteps approaching at a run, and Kallik's voice: "This way! Those birds have found some prey."

"Oh, thank Arcturus!" Lusa exclaimed. "Kallik! Toklo! Help!"

Toklo came galloping up. "It's not prey; it's Lusa!"

"Get me out of here!" Lusa begged. "My paw is stuck."

Kallik plunged down into the hollow to investigate, while Toklo reared up on his hindpaws, snarling and battering at the birds until they flew away. Their frustrated shrieking died into silence.

Lusa felt Kallik scraping at the ice beside her paw. "Try it now," the white bear said.

Lusa tugged at her paw again and felt it come free. Staggering slightly, she managed to stand up and haul herself out of the hollow.

"Is your paw hurt?" Kallik asked.

Lusa flexed her foot; it felt a bit sore, but she could put her weight on it and walk. "It'll be fine," she said. "Thank you for rescuing me. I thought I'd be stuck there forever."

"Just watch where you're putting your paws in future," Toklo grunted, giving her an affectionate push with his snout.

"Have you seen Nanulak?" Lusa asked as they headed back toward the den.

Kallik shook her head. "I thought he stayed with Yakone."

"No, he was out here," Lusa went on, indignation rising inside her. "I saw him and called out to him, but he just kept going and left me there. I guess he didn't see me," she added.

"Oh, that's awful!" Kallik responded. "I'm sure he'll feel terrible when he finds out."

I felt terrible when he left me, Lusa thought. *And I'm almost certain he saw me.*

When she pushed her way through the thorn thicket to the den they had made in the middle, Yakone and Nanulak were there together. Nanulak was curled up and looked half asleep.

"Nanulak, you left me stuck in the ice!" Lusa growled as soon as she saw the mixed bear.

Nanulak sprang to his paws. "I did what?"

His eyes were wide with shock. Lusa wondered whether he was genuinely appalled to hear what had happened, or whether he hadn't expected her to come back.

"I got my paw stuck," she explained. "I saw you and called out to you, but you just turned away."

"Well, I didn't see you," Nanulak replied, blinking at her. "I'm sorry, Lusa, but I really didn't."

He would say that, wouldn't he? "You looked right at me!" she retorted.

"Lusa, remember what it was like out there—dark, and you were down in that hollow," Toklo pointed out. "There was the noise of the wind, and those birds . . . It would have been difficult for any bear to see you."

Kallik nodded. "We wouldn't have spotted you if it hadn't been for the birds."

"I still think he saw me," Lusa muttered, frustrated at the way her friends were taking Nanulak's side.

"Why would Nanulak leave you stuck out there and then lie about it?" Toklo growled.

Lusa turned away with an angry shrug.

"I'm really sorry, Lusa." Nanulak's plaintive voice came from behind her, but Lusa ignored him.

She curled up at the edge of the den, with thorn branches scraping her back, and covered her head with her paws. She knew that if she said any more there would be a real quarrel, and she couldn't face it, especially when it looked as if no bear would be on her side.

I've been their friend for ages, she thought. *Why would they believe him and not me?*

Then she wondered whether perhaps she was making a mistake. It was so unlikely that any bear would leave another to die. Kallik was right that between the darkness and the noise of wind and birds, Nanulak might have missed her.

Still, she couldn't stifle a nagging suspicion of the young mixed bear. She had made eye contact with him over the edge of the hollow; he must have seen her as clearly as she'd seen him. *I don't care what the others think. I'm keeping an eye on him from now on.*

CHAPTER TWENTY-ONE

Toklo

I have to keep Nanulak safe, Toklo thought. *Nothing else matters.*

After their frantic escape from the ice cap, and Lusa's accident, the bears had spent an extra day resting in the thorn thicket. Toklo had made sure that one of them was always on watch. They hadn't seen any more bears, white or brown, but he knew they were roaming around everywhere on the island.

The white bears really are hostile to brown bears, he thought. *Tikaani must have been an exception.*

"We need to get off the island as soon as we can," he said softly to Kallik and Yakone. Lusa was asleep, and Nanulak crouched at the edge of the thicket, keeping watch.

Kallik nodded. "I don't feel comfortable here," she agreed. "There's something not right about it. The sooner we leave it the better."

"And I think we should travel at night," Yakone suggested. "That way we're less likely to meet hostile bears."

"Good idea," Toklo grunted. "We'll start tonight."

They set out after sunset and plodded on through the

darkness. Toklo's senses were alert for the first signs of other bears approaching, but he could pick up nothing but the scent of frost, hear nothing except their own pawsteps.

Night followed night as they traveled along the topmost ridge of the island. Sometimes they could see the ice cap glimmering in the distance, but after the encounter with the old white bear they kept well away from it. Each day as dawn broke they would find a hiding place, or dig out a den in the snow, and stay sleeping uneasily until the light faded again.

I'm so tired my paws are going to drop off, Toklo grumbled to himself. *And my belly thinks my throat's been clawed out!*

Hunting was harder at night, especially as they didn't dare split up and the pickings along their trail were slim.

I'd give anything for a musk ox, or a caribou. Toklo's mouth watered at the thought. *These scrawny hares wouldn't fill a hollow tooth! And Tikaani's hunting tips don't work as well in the dark.*

Toklo's only relief was to look up at the sky and see Ujurak's shape shining among the stars. And even that was a bleak kind of comfort, when he remembered how his friend had walked away from him in his dream.

Yakone and Kallik were padding side by side, their pelts brushing, their heads close together as they talked quietly. "I can't wait to see the Frozen Sea," Yakone was saying. "Is the hunting good there?"

"There are plenty of seals, until the ice melts," Kallik replied. "Oh, I wish I could fill my belly with seal meat right now!"

Lusa, awake for once, was perched on Yakone's shoulders,

but she didn't join in the conversation.

I wonder if she feels left out, Toklo thought. *I'll make sure that she finds a place with trees and other black bears. A place where she'll be safe, and where it's easy for her to live. And then I can travel on with Nanulak.*

Deep satisfaction flooded through Toklo as his thoughts returned to the younger bear. He felt warm from his ears to his claw tips.

I was buried underground, under sticks and earth, he thought, remembering the fear and despair he had felt in the tunnels. *I nearly died. And now I feel like I'm alive again.* I know *Ujurak sent Nanulak to me, to give me a reason for surviving.*

Toklo didn't feel as tired or hungry while he made plans about how he would teach Nanulak the way that brown bears lived. *I'll show him how to dig out a den, and how to mark his territory. He'll have the territory next to mine, and then we can look out for each other. I'll help him if other bears attack him. We can share prey. . . . It'll be almost like having Tobi back.*

Toklo sighed. Everything would be better once they got off this spirit-forsaken island. But the ridge still stretched out ahead of them with no sign of coming to an end.

One day . . .

A grassy meadow lay in front of Toklo, sloping down to where sunlight glittered on a swift-flowing river. In the shallows close to the bank a brown she-bear was teaching her cub how to catch salmon.

As Toklo watched, letting the warmth of the sun soak into his fur, an eagle circled above his head and alighted on the grass nearby. Toklo stared in astonishment as the bird's body filled out and its feathers vanished to be replaced by brown fur, and Ujurak dropped to four paws in front of him.

"Hi, Toklo," he said.

"Ujurak!" Toklo exclaimed. "I must be dreaming, right?" he added, feeling a stab of sadness that he would never meet his friend again in the waking world. "You're not really here."

"Of course you're dreaming," Ujurak replied cheerfully. "But that doesn't mean I'm not here with you. Race you to the river!"

He took off across the meadow, his paws skimming the grass, and Toklo galloped after him. Suddenly it didn't matter that this was a dream: For a little while he had his friend back again.

At the river the mother bear and her cub still stood in the shallows, watching intently for a salmon. Ujurak halted on a flat rock that stuck out into the current a couple of bear-lengths away.

"Toklo, will you teach me how to catch salmon now?" he asked.

He glanced back over his shoulder as Toklo caught up. Toklo halted in confusion. The bear in front of him wasn't Ujurak anymore; he was Nanulak.

"Sure I'll teach you," Toklo replied, padding out onto the rock beside Nanulak. He was disappointed to have lost Ujurak again after such a short time, but he tried to hide it.

Just then, the cub fishing with his mother leaped forward; glittering drops splashed up all around him. He thrust his snout into the water and raised it again with a salmon wriggling in his jaws.

His mother's eyes shone with pride. "Well done!" she barked.

Suddenly Nanulak launched himself off the rock. Landing in the river beside the cub, he cuffed him hard over the head with one paw. The cub let out a squeal of pain, dropping the salmon. Nanulak snatched it up before it could fall into the water, and gave the cub a hard shove.

The cub staggered, lost his footing, and rolled over into deeper water. He let out a terrified wail as the current carried him away. The mother bear roared in outrage, but instead of coming after Nanulak she swam after her cub.

Nanulak scrambled out onto the rock and dropped the fish at Toklo's paws. "*That's* how to catch a salmon!"

Toklo jerked in shock and opened his eyes in the darkness of the snow-den. Nanulak was curled up next to him, Lusa on his other side; Kallik slept in a mound of white fur, while Yakone was on watch, crouched at the mouth of the den.

Toklo tried to steady the pounding of his heart. *It was only a dream,* he told himself. *Nanulak would never do anything like that.*

Toklo wondered what the dream meant. Maybe it didn't mean anything. Maybe he wasn't supposed to compare the two brown bears. Ujurak had found his destiny and gone, except for a fleeting, unreliable contact in dreams. One bear was real; the other wasn't.

Now I have Nanulak to look after.

* * *

Toklo curled up with his nose on his paws. But the memory of the dream was too strong, too disturbing, for him to go back to sleep. Instead, careful not to disturb the others, he rose to his paws and slipped past Yakone, out of the den. The snowy landscape stretched all around him, with the ice cap glimmering in the distance, beneath a sky thickly frosted with stars.

If it's night, why aren't we moving on? Toklo wondered. "Hey," he said aloud, turning back to Yakone, "you should have—"

He broke off. Yakone and the den had vanished. Toklo was alone in the snow.

I'm still dreaming, he thought. *Can't I just dream a nice, plump hare?*

But the whole landscape was empty of prey. Instead, Toklo looked up to see that some of the stars were moving. His paws tingled with anticipation as Ujurak's shining shape formed in the air and cantered down the sky toward him.

"Toklo." Ujurak landed and stepped up to him; his paws left no prints in the snow. Toklo felt a jolt of energy run right through him as star-Ujurak touched noses with him. "Toklo, look."

Ujurak raised a paw to point. Gazing in that direction, Toklo spotted a brown bear curled up in the snow, under a rocky overhang. As he looked closer, he recognized Nanulak. He was sleeping peacefully.

"Nanulak can take care of himself," Ujurak said. "He doesn't need you. What matters most is for you to find a home."

"But—" Toklo turned to Ujurak in confusion. "I thought you sent Nanulak to me, so I could look after him."

Ujurak shook his head. "No, Toklo. He is not your destiny."

"But he needs me!" Toklo burst out. "You're wrong, Ujurak. Nanulak needs me!"

Ujurak gazed at Toklo with stars in the depths of his eyes. "Toklo, it's you who are wrong. You should leave Nanulak here, where he belongs."

"He doesn't belong here! His family drove him away. White bears attacked him." Anger surged up inside Toklo. "I see what the problem is!" he growled. "You're jealous of Nanulak! You're jealous because I've found another friend."

Ujurak let out a sad sigh. "Toklo, that's not true."

"If you wanted me to be your friend, you should have stayed with me!" All his grief and bitterness burst out. "But no, you had to go off into the stars. And that means you don't get to tell me what I should do anymore."

Toklo glared at Ujurak, waiting for a reply, half afraid of his own fury. He wanted Ujurak to say something that would make everything all right again.

But Ujurak only bowed his head and turned away. Without another word, he padded off across the snow, his starry shape growing smaller and smaller until it was only a faint glimmer on the horizon. Then he was gone.

Toklo jumped awake from the dream, shocked to find Nanulak lying close beside him, deeply asleep. Ujurak's voice still echoed in his ears, but now Toklo knew that he wasn't dreaming anymore. He was lying in the snow-den that Kallik and Yakone had dug out earlier as dawn had broken; Lusa was blinking up at him, clearly just waking up.

"Are you okay, Toklo?" she asked. "You were saying Ujurak's name in your sleep."

"I don't want to talk about it," Toklo retorted, turning his back on her.

There was silence from Lusa. Toklo knew that he shouldn't be grumpy toward her, but he was still shaken from what he had seen in the dream.

I don't want to think about it, he decided. *If Ujurak says that Nanulak isn't part of the plan, he's wrong, that's all.*

CHAPTER TWENTY-TWO

Lusa

Tumbling off Yakone's shoulders, Lusa found it hard to stay on her paws. Traveling by night made her feel as if every hair on her pelt were withering from exhaustion, even when she was riding on the white bear's back. Her muscles ached, and it was an effort even to keep her eyes open.

And I'm so hungry! It's so hard to find moss and leaves under the snow in the dark. Besides, there's so little time to stop and look when we're hurrying to escape from the white bears.

On the distant horizon, a line of pale light showed where the sun would rise. A nearby rocky outcrop cast blue shadows across the snow, where lines of tiny pawprints broke up the smooth white surface.

"It looks as if there might be more prey around here," Toklo said to the white bears, sniffing the air. "Let's hunt."

"Okay," Kallik replied. "Yakone, that looks like a frozen stream over there. Let's follow it."

"I'll go this way, then." Toklo padded off along the ridge in the direction they were heading.

"Wait for me!" Nanulak squealed, bounding across the snow to catch up with Toklo.

Toklo turned to face the younger bear. "No, we can't leave Lusa by herself. Besides, you need to stay in hiding so the white bears don't find you. Stay here and dig out a den, so it's ready for when we get back."

"But—" Nanulak began to protest, then seemed to realize there would be no point. He padded back to Lusa, his head down, his paws kicking up the snow.

Lusa wasn't sure she wanted to be left alone with Nanulak, but she told herself not to be mean. *Maybe I was wrong to think he left me stranded that night. Besides, he's Toklo's friend, so he should be my friend, too.*

"Come on, Nanulak," she said, trying to sound cheerful in spite of her tiredness. "I'll help you build the den."

"Okay. Under here would be a good place." Nanulak headed for the snowdrifts at the bottom of the rocky outcrop and began to dig.

For a moment Lusa admired the strong swipes of his paws, before coming to dig alongside him. "Your paws are just like Kallik's," she said. "It's great that you have strengths from different kinds of bear."

Nanulak just grunted.

"You remind me a bit of Ujurak," she went on, hoping she could make Nanulak talk to her. "In a way, you've got different shapes, just like him!"

Nanulak paused in his digging for a moment to look at her. "What do you mean?" he asked. "You all keep mentioning

Ujurak, but I don't see why he was so important."

"Oh, Ujurak was great!" Lusa replied enthusiastically. "He was a brown bear most of the time, but he could change his shape and be whatever he wanted."

Nanulak's eyes stretched wide. "He could do *what?*"

"Change his shape." Lusa realized that maybe she should be more careful about what she told Nanulak. She didn't want him to think that she was telling lies. *Nanulak isn't likely to believe that Ujurak could turn into a flat-face!* "Like . . . if we needed to know which way to go, he could change into a bird and spy out the land. Or once he changed into a mule deer and led some wolves away from us."

Nanulak paused for a moment, then began scraping at the snow again. Lusa carried on digging beside him, but she found the silence awkward.

"Ujurak always knew which way to go," she went on at last. "He could read signs in the landscape."

"What sort of signs?"

"Oh . . . like the way bushes were growing, or how rocks were placed." Lusa guessed that Nanulak would find that hard to believe, too. She didn't mention the stranger signs Ujurak could interpret, like the way the wind blew the clouds. "He taught me how to do it," she added, "but I was never as good at it as he was."

"Weird," Nanulak commented. "I guess Toklo didn't like that."

Lusa let out a little snort of amusement. "Not at first," she admitted. "But he learned to trust Ujurak, just like Kallik and

I did." Then her amusement faded as she realized something was strange about Nanulak's remark.

"Why do you think Toklo wouldn't like it?" she asked curiously.

Nanulak shrugged. "Signs and stuff . . . it's not what brown bears do. But then, it sounds like Ujurak wasn't really a brown bear."

"Yes, he was!" Lusa retorted, stung. "I told you, most of the time he was a brown bear, and that's the way he felt most comfortable."

"Okay . . ." Nanulak kicked a shower of snow behind him from the hollow where the den was taking shape. "How did Toklo meet Ujurak?"

"I'm not sure," Lusa replied. "I wasn't with them then. But I think he helped Ujurak when he was . . . when he was in another shape." *I won't tell Nanulak that he was a flat-face!* "Ujurak was quite young then."

"I see." For some reason Nanulak sounded pleased. "I guess Toklo was sorry for him."

Lusa wasn't sure what to say. She knew that Nanulak had it wrong. Toklo had felt protective toward Ujurak, but never sorry for him. *Angry, exasperated, worried . . . but never sorry.* But she didn't know how she could explain that to a bear who had never known Ujurak.

"Ujurak wasn't helpless," she said. "Sometimes he got into stuff he couldn't handle, but we've all done that. Sometimes I think Ujurak was the strongest of all of us."

Nanulak let out a snort, as if he wasn't about to accept that.

"Maybe he made you think so." He paused, then added, "A creature like that couldn't be Toklo's *real* friend."

Lusa stopped digging and gazed at Nanulak, biting back an angry response. She didn't know what to say in reply; she wanted to defend Ujurak, but she could tell that Nanulak wasn't going to believe her. Awkwardly she scuffled her paws in the snow.

A tide of relief washed over her as she heard pawsteps behind her, and Toklo padded up with a hare in his jaws. Several minutes later, Kallik and Yakone appeared at the top of the outcrop; Kallik was carrying a goose.

"Toklo, great catch!" Nanulak exclaimed, bounding over to the brown bear and gazing at the hare with admiring eyes.

Lusa couldn't help noticing that he completely ignored Kallik and Yakone. "That's a good catch, too," she told Kallik as the white bears padded down to join the others. "We'll eat well for once."

"I'm sorry we didn't find any plants for you, Lusa," Kallik said, dropping the goose.

"Never mind. I can eat meat." Lusa tried to sound cheerful, although her belly heaved.

Part of her wanted to tell her friends about the odd conversation she had shared with Nanulak. But after a moment's thought, she kept it to herself. *I might not understand either if I hadn't known Ujurak.*

Crouching down to take a mouthful of the goose, gagging on the fatty meat, all Lusa really wanted was to keep going until she could find some trees, more black bears, and a place that felt like home. She imagined sunlight on her fur, and the fresh taste of berries bursting in her mouth.

I never want to see another snowflake for the rest of my life!

When they had swallowed the last mouthfuls of prey, the bears curled up in the den. Lusa slept uneasily, dreaming in snatches about the Bear Bowl. Then she found herself on the mountainside on Star Island once again, with the avalanche thundering down toward her.

"Ujurak!" she squealed.

Terror jerked her awake, and she realized that she was alone in the den. Red light was angling through the entrance, turning the snow outside the color of blood.

Lusa scrambled to her paws and padded out into the open. Kallik and Yakone stood close together a couple of bear-lengths away, sniffing the air. Toklo and Nanulak were talking together a little farther off.

Toklo broke off as he spotted Lusa. "Good, you're awake," he grunted. "Now we can get going."

Feeling a bit guilty about how often she had traveled on Yakone's back, Lusa padded along beside Kallik as they set out. The sun was going down into a mass of ragged cloud. The cold air was like claws in Lusa's throat, but it didn't look as if there was more snow to come.

The red light of sunset was still in the sky when the bears reached the rim of a shallow valley on the edge of the ice cap. Thornbushes were thickly massed in the valley bottom; Lusa guessed there might be a stream or a pond down there, frozen and covered with snow.

"I'm going to run ahead for a bit," she told Toklo. "I want to get some bark off those bushes, and there might even be a few berries."

Toklo nodded. "Okay. But be careful."

Lusa headed off, kicking up the snow as she bounded through it. Then she remembered how she had been trapped in ice after not looking where she was going, and slowed her pace to a brisk trot.

A scatter of feathers on the snow slowed her still further. *It looks as if a bird was killed here,* she thought. *Maybe there are bears around. Should I go back and warn the others?*

But the bushes were quite close now, and Lusa's jaws were watering. *Just a few mouthfuls,* she promised herself, padding up to the nearest one and beginning to strip off the bark.

Then movement caught her eye; beyond the thorns she spotted a white bear loping along with a half-grown cub by her side. Lusa froze, thankful for the bushes that concealed her from them. *I should never have left the others. I was so bee-brained!*

Then another smaller cub bounced out of the thicket and ran after the she-bear. Lusa stifled a gasp of astonishment. *That cub is brown!*

Looking more closely, Lusa realized that the small cub could have been Nanulak's younger sister, with the sloping shoulders and muzzle of a white bear. And now she noticed that the mother bear had the shorter snout of a grizzly, while the older cub had patches of brown fur on his white pelt.

They're all mixtures, just like Nanulak!

When the bear family had passed by, Lusa emerged from hiding and pelted back to her companions, who were still making their way slowly down into the valley.

"There you are!" Toklo exclaimed as she dashed up to them. "You need to stay with us now. We—"

"There are white bears around!" Nanulak announced, wide-eyed with fear. "We saw their droppings."

"I've seen the bears," Lusa replied. "They're not white bears; they're mixtures, just like you. Three of them: a mother bear and two cubs."

To her surprise, Nanulak didn't look pleased at her news, though Kallik and Yakone exchanged an interested glance.

"We should go meet them," Kallik suggested. "They might know your family, Nanulak."

Nanulak shrugged uneasily. "I don't want to meet them. I'm a brown bear now."

"Well, if we head this way, we're likely to come across them," Toklo said. His voice was decisive, as if he was nipping a possible argument in the bud. "There's nothing to worry about, Nanulak. It was white bears who attacked you, right?"

"Right," Nanulak muttered, with a sulky look.

Yakone led the way down into the valley, tracking Lusa's pawsteps. Before they reached the bushes at the bottom, Lusa spotted the mother bear and the two cubs examining something in the snow a little way off.

"Hello there!" Yakone called out, veering in their direction. Lusa and the others followed, though Lusa could see that Nanulak was dragging his paws.

The mixed bears looked up at the sound of Yakone's voice and trotted over to meet them, the small cub keeping very close to his mother.

"Hi." Toklo spoke warily, stepping in front of Yakone so he was the first to encounter the new bears.

"Hi." The mother bear spoke first. Her gaze traveled over the others with friendly interest, though her eyes widened with surprise when she spotted Lusa. *I don't suppose she's ever seen a black bear,* Lusa thought.

"I don't think we've met before," the she-bear went on.

"No, we're just passing through." Kallik stepped forward to Toklo's side and dipped her head politely. "We're on our way to the Frozen Sea."

"Oh, I've heard about that!" the she-bear said. "It's supposed to be a really good place for white bears."

"You know it!" Kallik looked overjoyed. "Is it far?"

The mother bear shook her head. "That I couldn't tell you. I don't travel much," she added apologetically. "I'm happy here in this valley. My mate is always traveling, though. We don't see much of him during snow-sky. I don't think he's ever visited the Frozen Sea himself, but he's met other bears who have."

"We know we have to get off this island and cross the sea again," Yakone said. "Are we going in the right direction?"

"Yes, you're fine," the brown bear told him. "Keep going along the ridge, and when you get to the end, veer in that direction." She gestured with a paw. "Pretty soon you'll come to a deep gully, and that leads to a slope that takes you right down to the coast. Or so my mate tells me."

"Great, thanks," Yakone replied.

While the other bears were talking, Nanulak kept to the back of their group, as if he didn't want to be seen. Lusa was still surprised that he wasn't more excited to see bears who were mixtures like him.

"Hey, look!" She gave Nanulak a shove forward. "We're traveling with a bear who's just like you!"

Nanulak's paws skidded in the snow as he resisted, and he gave Lusa a glare. Lusa blinked back in astonishment. *What did I do?*

The she-bear padded up to Nanulak and gave him a sniff. "It's good to meet you," she said.

Nanulak grunted something inaudible in reply.

"Nanulak's had a bad time," Toklo explained. Lusa thought he sounded defensive, as if he wanted to apologize for Nanulak's unfriendliness. "His brown-bear mother drove him away when there wasn't enough prey, and then white bears attacked him."

"That's really tough!" the older cub exclaimed.

The little cub let out a growl. "If I got my paws on them, they'd be sorry." She reared up on her hind paws and batted fiercely at the air.

"Nanulak, I'm so sorry that happened to you." The she-bear bent her head to touch Nanulak on the shoulder. "We're lucky, I suppose. No bear has ever treated us badly." She hesitated, glancing at her cubs, then added, "If you want, you can come and live with us. There's not much room, and not much prey this time of year, but you're welcome to share what we have."

The little cub let out a squeak and gave a bounce of excitement, spraying up snow, but Lusa saw that the older cub was looking sulky, as if he didn't agree with his mother's offer. He looked about the same age as Nanulak; maybe he saw Nanulak as a rival.

Nanulak's eyes widened with shock, and he opened his jaws to reply. Lusa was certain he was going to say something rude and maybe antagonize these friendly bears.

But before Nanulak could speak, Toklo gave him a warning shove. "No, thank you," he replied, as if the she-bear's invitation had been extended to all of them. "We won't take up any of your territory. I'm sure you need all the prey you can catch for your own family."

"Stay for tonight, at least," the mother bear suggested. "Our den is in the thicket over there."

Toklo hesitated. Lusa guessed he was unwilling to tell the she-bear they were traveling by night, in case she asked why. "Okay, thanks," he said at last. "We'll help you hunt first, though. You shouldn't have to feed so many extra mouths."

"Great!" The older cub looked a bit less sulky now that he wasn't expected to share his food. "We found traces of a hare over there; we were going to follow its scent."

Lusa stayed among the thorns as the other bears set off on the hunt. She had managed to eat her fill of leaves and bark by the time they returned through the darkness. The mother bear was carrying a hare, while Kallik was dragging along an

Arctic fox, and Toklo had caught a small bird with speckled brown and white feathers. For once every bear had a full belly by the time they settled down for the night.

Maybe Nanulak should stay here, Lusa thought drowsily as she curled up in the mixed bears' den. *These bears are friendly, and just like him.* Feeling a bit guilty, she admitted to herself, *And we wouldn't be responsible for him anymore.*

A ray of sunlight angling through the thorns woke Lusa the next morning. Blinking, she lifted her head to see that Kallik and Yakone had already left the den. The mixed-bear family was still sleeping in a heap of mingled brown and white fur. On the other side of the den, Toklo and Nanulak were awake, their heads close together as they talked.

"You could stay here," Toklo murmured. "It's okay . . . I'll understand if you'd rather be with them."

"No!" The word burst out of Nanulak, and he pressed himself closer to Toklo's side. "I'm not like these bears! I'm like *you*. I'm a brown bear now. I want to stay with you."

"But—" Toklo began.

"Please don't leave me here!" Nanulak's voice rose to a shrill wail. "Brown bears don't belong on the ice. We belong in the forest, like you said!"

His loud voice had roused the mixed bears, who looked up with expressions of mingled surprise and hurt.

"Whoa, have it your way, then," the older cub growled. "I didn't want you to stay, anyway."

Lusa felt her belly cramp at the awkwardness of the

moment. She thought she ought to apologize for Nanulak, when the mixed bears had been so welcoming, but she didn't know what to say.

"It's all right, Nanulak." Toklo rested a paw on the younger bear's shoulder to calm him.

The mother bear nodded. "The little one knows his own mind," she said. "I wouldn't want to stand in his way."

"We'd better go," Toklo muttered.

He and Nanulak pushed their way out through the thorns into the open, and Lusa followed. Kallik and Yakone were sitting a bearlength away, and they rose to their paws as Toklo and the others emerged.

"Thank you for letting us stay," Lusa said to the mother bear, as she joined them outside. "I'm sorry that—"

The she-bear raised a paw to interrupt her. "There's nothing to be sorry for, small one. I understand."

With a few words of farewell Toklo led the way farther across the valley. Lusa turned to look back at the she-bear and her cubs, feeling rather sad as their shapes dwindled into the distance. *They were nice. I wish we could have been friends.*

"Hey, Lusa!" Toklo had paused to look around for her. "Are you coming?"

"Isn't it odd about these mixed bears?" Kallik was saying as Lusa bounded up to join them. "We've never met any before, and now we've seen four of them."

Toklo shrugged. "Not so strange," he replied. "We haven't been in many places where brown bears and white bears live together."

"I hope we don't see any more," Nanulak said in a resentful tone as all five bears padded on. "Those bears back there should make up their minds what sort of bear they want to be. Anything else is just stupid. *I'm* a brown bear; isn't that right, Toklo?"

"If that's what you want," Toklo responded.

Lusa was shocked that Nanulak was so dismissive of the bears, when they had been so kind and offered him a place to live. "But that's no excuse for being rude," she told Nanulak, her exasperation spilling over. "When you've traveled as far as we have, you'll learn that you can't afford to turn down friendliness, wherever you find it."

Nanulak halted, glaring at her. "Are you saying you want to get rid of me?"

"I'm fine with you staying with us if that's what Toklo wants," Lusa replied. "Just don't do anything to offend other bears."

"She's right," Kallik said firmly. "Now let's keep moving."

Ujurak could be anything he wanted to be and was often unsure about what he was, Lusa thought. *But he never let it make him angry and bitter like Nanulak.*

I feel bad when Nanulak has had such an awful time, she added silently to herself, *but I'm not at all sure that I like him.*

CHAPTER TWENTY-THREE

Kallik

The bears returned to traveling by night as they trekked along the ridge. Kallik's excitement began to rise. With the information the mixed bears had given them about the direction they should take, she was certain it wouldn't be long before they could leave the island.

"I can't wait to show you the Frozen Sea!" she said to Yakone. "I just hope we can get there before the ice melts."

"Yeah, I want to see it, too," Nanulak broke in, surprising Kallik by the enthusiasm in his voice. "Anywhere, so long as it's off this island!"

"There'll be a lot of white bears at the Frozen Sea," Yakone warned him. "Are you sure you won't be scared?"

"I'm a brown bear," Nanulak informed him loftily. "I'm not scared of *anything*."

Kallik thought back to the day when they had found Nanulak. He had been scared then, and later terrified that the white bears would spot him. Even though she wanted to take care of Nanulak and make sure that he found a safe place to live, she didn't like the way he was lying, or the thinly veiled hostility with which he spoke to Yakone.

"Besides," Nanulak went on, before Kallik could decide if she wanted to respond, "we won't be staying there long, will we, Toklo? We'll travel on and find the right place for brown bears to live."

Toklo glanced sideways at him, hesitating. "We'll see how things turn out," he replied after a moment.

Kallik understood Toklo's reluctance. She knew, just as they all did, that sooner or later their journey together must come to an end. But her pelt prickled with irritation at Nanulak's dismissive tone, as if their final parting were something that didn't matter.

"Let's press on ahead for a bit," she murmured to Yakone. "Otherwise I'm going to give that bear a swat over the ear!"

As Kallik took the lead with Yakone beside her, she cast a glance back at Lusa. The black bear hadn't reacted to Nanulak's words; she was trudging along with her head down, her snout almost brushing the snow.

She's been quiet for a while, Kallik thought. *I hope she's okay. Maybe she's still fighting the longsleep. And we can't give her the sort of food she needs. But when burn-sky comes, she and Toklo will have all they want to eat. It's Yakone and I who'll have problems, if we can't get to the Frozen Sea in time to fill our bellies before it melts.*

Picking up the pace, Kallik realized that the land was beginning to slope downward. The edge of the ice cap, which they had been following for several days, was curving away from them. Ahead of them, the ground fell away in fold after fold of snow-covered hills.

"We're almost at the other side of the island!" Kallik exclaimed, peering forward to see if she could detect the sea.

Yakone halted beside her, sniffing the air. "Not far now," he said with satisfaction.

Kallik turned and looked back along the ridge. Toklo and Nanulak were padding together a few bearlengths behind, while Lusa plodded along in their pawsteps.

"Come over here!" Kallik called. "We've found the way down!"

Instantly Toklo and Nanulak broke into a gallop, and even Lusa looked more alert and quickened her pace.

"At last!" Nanulak exclaimed as he halted beside Kallik.

Toklo gave a grunt of appreciation as he looked out at the rolling hills. "This way," he said, veering down the slope at an angle. The she-bear said there'd be a gully."

Nanulak followed him closely, bounding and slipping through the snow like a cub. As Lusa came toiling up, Yakone crouched down for her. "Come on," he invited her. "Ride on my back again. You look exhausted."

Lusa blinked at him in gratitude. "Thanks, Yakone." She clambered up onto the white bear's shoulders and wriggled down into his fur until she was comfortable. "That's nice," she murmured sleepily.

Once Lusa was settled, Kallik and Yakone padded after Toklo, who was heading purposefully onward. Nanulak frolicked around in the snow, though he never ventured far from

Toklo's side. Suddenly he let out a startled yelp and slid down out of Kallik's sight.

"Oh, no!" she gasped, starting to run. "He's fallen down a hole, just like Toklo!" Raising her voice, she called, "Toklo, what happened?"

Toklo had halted and was gazing calmly downward. As Kallik came panting up to him, she spotted Nanulak scrambling to his paws at the bottom of a deep fissure in the ground. He had landed in the middle of a clump of thorns and was struggling to tear himself free.

"Nanulak found the gully by slipping into it," Toklo replied. There was a rumble of amusement in his voice that Kallik hadn't heard for a long time.

"It's not funny!" Nanulak squealed from down below. "Come and help me out!"

"Okay, we're coming!" Toklo responded, beginning to edge carefully down the steep slope that led into the gully. "Follow me," he added to Kallik. "This is the way we have to go."

By the time Toklo and Kallik reached the floor of the gully, with Yakone and Lusa following more cautiously, Nanulak had escaped from the thorns. He shook mud and snowmelt from his fur, spattering Kallik, then examined each of his pads with minute attention.

"I think I have a thorn stuck," he complained, holding out a forepaw to Toklo. "See if you can get it out."

It was Kallik who seized his paw with her own and turned it over to inspect the surface of his pads. "There's no thorn," she said after a moment. "You're fine."

"But it hurts!" Nanulak put his paw to the ground, wincing. "I can't walk like this."

Kallik tried to suppress the memories of their own injuries on their long journey. They had been attacked by firebeasts, shot at by no-claws with firesticks, hunted by hungry orca . . . *But we never made a fuss like this.*

"We have to keep going," Yakone said, coming up with Lusa in time to hear the last of this exchange. "Dawn is breaking over the hills. We'll have to find shelter soon. You can rest your hurt paw then, Nanulak," he added sharply. "Meanwhile, you'll just have to put up with it."

Nanulak gave Yakone a sulky glare and looked at Toklo for support.

"Yakone's right," Toklo responded. "We have to get into hiding before daylight. Come on."

Muttering under his breath, Nanulak followed. He was limping heavily; Kallik started to feel sorry for him until she realized that he was favoring the other forepaw, not the one that was supposed to have the thorn. Letting out a small sigh, she decided not to say anything. *He's never been on a journey like this before. But he'll learn.*

As the dawn light grew brighter, they found a shallow cave in the side of the gully and crowded into it to sleep the day away. Lusa scraped a few scraps of lichen off the rocks at the entrance and chewed them stoically.

"Better than nothing," she muttered.

"I'm hungry, too. When are we going to hunt?" Nanulak asked. "I want to come this time."

"Maybe later." Toklo's jaws stretched wide in an enormous yawn. "Right now I want to sleep."

Kallik was prepared for more protests from Nanulak, but the younger bear just curled up close to Toklo. Trying to forget the gaping hole in her own belly, Kallik settled down beside Yakone. As she closed her eyes, she thought she heard the distant rumble of thunder, but the sky was clear.

I must be imagining things, she thought as she drifted into sleep.

Hunger woke Kallik when it was still light outside. Lusa was curled up in the den, but she could hear the others moving around outside.

"I know you're hungry, Nanulak," Yakone was saying in an exasperated voice. "We're *all* hungry. What do you think, Toklo? Is it safe to hunt?"

"I'd like to get moving," Toklo replied as Kallik emerged, blinking, into the open. "We can hunt on the way. The gully is pretty sheltered," Toklo pointed out. "And I haven't noticed any bear tracks. I think we can risk it."

"Let's do that," Kallik begged; every hair on her pelt was sick of plodding along in darkness. When Toklo nodded, she ducked back inside the den and nudged Lusa awake. "Come on, we're going to travel in daylight for once."

"Good," the black bear mumbled, heaving herself to her paws and stumbling outside to where the others were waiting.

With Toklo in the lead, the bears set off down the gully. The bottom gradually grew wider, though the sides still rose steeply, cutting out any view of the hills. Kallik had no idea if they were going the right way, but she trusted the she-bear's directions, and she felt as if they were making good progress.

"At this rate, it won't be long before—" she began. She broke off at a loud squeal from Nanulak.

"A hare! Look—a hare!"

Kallik spotted the telltale black tips of its ears as the hare sprang up from the shallow scrape in the ground and fled with huge bounds. Nanulak pelted after it. Suddenly the hare changed direction and ran right into Yakone's paws. The white bear killed it with a swift blow to the neck.

"Good catch!" Kallik exclaimed.

Nanulak glared at her. "I sent the hare into Yakone's paws. It's *my* prey, really."

"Yeah, right," Yakone murmured, rolling his eyes at Kallik.

One Arctic hare shared among five didn't satisfy any bear's hunger, but Kallik felt new strength in her paws as they headed down the gully again. Gradually it grew wider and shallower, and it began to twist, so that they couldn't see very far in any direction.

"I'll be glad to get out of this," Yakone muttered into her ear. "I like to see where I am. Anything could creep up on us down here."

Kallik felt an uneasy prickle in her fur as he spoke, but she had no time to reply before Toklo halted and exclaimed, "I can smell flat-faces!"

"What, up here?" Lusa asked, darting swift glances all around.

"Somewhere ahead," Toklo said. "We'll carry on, but keep quiet."

Setting her paws down carefully, Kallik followed the brown bear around the next curve in the gully. Suddenly he stopped again, peering around a huge boulder.

"Great spirits!" he whispered.

"What is it?" Nanulak gave an excited bounce as he tried to push past Toklo and see what lay ahead.

Toklo blocked him with his shoulder. "Keep back."

By now Kallik had caught up to Toklo and could gaze around the boulder. She gasped with astonishment, hardly able to believe what she was seeing.

Ahead of her, the gully flattened out into a wide bowl. Instead of unbroken snow, scars of raw earth and stones stretched across it from edge to edge. It looked as if some enormous creature had rampaged across it, tearing up the land with its claws.

On the far side of the bowl a big orange firebeast was sleeping. Three or four no-claws stood near it. One of them was bent over something that looked like a firestick stuck upright in the ground. He gestured to the other no-claws, who went behind the firebeast. Then he seemed to push the firestick down into the ground.

"What is he—?" Lusa began.

Her words were drowned in a clap of sound, so loud that Kallik thought her ears would burst. It was louder than firesticks, louder than thunder, louder than the metal bird that had hunted them near the no-claw denning place. At the same moment, the earth and stones at one side of the bowl fountained up into the air. They hung there for a moment, blocking out the sunlight, then fell down again. Some of the debris pattered to the ground around the bears. Kallik flinched as some of it landed on her pelt.

"That stings!" she exclaimed.

Nanulak had pressed himself to the ground, his paws wrapped over his head. Lusa was shaking. Kallik felt her heart pounding as she gazed at Toklo and Yakone, then back again at the stretch of earth that now displayed a new wound.

That was what I heard last night, she realized, remembering the mysterious rumble of thunder. The sound died away, but for a few moments Kallik felt as though her ears were still vibrating with its power. Toklo's jaws were moving, but at first she couldn't hear what he was saying.

What if I never hear anything again? she thought, on the verge of panic.

Then Toklo's voice gradually faded in, as if he were approaching from a long way away.

". . . can't go this way," he was saying. "We'll have to go back up the gully and find somewhere we can climb out."

"Why are the flat-faces tearing up the ground?" Lusa asked, her eyes round with fear. "What are they doing?"

"Why do flat-faces do anything?" Toklo echoed. "They're always weird. And this is *seriously* weird. Come on, Nanulak."

The younger bear was still quaking on the ground. Toklo nudged him gently with one paw. "Come on," he repeated. "It's over now. Let's get away before they do it again."

In response to his urging, Nanulak stumbled to his paws and pressed himself close to Toklo as the grizzly headed back up the gully.

"Are you okay, Lusa?" Kallik asked.

Her friend nodded. "Just a bit shaken. I'll be fine."

The sun was going down, casting deep shadows across the bottom of the gully. Overhead the sky was stained with scarlet, and the first of the star spirits were beginning to appear. Kallik looked in vain for the outline of Ujurak; that part of the sky was hidden by the side of the gully.

"Let's find somewhere to rest," she suggested. She was still quivering from the shock of the blast and wondered how long her paws would go on supporting her. "The slopes are too steep to climb in the dark, anyway."

"Makes sense," Toklo grunted.

But he led the bears on until they were well away from where the no-claws were tearing up the earth. Kallik stayed alert for the sound of another thunderclap, but heard nothing except the ordinary sound of wind and the scuttering of small prey. As darkness gathered, she guessed that the no-claws would have gone back to their dens.

Finally Toklo halted at the foot of the slope, where an overhanging rock gave a little shelter. "This will have to do," he said.

"Thank Silaluk!" Kallik exclaimed, letting herself flop to the ground.

Yakone settled beside her and touched his muzzle comfortingly to her shoulder. "You were very brave," he murmured.

Kallik shook her head. "I was terrified. But at least we don't have to go that way again."

"That's what bothers me," Yakone admitted. "The she-bear told us that's the way down to the sea. Now that we have to avoid the no-claws, it's going to be much harder to get there."

The next day dawned gray and chilly; the sky was covered with threatening cloud, and a raw, damp wind funneled down the gully.

"I think the wind is looking for us," Lusa grumbled. "I feel as if it's going to blow my fur off!"

Toklo walked in front again as the bears headed back the way they had come. Soon they came to a spot where part of the side of the gully had crumbled away. Huge boulders were piled at the bottom; above them thorn trees were rooted in cracks in the rock.

"We should be able to climb up there and go around where the flat-faces are," Toklo said, eyeing the broken surface. "It'll be better than going all the way back to the top."

He started to climb before any bear could comment, hauling himself upward by gripping the trunks of the thorn trees. Grit and small stones showered down as he scrabbled to find pawholds.

Yakone nodded at Nanulak. "You next," he directed. "And I'll be right behind you if you slip."

"I won't slip!" Nanulak retorted. "I can climb as well as any bear."

Without hesitating, he began to scramble up the slope after

Toklo. Yakone followed; Kallik boosted Lusa over the boulders and brought up the rear.

At the top of the gully, Kallik found herself standing on wind-scoured rock scarcely a bearlength wide. On the other side, a sheer cliff fell away into a deep ravine. Instinctively she tried to dig in her claws, half afraid that the wind would blow her off the precarious stone path.

"This is scary!" Lusa muttered.

With Toklo in the lead once more, the bears padded single file along the rock. The wind felt like the buffeting of a huge paw, flattening Kallik's fur to her sides and making her set her paws down as firmly as she could.

I really don't like this, she thought. *And am I imagining things, or is this rock path getting narrower?*

At the same moment, Toklo called out, "Stop!"

"What's the matter?" Yakone asked, craning his neck to peer past Nanulak.

"This path just came to an end," Toklo explained. "And we've got cliffs on both sides."

Kallik glanced around. On one side was the gully they had followed before, on the other the ravine, which had shrunk to little more than a deep fissure in the rock. The opposite side was only a bearlength away.

"We could jump over there," she suggested. "There's no point in trying to climb down into the gully again. We'd still be cut off by the no-claws."

"Good idea," said Yakone.

"But I'm scared!" Nanulak's voice rose over Yakone's. "I might fall."

"Do you want to get off this island or not?" Yakone asked. His voice was irritated, and however much Kallik sympathized with Nanulak, part of her couldn't blame Yakone.

"Toklo, you won't make me do it, will you?" Nanulak begged.

"Lusa's the only one who might have problems," Yakone argued, before Toklo could reply. He glanced back over his shoulder at the black bear. "What do you think, Lusa?"

Lusa measured the gap with an intent gaze before replying. "I'm fine with it," she said.

"Okay, then," Toklo said decisively. "Nanulak, if Lusa can manage, then so can you," he added, cutting off another wail from the younger bear.

"Yes, you're not telling me a black bear can outjump you, are you?" Yakone teased.

Nanulak didn't reply. Kallik couldn't see him—Yakone's body was blocking her view—but she could imagine his offended expression.

Kallik watched as Toklo launched himself into the air, clearing the gap with pawlengths to spare. "It's easy," he said, turning back to the others. "Come on, Nanulak."

"Lusa first," Nanulak said sulkily.

"Okay." Lusa sounded determined. "I'll be glad to get it over with. Toklo, be ready to catch me."

Unhesitatingly the black bear bunched her muscles and

pushed off, her paws splayed, reaching for the opposite side of the ravine. She landed with her hindpaws dangling, scrabbling at the cliff face. Toklo sank his jaws in her shoulder and hauled her up to stand, panting, on the far side.

"Great, Lusa!" Kallik called.

Without letting herself think about it for too long, she made her own leap, landing neatly beside Lusa. Turning back, she saw Nanulak and Yakone standing side by side on the spur of rock.

"I'm coming next!" Nanulak announced. "Keep back, all of you, and give me space."

Kallik and the others took a few paces backward, though Kallik could see that Toklo was ready to spring forward and grab Nanulak if he looked like he was falling.

Nanulak fussed around for a moment, getting into exactly the right position to jump, then let out a roar as he hurled himself at the far side of the ravine in a great leap.

He landed well away from the edge, stumbled, and righted himself. "See?" he said, looking around at the others. His eyes shone. "I'm a great jumper!"

"So you are." Toklo touched the younger bear's shoulder with his muzzle. "I knew you would be."

When Yakone had joined them, the bears set off again, trying to follow the line of the gully and skirt around the area where the no-claws were tearing up the earth. But they found themselves in a landscape of deep crevasses, where they had to keep turning away from the path they wanted. Sometimes they could jump across the cracks; sometimes they had to climb laboriously down one side of a ravine, only to toil up the other. Kallik's paws felt as heavy as rocks, she was so tired.

"This is hopeless," Yakone said at last, as they hauled themselves out of yet another gorge. "We're getting nowhere."

Toklo grunted agreement. "I'm not sure where we are anymore, but we must be skylengths away from where the she-bear told us to go. We don't even have the sun to guide us."

"What are we going to do?" Nanulak whimpered. "I'm so tired and hungry!"

Ujurak would know, Kallik thought. *Are you watching us, Ujurak? Please tell us which way will get us off the island!*

As the thought went through her mind, she spotted movement in the sky. A gull was hovering over a tumbled heap of boulders outlined against the horizon.

"Look!" Kallik exclaimed, pointing with her muzzle.

By the time the others had turned to follow her gaze, the gull had vanished.

"What?" Toklo asked, an edge of irritation in his tone.

"I saw a gull," Kallik replied. At the others' blank looks she added, "I think it was Ujurak, showing us which way to go."

"That way?" Yakone shrugged. "One way is as good as another, I suppose."

This time Kallik took the lead, heading in the direction where the gull had appeared. At first the going was easier, across gentle slopes of scree and thorn, and her optimism began to rise. She picked up the pace, only to halt in dismay as another ravine opened up in front of her paws, this one even deeper than the other.

The other bears joined her and stood looking down into the depths. The cliff face fell down in a series of huge steps, far deeper than a bear could stretch. These steps were slick, topped with snow. At the very bottom was a jumble of boulders with thorn trees growing among them; beyond that was what Kallik guessed was a frozen river, the surface covered with snow. As they stood gazing down, the first flakes of a new snowfall began drifting down.

"We have to climb down there?" Lusa asked doubtfully.

"I—I think so." Kallik was beginning to wonder if the gull had really been a sign from Ujurak. If any bear slipped and fell to the rocks below, they might be killed or badly injured.

"I think we could manage it if we're careful," Toklo said, crouching down to examine the cliff face.

Kallik half expected Nanulak to protest, but the younger bear remained silent, staring into the ravine with wide, scared eyes.

Yakone had padded a few bearlengths along the top of the cliff; now he turned back and called, "There's a sort of path here."

Kallik hurried to join him, with the others following. Yakone pointed with his snout to where the rock of the cliff face had crumbled, making a thin track that zigzagged down into the depths.

"If that's a path, then I'm a flat-face," Toklo muttered.

But they all realized that they had no other choice if they were to go this way. Yakone took the lead, edging his way down, followed by Lusa and then Nanulak.

"Go on," Toklo said to Kallik when they were left alone on the cliff-top. "I'll be right behind you."

Nervously Kallik ventured out onto the track. The loose stones shifted under her paws, making her feel that she would slip and fall countless bearlengths into the ravine.

If I slip, I'll probably bring at least one other bear down with me.

Kallik found that it was better not to look down. Thinking of how far she had to fall made her head swim and her legs shake. It was better to take each small step with her gaze fixed on her paws. Snow was falling more thickly now; it was harder to see ahead, and the stones under Kallik's paws grew slippery.

She was beginning to feel that she had been creeping downward forever when suddenly she had to stop to avoid bumping into Nanulak ahead of her. Risking a glance down, she saw that Yakone and Lusa had halted, too.

"What's the matter?" she called out.

"No more path!" Yakone replied.

From behind Kallik, Toklo let out a groan. "Don't tell me we have to climb back up this cliff!"

Kallik's heart began to pound as she twisted her neck to look back the way they had come. Through the whirling snow she saw that the cliff stretched above her head for many bearlengths; she guessed they were about halfway down. She knew they would never manage to climb back all that way. The daylight was fading, too, and in the dark they would have no hope of finding another path.

Nanulak glanced over his shoulder to glare at her. "This is

all your stupid fault!" he snarled. "You wanted us to come this way, and now we're stuck!"

Kallik wanted to snarl back at him, but guilt washed over her as she realized he had a point. "I'm sorry," she said. "I must have been wrong. Ujurak would never have sent us this way."

"What do we do now?" Lusa asked. Kallik could tell that she was trying to be brave, but her voice was quivering.

"Give me a moment," Yakone replied.

Kallik could see him a little way below, his claws digging into the shifting stones of the track while he peered down into the ravine.

"There's sheer rock here," he went on eventually. "But it doesn't stretch that far. And below it the path goes on again, wider this time. I'm pretty sure I can get down there, and then every other bear can slide down onto my back. What do you think?"

"It's worth a try!" Kallik agreed. "But for Silaluk's sake, be careful!"

"Yes, go for it," Toklo grunted, then added, "Thanks, Yakone."

Kallik knew how hard it must have been for Toklo to say that. She had no doubt that if Toklo had been in the lead, he would have made the same offer. But there was no way for him to get down to where the path ended until the other bears had cleared out of the way.

Every hair on Kallik's pelt prickled with tension as she watched Yakone lowering himself headfirst down the sheer face of the cliff. He reached out with his forepaws as if his pads could stick him to the rock, while his hindpaws remained at the end of the track. His body stretched out. Then with a sudden lurch he was sliding downward.

"Spirits, help him!" Kallik whispered, half expecting to see him go plummeting to his death.

But a heartbeat later Yakone landed on a ledge jutting from the rock. It was barely wide enough for him to stand, and he teetered on the edge for a moment before he regained his balance.

"I'm down!" he called.

"Good job!" Toklo responded.

Kallik was so relieved that she couldn't speak. *Thank you, Silaluk.*

"Okay, Lusa, you first," Yakone ordered.

The small black bear balanced herself at the edge of the track just above Yakone's head. Hardly seeming to hesitate, she launched herself down the cliff face and landed on Yakone's shoulders.

"Way to go, Lusa!" Kallik called, finding her voice again. "You make it look so easy!"

Lusa's voice came up faintly from below. "Yeah, I think I'll be a flying bear!" She clambered down from Yakone's back and withdrew a little way farther along the ledge, where Kallik could see that the track opened up again. Yakone had been right; it was much wider there. *If only we can get down there, we should find the rest of the climb a lot easier.*

Nanulak edged his way forward until he stood directly above Yakone. "Here I come!" he called.

Instead of sliding down, he jumped. Kallik gasped in horror, prepared to see him overshoot the ledge where Yakone waited and go hurtling down to the rocks below. But somehow Yakone swung his hindquarters outward, colliding with Nanulak as he fell and thrusting him back toward the cliff face. Instead of landing on Yakone's back, Nanulak crashed down onto the ledge.

"You moved!" he howled.

"If I hadn't, you would have been smashed to bits on the rocks," Yakone retorted. "Now go over there beside Lusa and stay out of the way."

Baring his teeth bad-temperedly, Nanulak did as he was told.

Kallik's heart beat faster as she crept down to the end of the track. Yakone's white pelt was almost invisible in the snow, but she could see his eyes gleaming as he gazed up at her.

"Come on," he encouraged her. "I won't let you fall."

Kallik remembered how he had stretched down the cliff face toward the ledge, and tried to copy him. She squeezed her eyes tight shut as she felt herself beginning to slip. A couple of heartbeats later she landed on Yakone's solid back, with his scent all around her.

"Thanks," she murmured as she scrambled down to the ledge. "Good catch!"

"I'll have bruises until burn-sky," Yakone said, a hint of amusement in his voice.

Kallik padded to the end of the ledge where Lusa and Nanulak were waiting. The new path led down steeply, but it was wider than the one they had just left, and her spirits began to rise again. *It won't be long before we're down.*

Toklo was crouched at the end of the upper track, preparing himself to slide down to where Yakone was waiting.

"Come on, Toklo!" Nanulak called. "It's easy!"

He bounded forward as Toklo slid down, as if he wanted to help break the grizzly's fall, jostling Kallik as he passed her. Kallik felt her paws slip on the loose, snow-covered stones of the path. The edge gave way under her weight, and she let out a terrified wail as she felt herself start to fall.

"No!" Lusa darted forward and fastened her teeth in Kallik's leg, but she was too small to drag her back to safety.

Kallik scrabbled vainly at the crumbling edge, but she knew she was toppling over, and could almost feel the wind of her fall and the crushing impact as she hit the rocks.

"Help me!" she cried.

Suddenly Yakone was there, his teeth in her shoulder, hauling her upward until she could set her paws firmly on the path again.

"You cloud-brained excuse for a bear!" he snarled, swinging around to face Nanulak. "Haven't you got any sense?"

Nanulak took a step back. "It wasn't my fault!" he wailed. "I was only trying to help!"

"There was no need for your help. I had Toklo just fine." Yakone spat each word out through his teeth. "Kallik could have been killed because you didn't think."

"Leave him alone." Toklo shouldered his way forward. "He's only a cub."

"He's not so young a cub that he doesn't know not to go pushing another bear when you're halfway up a cliff," Yakone retorted.

Nanulak shrank away, pressing himself into Toklo's side. "I didn't mean to," he muttered. "I'm sorry, Kallik."

Kallik was struggling to stop her paws from shaking, and the pounding of her heart was beginning to subside. She reminded herself that Nanulak was less experienced than the rest of them, and she remembered what Ujurak had said to her in her dream; that she had to be the peacemaker.

"It's okay," she said.

Yakone brushed her shoulder with his muzzle. "*I* don't think it's okay," he growled.

"There's no point in arguing," Toklo said. "No one got hurt. Let's go—unless you want to stand here all night."

CHAPTER TWENTY-FOUR

Toklo

A few flakes of snow whirled in the wind as Toklo stood on a boulder, scanning the hillside. Behind him, his companions huddled together, waiting for him to make a decision.

More days had passed as they toiled across the island, and still there was no sign of the coast. Every path they took would fall away into a sheer cliff or end in a huge wall of rock with no way to get through. Once they found themselves trying to cross another stretch of blasted earth with firebeasts crouching among the devastation. They were all famished and exhausted, their strength ebbing with every day that passed.

"We're lost, aren't we?" Nanulak demanded, jumping up to join Toklo on the boulder. "Admit it!"

"Calm down," Toklo responded. "We—"

"We have to get off this island!" Panic flared in Nanulak's eyes. "You promised!"

"Then shut up and let Toklo work out where to go," Yakone put in, giving Nanulak a hard stare.

Oh, great, Toklo thought. *Now I'll have a fight on my paws, as well as all our other problems.*

But Nanulak didn't reply, just glared at Yakone and stood beside Toklo with a sulky look on his face.

I wonder what Ujurak would do if he were here, Toklo thought. *Would he be able to spot a sign that would put us on the right path again?*

He examined the landscape ahead of him more intently, trying to see it through Ujurak's eyes. But between the rough terrain and the unnatural changes the flat-faces had made, it seemed impossible to find a way through. Just in front of Toklo, a clump of tall grass was blowing in the wind, the stalks bent backward in the direction they had come from.

"That's no good," Toklo muttered. "We've just been there! We want to go on."

The pawprints of some smaller animal—an Arctic fox, Toklo guessed—crossed in front of him and headed in the same direction, back toward the ice cap and the ridge down the middle of the island. Toklo frowned as he looked at them.

Would Ujurak say that these were signs telling us to go back? That's bee-brained!

The harsh cries of a gaggle of geese startled him, and he looked up to see their ragged triangle passing overhead. They too were heading toward the ice cap.

For a moment Toklo wrestled with doubt. *What if these are signs? What if something is telling us to go back?* Then he gave himself a shake.

"Nonsense!" he growled. "We're going on, and that's that!"

"Is something the matter, Toklo?"

Toklo jumped at the sound of the voice, then turned to see Lusa padding up closer to him.

"No, I'm fine," he retorted, then added more hesitantly, "I was trying to see signs like Ujurak used to, but I'm no good at it. Everything seems to be telling me that we should go back."

Lusa glanced back at the hills they had struggled to leave behind, and shuddered. "I hope not!" Then she paused and looked up at Toklo, her dark brown eyes round and questioning. "Suppose you're right?" she asked him quietly. "Maybe Ujurak *is* trying to tell you something. Maybe he doesn't want us to go this way."

"Why wouldn't he?" Toklo huffed. "We have to get off the island. If Ujurak was sending us signs," he went on, arguing with himself as much as with Lusa, "then the signs would make sense. What good can it possibly do us to go back to the middle of the island, when we're trying to get to the sea?"

"Ujurak would know." Lusa blinked at him. "Toklo, what if he is trying to help us? We have to listen to him!"

"You're not going on about Ujurak *again*!" Nanulak's voice cut across Lusa's last few words.

"We can talk about Ujurak if we want," Lusa snapped back at him. "He was our friend!"

Nanulak shrugged. "But he's gone now, and it's not like he was a real bear."

"He *was* real," Lusa insisted, turning away. "More real than any of us."

Toklo crushed down a stab of anger toward Nanulak. *He never knew Ujurak,* he reminded himself. *We can't expect him to understand.* "We thought Ujurak might be sending us signs to guide us," he explained.

"Why do we need signs?" Nanulak asked. "We know where we're going. We just need to find the way to the ocean!"

Toklo suppressed a sigh.

He was saved from finding a reply by Yakone, who had been studying the landscape. "I think I know how to find the way to the sea. Look at the shape of the snowdrifts," he pointed out. "They show us the way the wind blows. And we knew where the wind was coming from when we were traveling along the ridge."

"So we need to keep the wind blowing on us from the same direction!" Kallik exclaimed, grasping Yakone's idea. "That's brilliant!"

"It makes sense," Toklo grunted. "That means we go this way," he added, pointing with his snout at an angle down the hillside. "Let's go."

Signs or no signs, he reflected, *they'll never follow me if I try to lead them back to the ice cap.*

Though the bears made more progress that day, Toklo couldn't convince himself that they had made the right decision. There were no more dangerous ravines, but their journey was full of countless irritations. Sharp stones lay concealed beneath the snow. As they crossed a frozen stream, the ice gave way, plunging them into freezing water. It wasn't deep, but it left them cold and uncomfortable, even the white bears with their thick fur. Later, when they tried to hunt, there was no prey to be seen or smelled.

The whole world seemed to be full of signs pointing the other way: clouds scudding across the sky, thorns that pointed back the way they had come, wind that blew directly into their faces. Toklo felt that everything around them was shrieking, *Go back!* He couldn't take a pawstep without sensing that Ujurak was with him, sending him a message that they had to return.

But are these true signs? he asked himself over and over again. *Or am I imagining it because I want Ujurak to be with us? I don't want to go back, but I'd do it if I thought Ujurak wanted it.*

Toklo tried to work out why Ujurak might be telling him to go back. *If we do, we might come across Nanulak's family. . . . Hey, wait! Maybe that's it!*

Seeing the mixed-bear family had reminded Toklo that some families were good and kind and loyal to one another. Every bear, including Nanulak, deserved to have a family like that at the start of his life.

No bear should be driven away by his own mother, Toklo thought, with a sharp pang of pain as he remembered Oka. Indignation rose inside him as he imagined what he might say to the bears who had driven Nanulak away. His paws itched to confront them.

"Nanulak is worth caring for," he would say. "He's happy with us now. But you've lost him—you've lost an important part of your family. And I hope you're satisfied!"

If we go back, he thought, trying not to think about the long trek they would have to make, *it shouldn't be too hard to find Nanulak's family. Maybe Ujurak feels the same as I do: that we should put things straight with them before we take Nanulak away forever.*

But can I be sure that's what the signs are telling me? Toklo shook his head in confusion. *Will the others believe me? I can't expect them to trust me if I can't trust myself.*

"We'd better look for somewhere to make a den," Yakone said, as the sun went down.

Toklo gazed around. They were standing on a bleak hill-side that seemed to go on forever; there was no sign of shelter anywhere in the gathering shadows.

"No thorn trees, no boulders," Kallik muttered. "And the snow is starting again."

"Then where are we going to sleep?" Nanulak asked.

"Here." Toklo let himself flop down.

"In the open?" Nanulak protested. "But—"

"Do you have a better idea?" Yakone growled. "If you know of a den, show us where it is."

Toklo knew that he should defend Nanulak; Yakone didn't have enough patience with the inexperienced cub. But he was weary from the tip of his snout to his tail, and he simply didn't have the energy.

"Things will look better in the morning," he mumbled, wrapping his paws over his snout.

He felt Nanulak curl up beside him out of the wind, and Lusa press close on his other side. Gradually a little warmth spread through Toklo's body, and he drifted into sleep.

In his dream the unfriendly hillside where they had stopped to rest was transformed into a meadow of waving grass under bright sunlight. Toklo raced across it, reveling in the new strength in his paws.

Ahead of him was a mule deer; startled by the sight of him, it leaped away and fled. Toklo's jaws watered in anticipation as he sped after it, cutting the distance between them with powerful bounds. But as he was readying himself for a spring, the mule deer stopped and spun around. Its hooves and antlers disappeared. Its limbs thickened, and brown fur sprouted out of its sleek pelt.

"Ujurak!" Toklo yelped, skidding to a halt. "I wish you wouldn't do that! One day you'll get yourself killed, and—" He broke off, remembering with a jolt of grief that his friend was already dead.

Ujurak's eyes shone with affection. Giving Toklo a friendly poke with his snout, he said, "That was a great race, wasn't it? You're really fast!"

Toklo was swept back to the time when they had traveled together, in the early days before they'd met Lusa and Kallik, and he'd had to protect Ujurak and teach him the things a brown bear needed to know.

"I wish we could travel together again," he murmured. "But I know this is only a dream."

"Not *only* a dream," Ujurak corrected him. "Dreams are the way for me to talk to you now."

"Then you have something to tell me?" Toklo asked, suddenly hopeful.

Ujurak nodded, deeply serious now. "You have to go back to the place where you found Nanulak," he announced.

"Then I *was* right! You want me to find Nanulak's family and make them see what they did to him was wrong!"

Ujurak blinked thoughtfully. "Nanulak's story on this island is not over," he said at last.

Toklo stared at him, frustration driving out the brief flash of hope. "What do you mean by that? Am I right or not?" Struggling not to drive Ujurak away from him, as he had done in his previous dream, he added, "Are you deliberately blocking our way, to send us back over the ice cap?"

Ujurak dipped his head, sadness in his eyes. "Some things are meant to be."

"That's no answer!"

Toklo shivered as Ujurak stretched out his neck to lay his muzzle on his shoulder.

"Toklo, you're still my friend," the star-bear said softly. "Remember the good times we had together? Remember how we trusted each other? You have to trust me now."

Looking into his friend's eyes, Toklo felt his anger die. "It's like you're trying to make me choose between you and Nanulak," he choked out.

"I wouldn't ask that," Ujurak promised. "It's just that you have much more to learn before you can continue on your journey."

"And if we don't go back?" Toklo challenged him. "If we just keep on going toward the sea?"

Ujurak gave a tiny shrug as his form began to dissolve into mist. But Toklo didn't need a reply. The answer was already echoing in his head.

If we don't go back, we'll never reach the sea.

When Toklo woke, his memory of the dream was still clear, Ujurak's words running through his mind. He pulled himself to his paws to see Kallik and Yakone standing side by side, gazing across the hillside, while Nanulak sat a bearlength away, scratching himself vigorously. Only Lusa was still curled up asleep.

Gray dawn light was seeping over the landscape. The clouds were low and threatening, as if they held more snow. Toklo had a brief image of himself and his companions fighting their way through a blizzard.

"Okay, Ujurak," he sighed. "You've made your point." Prodding Lusa awake, he called to the others. "I had a dream last night," he announced as they gathered around him. "Ujurak told me we have to go back to the place where we found Nanulak. He said his story on this island is not over."

"What?" Yakone exclaimed, at the same moment as Kallik asked, "Oh, Toklo, are you sure?"

Toklo nodded. "That's why it's been so difficult," he explained. "All this time, we've been going the wrong way."

Lusa nodded as she stifled a yawn. "I see," she murmured. "So those *were* signs we saw yesterday." Shivering, she added half to herself, "All that way back again . . ."

"Well, I *don't* see." For a moment Nanulak had stood in outraged silence. Now his voice was high-pitched and angry. "I don't see why we have to slog all the way back, just because of what some dead bear told you in a dream!"

Toklo rounded on him, then bit back a furious response. *It's not his fault. He doesn't understand.*

"Well, for once I agree with Nanulak," Yakone said. "What's the point of going all that way? It's been hard enough to get this far."

"I told you," Toklo repeated, trying not to sound impatient. "It's been hard because we've been doing it wrong. Once we turn back, it'll get easier, I promise."

Yakone still looked doubtful. "I wish I could believe you, but . . ."

"I believe you, Toklo," Kallik said, then turned to the white bear. "Ujurak knows these things. If he told Toklo to go back, then that's what we have to do."

"I agree." Lusa moved closer to Toklo's side.

"But I don't!" Nanulak's eyes flashed with anger. "Toklo, I can't believe you want to take me back there! You know the white bears are looking for me."

"I won't let them hurt you," Toklo began, trying to reassure the younger bear. "Just let them try. I'll—"

"They won't get a chance to hurt me," Nanulak interrupted, "because I'm *not going.* Toklo, I thought you were my friend. But if you let me down, then I'll carry on to the sea by myself."

For a moment Toklo was tempted to give in. He hated the idea that he was letting Nanulak down. But his memory of Ujurak returned to give him strength in his resolve. "That's your choice," he said quietly. "But I want you to come with us.

We have to do this, to show your family they were wrong to drive you away when prey was scarce."

Nanulak's eyes widened in disbelief. "You'd really leave me alone?" He took a deep breath. "All right. I'll come. But whatever my family says, you'll still take me to the forests, right? I'm still a brown bear?"

"Of course," said Toklo.

CHAPTER TWENTY-FIVE

Lusa

Lusa toiled at the back of the group as they retraced their pawsteps toward the center of the island. She couldn't help wondering how long it would take any of them to notice if she disappeared. Kallik and Yakone were padding close together, while Nanulak kept near Toklo's side. Both pairs of bears obviously belonged together.

And I don't belong with either pair, she told herself sadly. *Sooner or later they'll split up, and then who will I go with? Maybe they don't want me, anyway.*

Kallik and Yakone would settle at the Frozen Sea, while Toklo and Nanulak would journey on until they found a forest where they could claim territory.

"I just want to be home," she whispered. "With sunlight, and green trees, and berry bushes . . ."

But that wasn't her home; the only home she had known before the journey had been the Bear Bowl, surrounded by animals that weren't bears, fed and watched by flat-faces, confined to a space smaller than some of the ice floes they had traveled on. However much Lusa missed her family—Ashia, King, Yogi, Stella—she knew she could never go back to the Bear Bowl. She had to find a new home, a place where black bears could live in the wild, far from flat-faces and silver cans of food scraps. For her, this journey had no ending, or at least not one that she knew of yet.

She accepted completely that Ujurak had spoken to Toklo in a dream and had told them to retrace their pawsteps. Still, Toklo's words to Nanulak about showing his family they were wrong had unsettled her. She couldn't stifle a nagging anxiety that Toklo was looking for revenge against the bears who had abandoned Nanulak. Surely that couldn't have been what Ujurak meant.

That is not our battle, she told herself. *Looking after Nanulak, helping him find a safe place to live . . . okay. But not deliberately looking for a fight.*

But for the time being they were far away from where they might expect to find Nanulak's family. They encountered no white bears, and Lusa's hopes began to rise. She wasn't sure if she was imagining it, but there seemed to be a tiny bit more light every day. The threatened snow never fell, and the skies cleared. Lusa felt as if every hair on her pelt were drinking in the sunshine.

Maybe the sun is on its way back? I've missed it so much! And trees . . . I'm hungry for trees.

The terrain was easier, too. Toklo had been right about that. Lusa had been afraid that they would have to struggle up and down the ravines again, but somehow they managed to find their way among the crags with no more than a short scramble or a bold leap. Thorn thickets seemed to part to let them through, and the soft snow was soothing for weary paws.

Food gradually became more plentiful. Lusa felt as if something was guiding her to the right spots to dig down and find leaves or lichen, and she found a few stray berries still clinging to the branches of the thorns. Toklo caught a plump Arctic hare, and Yakone spotted a fish beneath the surface of a frozen pool and broke the ice to hook it out.

But Nanulak's reluctance to return seemed to increase with every pawstep he took. He complained all the time about being tired, until even Toklo started to lose patience with him.

"I don't want to do this," he said one night as Kallik and Yakone were digging out a den. "Toklo, we don't have to stay with these bears. Let them go back if they want to. Let's go to the sea, just the two of us."

Lusa drew in a breath, shocked that Nanulak would even suggest this. *Doesn't he understand anything?*

"We can't do that, Nanulak," Toklo replied, with an edge to his voice that hadn't been there before when he spoke to the younger bear. "We're doing this because of you. Ujurak said that your story on this island isn't finished."

"Then he's wrong!" Nanulak insisted. "Why do you listen to him instead of me?"

"Because Ujurak knows these things," Lusa replied.

Nanulak whirled to face her. "What do you know about it? You're only a *black* bear!"

Lusa stared at him, hardly able to believe he'd said that.

"That's enough," Toklo growled. "We're going back, and that's that."

Nanulak opened his jaws to argue some more, then seemed to realize how angry Toklo was and thought better of it. He stayed in sulky silence until all the bears settled down to sleep.

As they drew closer to the ice cap, Nanulak's reluctance gave way to real fear. Lusa noticed that he was always on edge, casting nervous glances in all directions. Even though she didn't like him any better, she found herself feeling sorry for him.

"There's nothing to be afraid of," she said, falling into step beside him as they followed Toklo up a steep mountain slope.

"Yes, there is," Nanulak whimpered. "The white bears will get me, I know they will! We never should have come back."

"Toklo knows what he's doing," Lusa reassured him, deciding there was no point in mentioning Ujurak. "And he'll look after you."

"But the white bears are *big*!" Nanulak protested. "Bigger than Toklo."

"They might be bigger, but they won't fight as well as Toklo," Lusa told him. "Toklo's the best! He fought a white bear on Star Island. And back when we were at Great Bear Lake—and Toklo was much younger than he is now—he defeated a full-grown grizzly called Shoteka."

Nanulak blinked at her. "Really?"

"Really."

To Lusa's relief, Nanulak brightened up, as if he hadn't quite believed until then that Toklo could defend him from his enemies. Bounding forward until he reached Toklo's side, he exclaimed, "Toklo! Tell me about the time you killed a grizzly at Great Bear Lake!"

"Later," Toklo replied. "I'm going to hunt now. And I didn't kill him."

"Why not?" Nanulak persisted. "It's good to kill your enemies."

Toklo let out an exasperated sigh. "No, it's not. Not when you can defeat them without killing them. I'll tell you all about it when I get back from hunting."

"I want to come with you," Nanulak announced, following in Toklo's pawsteps as he drew aside from their path and began to sniff the air. "I only feel safe when I'm with you."

"Yakone and Kallik will look after you," Toklo told him; Lusa could tell that he was trying hard not to sound annoyed.

"But they're white bears!"

Toklo sighed again. "Okay, you can come. But you have to keep quiet. No stories until we've caught something, okay?"

"Okay!" Nanulak said happily, bounding at Toklo's side until the two of them vanished behind a tumbled heap of boulders.

Kallik took the lead as the remaining bears headed up the hillside. Yakone padded along at her shoulder, then dropped back until he was walking beside Lusa.

"I want to ask you something," he announced.

Lusa blinked up at him curiously.

"What do you think about the way Toklo treats Nanulak?" the white bear went on. "Why is he so close to him? They're not kin."

Lusa thought for a moment. "You need to understand what it was like for Toklo when he was a cub," she said at last. "He had a brother, Tobi, who was weak and sick, and eventually he died. Toklo feels guilty that he wasn't able to save him."

Yakone nodded. "So he wants to save Nanulak . . ."

"There's more," Lusa said. "Toklo's mother, Oka, was so grief-stricken after Tobi's death that she drove Toklo away. He had to fend for himself when he was really too young. So I think he feels very close to Nanulak because he was driven away by his family, too."

"That makes sense," Yakone said.

"That's why Toklo became so close to Ujurak, too." Lusa felt a renewed stab of grief. "They were such good friends."

"Toklo needs to be needed," Yakone said. "That's good. But I wish I could believe that Nanulak deserves him."

Lusa grunted in agreement. Talking to Yakone had cleared her own mind. It did make sense that Toklo would try to fill the yawning gap left after his brother, Tobi, had died, and his mother, Oka, had driven him away. She knew that Toklo had to miss his family the same way that Kallik missed hers, and that he surely longed for a new family the same way Lusa longed to see the bears in the Bear Bowl once more.

We're a family now, Lusa thought. *Maybe we don't always like it, or understand it, but that's what we are. We have to stick together if we're going to survive.*

CHAPTER TWENTY-SIX

Kallik

The journey back along the ridge didn't seem to take as long as the outward trek, and Kallik found the going much easier when they could travel by day.

"We're not hiding anymore," Toklo had said stoutly. "We've done nothing wrong."

Besides, the slightly longer days gave more time for hunting and walking. Kallik still didn't like the island: There were too many shadows, too many unfamiliar things, and she couldn't shake the feeling that there was something not quite right about it. But she knew that she could survive there for as long as it took to find Nanulak's family and make them face up to what they had done.

And I have Yakone with me, she reflected. Warm happiness flooded through her from ears to paws as she looked at the reddish-pelted bear. *I can cope with anything as long as we're together.*

All that worried Kallik was the fact that every pawstep was taking them farther away from the Frozen Sea. "At this rate, we'll never get there before the ice melts," she confided to Yakone. She was feeling hungry and tired, and so far that day Toklo hadn't stopped to hunt at all. "And then we'll have to survive with empty bellies through the whole of burn-sky."

Yakone touched her ear with his nose. "It'll be okay," he reassured her.

Kallik quickened her pace a little, then realized that Yakone had dropped back. She looked around for him, but there was no sign of him.

"I shouldn't have been so grumpy," she muttered. "Oh, spirits, don't say I've driven Yakone away!"

Her heart sinking into her paws, she trudged after Toklo and Nanulak, all the while glancing around to see if Yakone was coming back. At last she spotted him, galloping up behind them with something dangling from his jaws. As he drew closer, she saw that it was a goose. Yakone's eyes were alight with triumph.

"Here," he said, dropping his prey at her paws. "I caught it just for you." Awkwardly he added, "You deserve to be looked after."

Gratitude overwhelmed Kallik so that she hardly knew what to say. "Thank you," she whispered, stretching forward so that she could touch noses with Yakone.

Then something made her fur prickle; she jumped back when she saw Nanulak watching them, his eyes dark and unreadable.

Kallik lost count of the number of days they spent trekking back to the middle of the island, though she knew it was taking far less time than their struggle toward the sea. Finally they stood on the rim of the little valley where they had found Nanulak, and gazed down. Fresh snow had fallen since they left, but it was softer than before, and not as deep; it was also trampled with the pawprints of white and brown bears.

Well, here we are, Kallik thought. *Now what?*

She glanced around for Yakone, but he had disappeared once again. Kallik spotted his tracks leading farther along the edge of the valley and vanishing behind a jutting rock. A worm of uneasiness twisted in her belly at the thought that he had gone exploring on his own.

We don't know what danger might be waiting for us here.

"I don't like it here," Nanulak said, echoing Kallik's apprehension. "How long are we supposed to stay?"

"I don't know," Toklo admitted. He was standing next to Kallik and Lusa, staring down into the valley as if the mess of bear tracks down there might tell him something. "I can't see why Ujurak sent us back here," he added to Kallik in a lower voice. "There's nothing to find."

Kallik nodded. "I've been thinking," she began. "I can't help wondering why the white bears attacked Nanulak. If white bears and brown bears can live so closely that they have cubs together, why would they turn on each other?"

Toklo shrugged. "Maybe there wasn't enough prey to go around," he guessed. "That's why Nanulak's family drove him away."

Kallik wasn't sure. She peered intently down into the valley again, studying the rocky slopes, the snow, and the boulders that littered the valley floor. *There must be a sign down there. Something to tell us what we have to do now. Ujurak wouldn't have sent us back here if it wasn't important.*

Suddenly she realized that Yakone had reappeared and was bounding along the top of the valley toward her. There was urgency in his face, but he didn't speak until he reached Kallik and the others.

"White bears!" he panted. "Several of them, over there." He jerked his muzzle in the direction he had come from.

"No!" Nanulak whimpered, pressing himself against Toklo's side. "They'll find me and kill me. I knew we should never have come."

"Did they see you?" Toklo asked Yakone.

The white bear shook his head. "No. But maybe we should get out of here."

"Without finding out why Ujurak sent us?" Lusa argued.

Kallik understood her friend's reluctance, but she didn't want to stay near the valley if it meant a fight with white bears. "We're supposed to be finding Nanulak's family," she argued. "But they're not here. I vote we find somewhere close by to hide, and come back when the white bears are gone."

"Good idea," Toklo said. "We—"

"No!" Nanulak exclaimed. "I'll be brave, Toklo. You were right. I should face up to my enemies."

Kallik saw her own surprise reflected in Toklo's eyes. *Why should Nanulak suddenly change his mind?*

Toklo stared down at Nanulak. "You *want* to confront these white bears?"

Nanulak nodded vigorously. "I want revenge!" he insisted. "I want those white bears to pay for what they did to me. You'll do it for me, won't you, Toklo?"

Kallik could tell that Toklo was uneasy; he hesitated for a long time before replying.

"How can you be sure these are the same bears?" he asked eventually. "You haven't even seen them."

"The bears who attacked me lived around here," Nanulak replied. "They must be the same."

Toklo exchanged a glance with Kallik, still clearly uncertain.

"You said you would help me!" Nanulak reminded him.

Toklo nodded. "All right. But we need to get a good look at these bears first. I'm not fighting them if they're not the ones who attacked you."

Nanulak looked sulky, as if he wasn't satisfied with Toklo's answer, but he said nothing more.

"Yakone, show us where you saw the bears," Toklo said.

The white bear led the way back along the valley's rim. Rounding the heap of boulders, Kallik saw a confused mass of tracks leading into the distance, but no sign of any white bears.

"They're gone!" Nanulak exclaimed. "Come on, we have to follow them!"

Kallik thought how strange it was that he sounded determined to find the bears, when up until now he had been so desperate to avoid them. She spotted Lusa giving him a surprised look, too, as if she was wondering what was going through Nanulak's mind.

Toklo took the lead as they followed the tracks away from the valley, across a narrow frozen stream, and up a steep slope beyond. Reaching the top of the slope, Kallik spotted a group of white bears heading away from them, trekking across a shallow dip beyond the ridge. A huge male was in the lead, followed by two younger bears, a male and a female, with a very old she-bear bringing up the rear.

"Well?" Toklo asked. "Do you recognize them?"

"Yes." Nanulak's eyes were full of anger. "That big bear—he's the one who attacked me!"

"Are you sure?" Lusa asked, looking worried.

Kallik shared her anxiety. The white male was far bigger than Toklo, and he looked tough. She didn't know if Toklo could beat him in a fight.

"I'm sure!" Nanulak snarled. "Do you think I could ever forget what that bear did to me? He's a vicious bully, and he deserves to die!"

Kallik shivered. Something about this didn't feel right.

"Okay, let's go for it." Toklo squared his shoulders and headed after the group of white bears.

Kallik and the others followed. Kallik noticed that Nanulak was keeping well to the rear, where the white bears wouldn't spot him right away.

Lusa was trotting beside Kallik. "Do you think this is why Ujurak sent us back?" she whispered. "To take revenge?" She shook her head. "That doesn't sound like Ujurak at all."

Kallik had to agree with her, but there was nothing she could do to stop the fight now. Toklo had given his word to Nanulak.

"Hey! You there!" Toklo roared as they began to catch up to the white bears. "Wait!"

The white bears halted and turned to stare at them. For a moment Kallik thought that Nanulak had disappeared, until she spotted him hiding behind a boulder, peering around it to get a good view without being seen.

As Toklo approached, the biggest white bear signed to his companions to stay where they were, and strode out to face Toklo. He had a wary look, as if he was ready for trouble. Kallik exchanged a glance with Yakone. Without needing to speak, the two of them began circling in opposite directions, to place themselves between the big white male and the bears with him.

This is going to be a fight between two bears, Kallik thought determinedly. *This bear's friends aren't going to help him against Toklo, not if Yakone and I have anything to do with it.*

"What do you want?" the male bear asked.

"You." Toklo halted, his snout thrust out aggressively. "I heard you've been attacking smaller bears. But now you've got me to deal with."

"What?" The white bear sounded startled. "I don't know what you're talking about. I haven't attacked any bear."

"You would say that," Toklo sneered. "You're a coward.

You're too scared to face up to a bear your own size."

"You're not my own size." The white bear loomed over Toklo, and his voice deepened to an angry growl. "But no bear calls me a coward. If you want a fight, you can have it."

CHAPTER TWENTY-SEVEN

Toklo

Toklo braced himself, holding the white bear's gaze. *How did I get here?* he wondered. He didn't want to fight. He knew that if he was injured, it would make their journey much harder. And yet he also knew that Nanulak was watching.

Maybe this is my destiny, he thought. *Maybe I'm here to teach this white bear that he can't bully bears smaller and weaker than himself.*

He tried to imagine Ujurak by his side, supporting him and urging him on, but he had no sense of his friend's presence. *You brought us back here,* he thought, *so now where are you?*

While he hesitated, the white bear let out a roar and lunged at him. Toklo ducked under his outstretched paws and rammed his head hard into the white bear's belly. Dodging aside, he felt a violent blow on his shoulder, and for a heartbeat his whole leg went numb. He almost lost his balance, and in that moment the white bear was upon him.

Toklo flinched as his opponent raked his claws along his side. Staggering, he aimed a blow at his shoulder, but his claws passed harmlessly through the white pelt. He saw scarlet drops of blood spatter on the snow. While he was still off balance, the white bear gave him a hefty shove; Toklo barely managed to stay on his paws.

"You can't win," the white bear growled. "Get out of here, or I'll rip your pelt off!"

Toklo lurched to his hindpaws and advanced on the white bear, his forepaws splayed out and his jaws gaping as he roared a challenge. He dropped forward onto the white bear's shoulders, slashing his claws over and over again, feeling a savage satisfaction as they dug into flesh.

The white bear let out a yelp of pain. Suddenly he went limp, dropping Toklo to the ground and rolling on top of him. Crushed, half smothered in white fur, Toklo struggled to throw him off. His senses were reeling, the world beginning to dissolve into sparkling darkness. With a massive effort, Toklo brought up his hindpaws and battered at the white bear's belly. He caught a glimpse of dripping jaws and sharp white fangs as the white bear lunged for his throat.

Summoning all his strength, Toklo dragged himself from underneath the white bear. The hot reek of blood was in his nose, and blood was trickling into his eyes from a scratch on his forehead. Panting, he realized that he would have to finish the fight quickly.

"Come on, fish-breath!" he taunted. "Is that all you've got?"

The white bear sprang at him again. Toklo slipped to one side, landing a couple of good blows on his enemy's rump. The white bear turned to strike back, but he wasn't fast enough. Toklo charged into him from the other side, carrying him off his paws. Leaping on top of him, he held him down with one paw across his throat, while he bared his teeth, ready to rip at his flesh.

"Had enough?" he snarled.

The white bear nodded. "You win," he rasped, blinking blood out of his eyes. "You fight well."

Toklo relaxed his grip, intending to let the white bear stand up, but before he could, he heard Nanulak shriek.

"Don't let him go! Kill him!"

At the sound of Nanulak's voice, the white bear let out a gasp. He turned his head to see Nanulak running up, his lips drawn back in a snarl and a gloating look in his eyes. Toklo hardly recognized him.

"Kill him!" Nanulak repeated.

Toklo opened his jaws, but the white bear spoke first.

"Nanulak! Son!"

"What?" Toklo staggered back. "Nanulak, this white bear is your *father*?"

"No!" Nanulak spat the word out. "He's *nothing* to me. I'm a brown bear now."

The white bear staggered to his paws and shook the snow from his pelt. His eyes were full of sorrow. "I am his father," he told Toklo. "His mother is a brown bear. We love Nanulak very much, but he—"

"You never loved me!" Nanulak growled. "You never understood me. My mother kept telling me that I was different and special because I was half white bear. But I'm *not*! I *won't* be! I'm a *brown* bear."

The white bear shook his massive head, scattering lumps of snow and scarlet drops onto the ground. "I don't understand this," he said. "Who are these bears? Where have you been? We all thought you were dead!"

"As if you care!" Nanulak sneered.

"You know we care." The white bear's voice was quiet. "Your mother and your half brother and sister have been looking for you. So have I, and my white-bear kin here were helping me. We were worried about you."

"What?" Lusa bounded up behind Nanulak, gazing at him with wide, disbelieving eyes. "You told us your family drove you away!"

Nanulak's father glanced at her, looking faintly surprised at the sight of a black bear. "None of us would do that," he said. "We took care of Nanulak while he was with us. Until now we've been grieving for him."

Toklo felt as though the white bear's words were clawing into his heart, more painful than any of his wounds from the fight. Kallik and Yakone padded up, with the other white bears behind them.

Nanulak didn't stop staring at his father with hatred in his eyes. "You know *nothing* about me!" Suddenly he whirled to confront Toklo. "I thought you were going to help me," he snarled. "But you let me down. I wanted you to kill him for me!"

Toklo blinked through the blood clotting in the fur around his eyes. "You lied to me," he said hoarsely. "Over and over again. You told me your family had driven you away. You told me this bear had attacked you. You would have made me kill your own father!"

Nanulak flattened his ears, fury giving way to confusion. "But we're friends, Toklo. We're both brown bears, right? Isn't that what friends do for each other?"

Toklo felt a surge of anger rise in his belly. *Nanulak can't even see that what he did is wrong!* "Friends tell each other the truth," he growled. "Instead you used me. You're no friend of mine."

"But . . . we're going to travel together," Nanulak stammered. "We're going to find territories side by side. You said so."

"I made that promise to another bear," Toklo murmured, sorrow welling up inside him. "A bear who really did need me. Not one who lied to me and tried to make me kill an innocent bear. An innocent bear who is his *father.*"

Nanulak took a pace back. "I get it now," he said, his voice hardening again. "You're against me, like all the others, because I'm half white bear and half brown."

"That's not true," Toklo said.

"He's always been like this." It was the younger male white bear who spoke. "Right from when we were little cubs. My sister and I tried to play with him, but he never wanted anything to do with us."

The young she-bear nodded. "He always went off by himself instead."

Nanulak raked the group of white bears with a cold gaze. "You're all against me," he hissed. "It's not my fault that I'm half white and half brown."

The old white she-bear stepped forward until she stood in

front of Nanulak, looking down at him. She was scrawny with age, and her fur was patchy, but Toklo could see wisdom in her cloudy eyes. She reminded him of Aga, the ancient she-bear on Star Island.

"No bear cares about that but you," she told Nanulak.

"It's true." Nanulak's father padded to his son's side and bent his head to touch his shoulder with his muzzle, only to leave the movement unfinished. "Your mother and I love each other," he said. "And we want to love you. Can't you let us?"

Nanulak turned a look of freezing contempt on his father. "I don't care about you," he snarled. "I'm better than any of you. I'll live alone, like a true brown bear. Will you travel with me, Toklo? You promised, remember? Just you and me, brown bears together."

CHAPTER TWENTY-EIGHT

Toklo

Toklo stood rigid, unable to reply. He wondered if Nanulak really meant what he was saying. *After all that's happened, does he really think I'll leave my friends and go with him?*

Before he managed to find words, a yelp came from behind him.

"Nanulak!"

Toklo spun around to see three brown bears approaching over the rim of the valley: a full-grown she-bear and two cubs about his own age. One of the white bears was with them.

It was the she-bear who had called out. She raced down the slope and thrust her way through the crowd of bears until she stood facing Nanulak.

"My son!" she cried. "I thought I'd never see you again."

Toklo exchanged a shocked glance with Lusa and Kallik. Here was more proof that Nanulak's brown-bear family had never driven him away.

"You let your mother think you were dead," Lusa hissed. "How could you do that?"

Nanulak whirled around to look at her, his teeth bared in a snarl. "You have no right to question me, you . . . you *black* bear! You don't even belong here, but they all accept you, more than they've ever accepted me!"

"I've always accepted you," Nanulak's mother said.

"Didn't you care that you made your mother grieve for you?" Kallik asked. "Did you really hate her so much?"

"Yes!" Nanulak's voice had risen to a shriek. "She betrayed me! I didn't ask to be half a bear, not white and not brown."

Nanulak's mother shook her head. "But your father and I were so proud to have you. You are not the only bear like this on the island. How can you hate us for having you?"

Nanulak let out a yelp of rage. "I hate you! And I hate them!" he growled, jerking his head at his fully brown half brother and sister. His voice suddenly shaking, he added, "I just wanted to be one type of bear."

"You are one type of bear," his mother responded. "You are yourself. You are my son, and I love you. We are your family, and always will be."

Suddenly Toklo understood what Ujurak had meant when he'd said, *Remember what truly matters.* Family was the most important thing in the world, but it didn't have to be the family you were born into. He and the others had created a family for themselves: this ragtag band of bears, thrown together by luck or by the spirits, yet trusting one another with their lives.

Toklo knew what he had to do. He padded up to Nanulak, who was still glaring at his mother, still quivering with anger and hatred. "Nanulak, don't do this," he urged. "Come with us, if that's what you want. Your anger will destroy you, and if you go off alone, you won't survive."

"What?" The sharp exclamation came from Lusa. "You'll let this . . . this liar come with us?"

She crowded up to Toklo on one side, while Kallik pressed against him from the other.

"Toklo, what are you doing?" Kallik asked. "Nanulak might look like a brown bear, but he's not a replacement for Tobi or Ujurak."

"I know," Toklo replied quietly. "But we've always found room for bears to join us, however difficult they might seem to be at first. We forgive mistakes—that's what makes us the family we are. Nanulak," he went on, turning back to the younger bear, "you can belong with us if you really want to. We'll give you all the help you need."

Nanulak swiveled to glare at Toklo. "You're not a true brown bear," he retorted. "If you were, you'd come with me and leave these others behind. No wonder Ujurak left you!"

Toklo heard a gasp from Lusa and Kallik; he knew they expected him to explode with anger, but he made himself stay calm.

"I hope you find peace on your travels," was all he said. "Or you're going to come to a nasty end."

"Are you threatening me?" Fury flared in Nanulak's eyes. "If I have to fight to prove what I am, then I will."

Drawing his lips back in a snarl, Nanulak aimed a blow at his mother, who leaped out of range, not trying to defend herself. Nanulak whirled and lashed out again, at Toklo this time;

Toklo blocked the blow with a firm paw.

"Nanulak, this is ridiculous," he sighed. "There's no need for fighting."

"It's what brown bears do, isn't it?" Nanulak growled. "We fear nothing, accept nothing but victory."

Toklo suddenly felt as if he were adrift in a rough sea. He had no idea how to get through to this troubled bear. He didn't even recognize Nanulak now, all fury and vengeance.

"You tricked me!" Nanulak spat. "You never wanted me to come with you. You changed your mind, and now you want me to stay with these bears."

"That's not true—" Toklo began.

"I can survive on my own!" Nanulak declared. "If no bear wants me, then I don't want them, either."

"Wait," his mother said, stepping forward again. "I want you."

"You're dead to me," Nanulak sneered. "You betrayed me by making me neither a white bear nor a brown bear. Can't you see that?"

There was a muffled gasp from his brown and white kin. Nanulak's mother bowed her head, and the white bear who was Nanulak's father padded to her side and pressed himself against her.

"Let him go," he whispered. "It's what he wants."

Nanulak had already turned away, thrusting himself between the bears who surrounded him. Toklo started after him, but Kallik stepped into his way.

"No," she said, her voice quiet but firm. "Nanulak has made his choice."

Reluctantly Toklo nodded, watching as Nanulak shouldered his way through the crowd and began to climb the slope. His mother gazed after him, her eyes full of regret and longing.

Toklo faced Nanulak's father. "I am truly sorry," he said. "If I hadn't believed Nanulak's lies, I would never have attacked you."

The white bear dipped his head. "It wasn't your fault. Thank the spirits that no great harm has been done."

But Toklo found it hard to accept his forgiveness. *I might have killed this bear. And I've lost Nanulak.*

No. I've lost the bear I thought he was.

He stood in the midst of the blood-stained snow, staring at Nanulak as he trudged up the hillside, growing smaller and smaller until he reached the ridge and disappeared. Grief tingled in Toklo's fur, and he had no idea what he was supposed to do now.

Lusa drew his attention by pressing her muzzle into his shoulder. "This is why Ujurak sent us back," she murmured. "We had to discover the truth about Nanulak."

"It wasn't his destiny to travel with us," Kallik said.

A faint warmth began to seep into Toklo's fur. He felt as if Ujurak was somewhere close to him, gazing at him with stars in his eyes.

You were so brave, Toklo, and so loyal to the bear you thought was your friend. You were right to offer him forgiveness. Now you can journey on, knowing that you did all you could for Nanulak.

Journey on? Toklo wondered. *Can I?* Even Ujurak's praise

wasn't enough to heal the wounds Nanulak had dealt to his spirit, so much deeper than those he had taken from Nanulak's father.

Yakone padded up to him and butted him gently in the shoulder. "Come on," he said. "We'll find a den for the night, and put some snow on those scratches."

"You're welcome to stay with us if you want," the old she-bear invited.

Toklo shook his head. "We're traveling to the Frozen Sea," he explained. "Thank you, but we must go on."

Dipping his head to the white and brown bears, he turned away. The first pawstep was the hardest, but as he got moving, it suddenly felt right to be journeying once again with friends he could trust. Lusa and Kallik walked close beside him, their fur brushing his. Toklo was comforted by his sense of his family near him.

Maybe I don't need another brown bear to make a territory next to mine. Maybe, for now, this strange family we've created is enough.

LOOK FOR

RETURN TO THE WILD

SEEKERS

BOOK 2: THE MELTING SEA

Toklo

Toklo's paws churned up snow as he hurtled across the ground, ice clogging his belly hair. He could feel his heart pounding. His breath came in hot gasps.

Glancing over his shoulder, Toklo saw Kallik on his tail. A wild light shone in her eyes as she pounded along. Yakone was racing after her shoulder, less than a snout-length behind. Forcing his aching legs to move even faster, Toklo faced forward again. A steep, rocky outcrop loomed up in front of him.

If I can only reach that . . . he thought.

Somewhere behind him he heard Lusa stumble and let out a yelp that was quickly muffled by snow. Toklo was sure the small black bear had fallen into a drift, but he didn't stop or even look back.

Lusa will have to look after herself. I need to keep going.

One set of the thundering pawsteps behind Toklo halted, and he realized that Yakone had dropped back to help Lusa.

The rocky outcrop was just ahead. With a mighty leap, Toklo flung himself at the lowest ledge, but his paws slipped on the icy surface and he fell back, rolling over in the snow in a tangle of flailing legs.

Kallik sprinted past him and sprang onto the rock, scrambling to the summit and sending a shower of yet more snow down onto Toklo.

"I won!" she roared.

Toklo hauled himself to his paws, shaking clotted snow out of his fur. "No, you didn't," he retorted, annoyance welling up inside him. "I got to the rock first. It's not my fault my paw slipped."

"First to the top of the rock, that's what we said." Kallik slid down to join him, giving him a friendly poke with her snout. "Don't be a sore loser."

Toklo just grunted. He was angry with himself more than with Kallik. *I should have won! If I'd just been a bit more careful . . .*

"Well done, Kallik!" Yakone called as he came puffing up with Lusa. "You're really fast. You too, Toklo."

"Thanks for checking on me—not!" Lusa added.

Toklo stifled a snort of amusement as he looked at the little black bear. She was covered in snow; even her ears were filled with it. "I know how much you like falling into snowdrifts," he said to her. "Besides, it could have been a trick to make me slow down."

Lusa shook her head from side to side, trying to dislodge the snow from her ears. "I never had a chance of winning," she murmured sadly. "My legs are so short."

Seeing her beginning to shiver, Toklo padded over to her and started to lick the snow out of her ears. "Cheer up," he comforted her. "You'd win in a tree-climbing race."

"I'm not sure I would." Lusa looked dejected. "I'm so out of practice. I can't remember the last time we saw a real tree!"

"True," Kallik agreed. "There's not much of anything on this island, and it seems to just go on forever. Are you *sure* this is the right way to the sea?"

"This is the way Nanulak's family told us to go," Toklo replied.

"And we trust them?" Yakone muttered. "After what Nanulak did?"

Yakone's words revived the pain of betrayal, as sharp as a thorn piercing Toklo's heart. He had believed that Nanulak was his friend, that he could teach and take care of the young bear just as he had taken care of Ujurak.

But all Nanulak wanted was to use me, to get revenge on his family.

The memory of Nanulak's father flashed into Toklo's mind so vividly that he almost thought that the huge white bear was looming over him. He saw blood patching the bear's white fur, and remembered the pain of his own wounds.

I could have killed him because Nanulak lied to me. How could I have been so wrong about Nanulak?

Kallik gave Toklo a gentle nudge, drawing him away from his hurtful memories. "Why don't we hunt?" she suggested. "It won't be light for much longer." Her eyes gleamed with amusement as she added, "I won the race, so I think you should all bring food for me!"

"In your dreams!" Toklo exclaimed, relieved that she hadn't mentioned Nanulak. He gave her a harder nudge in return. "You're so fast, you should be the one chasing prey!"

Toklo took the lead again as the bears headed onward, making for the crest of a low range of hills that lay across their path. His belly was bawling with hunger, but so far there was no sign of any prey. Snow-covered slopes rolled into the distance on every side, broken occasionally by jutting rocks or a few stunted thorn trees. For days they had been heading toward the setting sun, meeting scarcely any other bears. Even traces of flat-faces were rare in this desolate landscape: only the occasional small den, or thin tower poking into the sky.

Pushing the thought of Nanulak to the back of his mind, Toklo tried to relax and enjoy the company of his friends. The race had been fun, even though he had lost. Yakone, the reddish-pelted white bear they had met on Star Island, was settling into the group. And they had directions now that would take them to a narrow stretch of sea that divided this island from the mainland. Everything was looking good.

But the parting that was soon to come nagged at Toklo's mind like a rough pieces of ice between his toes. The whole point of this journey was to reach the Melting Sea, where Kallik and Yakone would stay with the other white bears who made their homes there. The little family they had created through so many difficulties and dangers would be broken up. Soon Lusa, too, would find bears like herself and live with them among the trees that were her true home.

If only Nanulak . . .

Toklo cut off the thought, stifling a sigh. Everything seemed to lead back to Nanulak. Once Toklo had believed that he would build a new life with the young mixed bear, living in adjoining territories so that he could teach Nanulak the ways of brown bears.

That's not going to happen now. I can't believe that treacherous bear had me fooled for so long. And suppose a bigger, stronger bear does that—one who could beat me if it came to a fight? Determinedly, Toklo shrugged off the worry. *No. I'll never make that mistake again.*

"I can't wait to get away from all this snow!" Lusa's voice came from just behind Toklo; she was trotting along between Kallik and Yakone, and sounded quite cheerful, as if she had forgotten all about Nanulak and the problems he had caused. "I'm just longing to see real trees again, and to find some other black bears!"

"I'm sure you will," Kallik responded. "Every pawstep is taking you closer."

The she-bears' confidence reminded Toklo of his own blank future. Kallik had Yakone, and might even meet her brother, Taqqiq, again once they reached the Melting Sea. And Lusa was so friendly, she would find it easy to be accepted by her own kind.

But what about me? Toklo wanted to wail like an abandoned cub, and instantly felt ashamed of himself. *You'll find a territory and live alone. That's what brown bears do.* But the prospect didn't seem as enticing as it once had.

By now the crest of the hill was only a few bearlengths away. As they approached it, Toklo heard a familiar clicking sound, though it took him a moment to remember what it was.

"Caribou!" he exclaimed.

"Oh, great!" Kallik bounded past him. Reaching the top of the hill, she glanced back and added, "A whole herd!"

Memories flashed through Toklo's mind of the first time they had seen caribou in the Last Great Wilderness, and then of the time they had driven a herd of caribou into a frantic stampede on Star Island, to trample down the flat-face oil rig that was destroying the wild and driving the spirits away.

He gave his pelt a shake in an effort to banish the recollections. *We've got more urgent things to worry about now,* he thought, gazing out across the landscape.

Beyond the caribou, the slope ended in a narrow stretch of flat, white ice. On the opposite side, mountains reared up, dark and bulky against the sky.

"That must be the crossing," Toklo said, angling his head toward the ice. "The Melting Sea should be really close now."

Kallik sniffed the air eagerly, then shook her head. "I can't pick up anything familiar," she told the others. "We're still too far away—but this must be the right way to go." With a sigh she added, "It was so much easier when we had Ujurak with us."

Toklo murmured agreement, struggling once again with a pang of loss. The small brown bear had always been certain of the path they should take, even when there was nothing to guide them. Now the bears had only their own instincts to trust, and any information they could glean from other bears. *And we just have to hope we're getting it right.*

DON'T MISS

DAWN OF THE CLANS

WARRIORS

BOOK 1:

THE SUN TRAIL

Gray Wing toiled up the snow-covered slope toward a ridge that bit into the sky like a row of snaggly teeth. He set each paw down carefully, to avoid breaking through the frozen surface and sinking into the powdery drifts underneath. Light flakes were falling, dappling his dark gray pelt. He was so cold that he couldn't feel his pads anymore, and his belly yowled with hunger.

I can't remember the last time I felt warm or full-fed.

In the last sunny season he had still been a kit, playing with his littermate, Clear Sky, around the edge of the pool outside the cave. Now that seemed like a lifetime ago. Gray Wing had only the vaguest memories of green leaves on the stubby mountain trees, and the sunshine bathing the rocks.

Pausing to taste the air for prey, he gazed across the snow-bound mountains, peak after peak stretching away into the distance. The heavy gray sky overhead promised yet more snow to come.

But the air carried no scent of his quarry, and Gray Wing plodded on. Clear Sky appeared from behind an outcrop of rock, his pale gray fur barely visible against the snow. His jaws were empty, and as he spotted Gray Wing he shook his head.

"Not a sniff of prey anywhere!" he called. "Why don't we—"

A raucous cry from above cut off his words. A shadow flashed over Gray Wing. Looking up, he saw a hawk swoop low across the slope, its talons hooked and cruel.

As the hawk passed, Clear Sky leaped high into the air, his forepaws outstretched. His claws snagged the bird's feathers and he fell back, dragging it from the sky. It let out another harsh cry as it landed on the snow in a flurry of beating wings.

Gray Wing charged up the slope, his paws throwing up a fine spray of snow. Reaching his brother, he planted both forepaws on one thrashing wing. The hawk glared at him with hatred in its yellow eyes, and Gray Wing had to duck to avoid its slashing talons.

Clear Sky thrust his head forward and sank his teeth into the hawk's neck. It jerked once and went limp, its gaze growing instantly dull as blood seeped from its wound and stained the snow.

Panting, Gray Wing looked at his brother. "That was a great catch!" he exclaimed, warm triumph flooding through him.

Clear Sky shook his head. "But look how scrawny it is. There's nothing in these mountains fit to eat, and won't be until the snow clears."

He crouched beside his prey, ready to take the first bite. Gray Wing settled next to him, his jaws flooding as he thought of sinking his teeth into the hawk.

But then he remembered the starving cats back in the cave, squabbling over scraps. "We should take this prey back to the others," he meowed. "They need it to give them strength for their hunting."

"We need strength too," Clear Sky mumbled, tearing away a mouthful of the hawk's flesh.

"We'll be fine." Gray Wing gave him a prod in the side. "We're the best hunters in the Tribe. Nothing escapes us when we hunt together. We can catch something else easier than the others can."

Clear Sky rolled his eyes as he swallowed the prey. "Why must you always be so unselfish?" he grumbled. "Okay, let's go."

Together the two cats dragged the hawk down the slope and over the boulders at the bottom of a narrow gully until they reached the pool where the waterfall roared. Though it wasn't heavy, the bird was awkward to manage. Its flopping wings and claws caught on every hidden rock and buried thornbush.

"We wouldn't have to do this if you'd let us eat it," Clear Sky muttered as he struggled to maneuver the hawk along the path that led behind the waterfall. "I hope the others appreciate this."

Clear Sky grumbles, Gray Wing thought, *but he knows this is the right thing to do.*

Yowls of surprise greeted the brothers when they returned to the cave. Several cats ran to meet them, gathering around to gaze wide-eyed at the prey.

"It's *huge*!" Turtle Tail exclaimed, her green eyes shining as she bounded up to Gray Wing. "I can't believe you brought it back for us."

Gray Wing dipped his head, feeling slightly embarrassed at her enthusiasm. "It won't feed every cat," he mewed.

Shattered Ice, a gray-and-white tom, shouldered his way to the front of the crowd. "Which cats are going out to hunt?" he asked. "They should be the first ones to eat."

Murmurs came from among the assembled cats, broken by a shrill wail: "But I'm *hungry*! Why can't I have some? I could go out and hunt."

Gray Wing recognized the voice as being his younger brother, Jagged Peak's. Their mother, Quiet Rain, padded up and gently nudged her kit back toward the sleeping hollows. "You're too young to hunt," she murmured. "And if the older cats don't eat, there'll be no prey for any cat."

"Not fair!" Jagged Peak muttered as his mother guided him away.

Meanwhile the hunters, including Shattered Ice and Turtle Tail, lined up beside the body of the hawk. Each of them took one mouthful, then stepped back for the next cat to take their turn. By the time they had finished, and filed out along the path behind the waterfall, there was very little meat left.

Clear Sky, watching beside Gray Wing, let out an irritated

snort. "I still wish *we* could have eaten it."

Privately Gray Wing agreed with him, but he knew there was no point in complaining. *There isn't enough food. Every cat is weak, hungry—just clinging on until the sun comes back.*

DOGS WILL RULE THE WILD IN

SURVIVORS

BOOK 1:
THE EMPTY CITY

Lucky startled awake, fear prickling in his bones and fur. He leaped to his feet, growling.

For an instant he'd thought he was tiny once more, safe in his Pup Pack and protected, but the comforting dream had already vanished. The air shivered with menace, tingling Lucky's skin. If only he could see what was coming, he could face it down—but the monster was invisible, scentless. He whined in terror. This was no sleep-time story: This fear was *real.*

The urge to run was almost unbearable; but he could only scrabble, snarl, and scratch in panic. There was nowhere to go:

The wire of his cage hemmed him in on every side. His muzzle hurt when he tried to shove it through the gaps; when he backed away, snarling, the same wire bit into his haunches.

Others were close . . . familiar bodies, familiar scents. Those dogs were enclosed in this terrible place just as he was. Lucky raised his head and barked, over and over, high and desperate, but it was clear no dog could help him. His voice was drowned out by the chorus of frantic calls.

They were all *trapped*.

Dark panic overwhelmed him. His claws scrabbled at the earth floor, even though he knew it was hopeless.

He could smell the female swift-dog in the next cage, a friendly, comforting scent, overlaid now with the bitter tang of danger and fear. Yipping, he pressed closer to her, feeling the shivers in her muscles—but the wire still separated them.

"Sweet? Sweet, something's on its way. Something bad!"

"Yes, I feel it! What's happening?"

The longpaws—where were they? The longpaws held them captive in this Trap House but they had always seemed to care about the dogs. They brought food and water, they laid bedding, cleared the mess . . .

Surely the longpaws would come for them now.

The others barked and howled as one, and Lucky raised his voice with theirs.

Longpaws! Longpaws, it's COMING. . . .

Something shifted beneath him, making his cage tremble. In a sudden, terrible silence, Lucky crouched, frozen with horror.

Then, around and above him, chaos erupted.

The unseen monster was here . . . and its paws were right on the Trap House.

Lucky was flung back against the wire as the world heaved and tilted. For agonizing moments he didn't know which way was up or down. The monster tumbled him around, deafening him with the racket of falling rock and shattering clear-stone. His vision went dark as clouds of filth blinded him. The screaming, yelping howls of terrified dogs seemed to fill his skull. A great chunk of wall crashed off the wire in front of his nose, and Lucky leaped back. Was it the Earth-Dog, trying to take him?

Then, just as suddenly as the monster had come, it disappeared. One more wall crashed down in a cloud of choking dust. Torn wire screeched as a high cage toppled, then plummeted to the earth.

There was only silence and a dank metal scent.

Blood! thought Lucky. *Death . . .*

Panic stirred inside his belly again. He was lying on his side, the wire cage crumpled against him, and he thrashed his strong legs, trying to right himself. The cage rattled and rocked, but he couldn't get up. *No!* he thought. *I'm trapped!*

"Lucky! Lucky, are you all right?"

"Sweet? Where are you?"

Her long face pushed at his through the mangled wire. "My cage door—it broke when it fell! I thought I was dead. Lucky, I'm free—but you—"

"Help me, Sweet!"

The other faint whimpers had stopped. Did that mean the other dogs were . . . ? No. Lucky could not let himself think about that. He howled just to break the silence.

"I think I can pull the cage out a bit," said Sweet. "Your door's loose, too. We might be able to get it open." Seizing the wire with her teeth, she tugged.

Lucky fought to keep himself calm. All he wanted to do was fling himself against the cage until it broke. His hind legs kicked out wildly and he craned his head around, snapping at the wire. Sweet was gradually pulling the cage forward, stopping occasionally to scrabble at fallen stones with her paws.

"There. It's looser now. Wait while I—"

But Lucky could wait no longer. The cage door was torn at the upper corner, and he twisted until he could bite and claw at it. He worked his paw into the gap and pulled, hard.

The wire gave with a screech, just as Lucky felt a piercing stab in his paw pad—but the door now hung at an awkward angle. Wriggling and squirming, he pulled himself free and stood upright at last.

His tail was tight between his legs as tremors bolted through his skin and muscles. He and Sweet stared at the carnage and chaos around them. There were broken cages—and broken bodies. A small, smooth-coated dog lay on the ground nearby, lifeless, eyes dull. Beneath the last wall that had fallen, nothing stirred, but a limp paw poked out from between stones. The scent of death was already spreading through the Trap House air.

Sweet began to whimper with grief. "What was that? What *happened*?"

"I think—" Lucky's voice shook, and he tried again. "It was a Growl. I used to—my Mother-Dog used to tell me stories about the Earth-Dog, and the Growls she sent. I think the monster was a Big Growl. . . ."

"We have to get away from here!" There was terror in Sweet's whine.

"Yes." Lucky backed slowly away, shaking his head to dispel the death-smell. But it followed him, clinging to his nostrils.

He glanced around, desperate. Where the wall had tumbled onto the other dog cages, the broken blocks had collapsed into a pile, and light shone bright through the haze of dust and smoke.

"There, Sweet, where the stones have crumbled in. Come on!"

She needed no more urging, leaping up over the rubble. Aware of his wounded paw, Lucky picked his way more carefully, nervously glancing around for longpaws. Surely they'd come when they saw the destruction?

He shuddered and quickened his pace, but even when he sprang down onto the street outside, following Sweet's lead, there was no sign of any longpaws.

Bewildered, he paused, and sniffed the air. It smelled so strange. . . .

"Let's get away from the Trap House," he told Sweet in a low voice. "I don't know what's happened, but we should go far away in case the longpaws come back."

Sweet gave a sharp whine as her head drooped. "Lucky, I don't think there are any longpaws left."

Their journey was slow and silent except for the distant wail of broken loudcages. A sense of threat grew in Lucky's belly; so many of the roads and alleys he knew were blocked. Still he persevered, nosing his way around the broken buildings through tangled, snaking coils torn from the ground. Despite what Sweet thought, Lucky was sure that the longpaws would return soon. He wanted to be far away from the destroyed Trap House when they did.

The sky was darkening by the time he felt it was safe to rest; Lucky sensed anyway that Sweet couldn't go much farther. Maybe swift-dogs weren't as good at long journeys as they were at quick dashes. He gazed back the way they'd come, shadows lengthening across the ground, hiding spaces emerging in dark corners. Lucky shivered—which other animals might be out there, scared and hungry?

But they were both exhausted from escaping the Big Growl. Sweet barely managed to tread her ritual sleep-circle before she slumped to the ground, laid her head on her forepaws, and closed her troubled eyes. Lucky pressed himself close against her flank for warmth and comfort. *I'll stay awake for a while,* he thought, *Keep watch . . . yes . . .*

Warriors: Power of Three

Firestar's grandchildren begin their training as warrior cats.
Prophecy foretells that they will hold more power than any cats before them.

Warriors: Omen of the Stars

Includes WARRIORS ADVENTURE GAME

Which ThunderClan apprentice will complete the prophecy that foretells that three Clanmates hold the future of the Clans in their paws?

Also available unabridged from HarperChildren's*Audio*

Warriors: Dawn of the Clans

Discover how the warrior cat Clans came to be.

HARPER
An Imprint of HarperCollins*Publishers*